BIG IN JAPAN

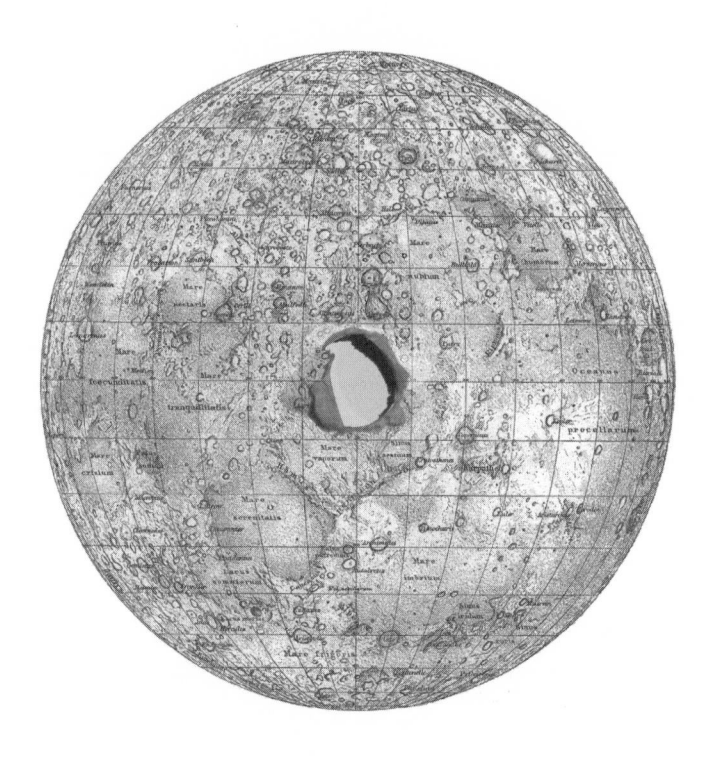

A GHOST STORY

BIG IN JAPAN

TRADE **CHIN MUSIC PRESS** MARK

AGENBITE

SPECIALLY MADE
FOR
EXPORT.

M. THOMAS GAMMARINO

CHIN MUSIC
PRESS

FALL 2009
CHIN MUSIC PRESS, *PUBLISHERS*
SEATTLE

kami
PAPERBACK
SERIES

PUBLISHER:
Chin Music Press
2621 24th Ave W
Seattle, WA 98199
USA

www.chinmusicpress.com

ISBN 978-0974199597

A Kami book
Kami is an imprint of Chin Music Press

First {1} Edition

BOOK DESIGN: Joshua Powell

COVER ART: *Memorial to Ichikawa Danjūrō VIII*, Utagawa Kuniyoshi
(1798-1861), courtesy of Scott Skinner at The Drachen Foundation,
www.drachen.org

Lunar image taken from *The Agile Rabbit Book of Historical and
Curious Maps*, published by The Pepin Press, www.pepinpress.com

Images from the *Gaki Zoshi* provided by The Tokyo National
Museum, TNM Image Archives, http://TNMArchives.jp/

Printed in the USA by McNaughton & Gunn Inc.

LIBRARY OF CONGRESS CATALOGING-IN-PUBLICATION DATA

Gammarino, M. Thomas, 1978-
Big in Japan : a ghost story : a novel / by M. Thomas Gammarino.
  p. cm.
"A Kami book."
ISBN 978-0-9741995-9-7 (alk. paper)
1. Rock musicians—Fiction. 2. Americans—Japan—Fiction.
3. Musical fiction. 4. Psychological fiction. I. Title.

To those who have yet to look beyond the name of our company: We advise you
to quickly peruse our website to confirm that we are book publishers and that
pitching us your latest rap demo over the phone (happened once) or sending
us your sheet music (also happened once) will get you nowhere. We are known
to accept sample CDs, however, and actually wouldn't mind receiving more,
especially from the likes of Terence Blanchard or Bill Evans. Oh, we like The
Clash, so that's good too. We can't guarantee anything will come of it except to
say that it may be considered for review on one of our many websites. Thank
you in advance.

CHIN MUSIC PRESS

登録 TRADE 商標 MARK

チン・ミュージック

"Curiously Bibliophilic."
(CMP–2004)

BOOKS MADE IN SEATTLE EXCLUSIVELY BY CHIN MUSIC PRESS, INC.

•

For my friends
(who are my family),
& my family
(who are my friends).

·

The hungry ghosts I see are real people.
—Ikkyū, 1461

Brain peered into Martina's hole. All he wanted was to play one more time through the Gregorian speed-polka power ballad he'd spent all day composing and didn't totally hate yet, but he hadn't foreseen dropping his pick in there like that, he certainly hadn't foreseen this minutes-long struggle to get it out, and if he didn't go for a drive at precisely 11:11, as promised to himself by himself several hours ago, then something bad was sure to happen. Tomorrow's flight would crash maybe, or his mom would die. Oh, he didn't *literally* believe that. Still, the instant his alarm clock flashed 11:10, he laid Martina down gently on his bed and hauled his impossibly scrawny ass up the stairs, across the darkened living room and out the back door.

With six seconds to spare by his infallible inner clock, he entered Volva and backed down the driveway. Now maybe he could relax— insofar as he ever could. He lit himself a cigarette and set to weaving webs of smoke through the backroads, thinking how much he loved this time of night this time of year, that back-to-school nip in the air, the rustling treetops, the ghosted moon… That decided it then. First thing in the morning, as soon as his bandmates arrived, he'd take his stand. "You'll just have to do without me," he'd say. They'd puff themselves up and go red in their prima donna faces, but he'd hold the line. "What about the band?" they'd say, as if the band were somehow greater than the sum of its shoddy parts—Brain himself believed that only about half the time—and he'd tell them what they could do with their band. In all likelihood they'd spill each other's blood for a few minutes then. Probably he could count on born-again Matt to sit out, but he'd still be outnumbered two to one, and in any case, the pain would prove temporary and worthwhile. Sooner or later they'd depart, Agenbite dissolved, and he could go off and pursue some better, freer, more lifelike life.

He lit another cigarette, relished a choir of crickets and performed the ritual of turns that led to the high school. He parked Volva in the deserted lot, got out and dashed across the sprinklered lawn. A sickly orange streetlight whanged its eternal lonely drone—a low G with Aeolian overtones. Brain had graduated from this place more years ago than he cared to count, but the night had drawn him back like some disgruntled revenant ever since, and now here he was peering into shadowy classrooms, revisiting Mr. D's history class, whence he'd gleaned the as-yet-unuseful bit of information that the ancients had once mixed honey with cow dung for a spermicide (it also happened to be where he'd first met Nick, which event the intervening years and a growing catalogue of resentments had relegated to the parentheses of memory), and Sweeney's lit class, where they'd tried to read *Ulysses* and come away with a name for their band, if not a lot else. He remembered the line by heart: *Agenbite of inwit: remorse of conscience. It is an age of exhausted whoredom groping for its god.* It still sounded badass. Maybe he would go with them after all.

He slinked past the auditorium and relived the Battle of the Bands they'd played there once, though in washed-out sepia tones now and with none of the giddy, orgiastic promise of being sixteen years old and what seemed like mere minutes from the big time. And he remembered his senior prom yet again and his blind date, Beth, who was Nick's girlfriend's piano-prodigy cousin, and how he'd stood with her by the fireplace as Nick's mother snapped their photos, how his fingers had grazed the down of her wrist and his head had seemed to fill with light and then stayed that way all through the limo ride and onto the dance floor, where he'd actually danced, and then into dinner when they took their seats and Beth excused herself to use the restroom, and then how it gradually became clear that something was amiss because Beth didn't seem to be coming back, and finally Lauren went to check on her cousin and found her not in the bathroom at all but at the piano in the band room playing "Moonlight Sonata," her mascara inking the keys because it so happened she'd made a long-distance call to her boyfriend from the payphone and he'd dumped her just like that because he'd thought about it long and hard, and all his friends agreed, it wasn't cool for your girlfriend to go to some other guy's prom if you'd asked her not to, even if it was just as a favor to her cousin, and she felt really bad about it but asked could she go back to Lauren's house now, and Lauren must have said okay because that's exactly what she did, though not without apologizing to Brain first for ruining his prom, and he'd said, "Not at all, not at all," while meanwhile the light seeped out of his head, and now here he was, all these years later, *God damn it*, still thinking about it.

•

Nick infiltrated Brain's basement at seven AM sharp. "You ready?"

"Almost," said Brain, who'd just played through his Gregorian speed-polka power ballad and decided it sounded like nothing so much as a prolonged splutter of watery stool.

Nick dropped onto the couch and riffled through Brain's latest issue of *Maxim*.

Brain finished packing up his cords and pedals, cradled Martina and Ibaneza in his left arm, Rolanda in his right, and made for the stairs. When Nick stood and tossed the magazine haphazardly onto the ottoman, Brain's first impulse was to sigh and go straighten it, but having just read an article in that selfsame issue of *Maxim* that cited anal-retentiveness as a major turnoff for beautiful women, he forced himself to turn a blind eye.

He flipped the light switch with his chin and led the way up the stairs. Before leaving for her job at the library, his mom had woken him, kissed him on the lips and wished him a great trip, but his dad had the day off for some reason and was sitting on his tawny spot on the couch, watching *Full Metal Jacket* for what had to be the seventy-fifth time. An awful lot of dying went on in the living room.

"Okay, Dad. We're going."

"Don't fall in love over there, *Brian*. We can't afford the phone bill."

"That's not my name," Brain said, *sotto voce*, shouldering his way through the screen door and making no effort to hold it open for Nick, who, even though he no longer had a job, was bound to get caught up in shoptalk about lasers or stealth bombers or the relative strengths and weaknesses of Raytheon and Boeing. If only Nick had been born in Brain's place, he might have added some joy to the old man's life. Nick, with his money and his mojo. Nick, who was the worst best friend a guy could ask for.

The sun greeted Brain like a flaming bag of shit. To make matters a little bit worse, Matt and Theo were sitting on the hood of his car.

"Good morning, Brain," Matt said.

"Get off of there," Brain retorted.

Matt complied. Theo finished lighting his cigarette first.

"Good morning to you too," Theo said when he was ready. "You psyched?"

"No," Brain replied.

"Why not?"

"Why would I be?"

"Because you're finally gonna get your balls wet, you son of a bitch. What's the matter with you?"

Nick emerged from the house and popped the trunk of his Range Rover with his keychain.

"You know," Brain said, "I think I may want to drive after all." Brain had agreed to this tour only on condition that he not have to do anything besides play music, but surrendering control had never been his forte.

"What difference does it make?" Nick asked.

"I just don't like being a passenger is all."

"You should do real great on the plane then," Theo said. "You'll only be a passenger for, what, like fifteen hours?"

Without waiting for anyone's approval, Brain began extricating their luggage from the Range Rover and building a puzzle of it inside of Volva. He had to start over twice before finding a way to fit all three of Matt's duffel bags.

"What the hell've you got in there anyway?" Theo asked.

"Literature," Matt said.

"*Moby Dick* and shit?"

"Pamphlets."

"Oh, right," Theo said. "Tracts."

Nick called shotgun and Theo called him a motherfucker while he and Matt jigsawed themselves around the luggage in the back seat. Brain twisted the key and popped in some Bulgarian folk music. The car had lurched halfway into the street when that cockeyed magazine flashed on his inner eye, leaving him no choice but to step on the brake and thrust the shifter into P.

"What the hell?" Theo said.

"Back already?" Brain's dad said while Brain went down the basement to re-arrange the magazine such that it now sat face-up, edges flush with the corner of the ottoman. This was eccentric behavior and Brain knew it, but he couldn't help the way he was wired, he certainly couldn't help it if no girl had ever seen fit to share her body with him, and if he was a good composer at all, he knew he probably had these same demons to thank. When he'd gotten the magazine just so, he flipped off the light and returned to his sputtering vehicle feeling twenty pounds lighter.

He lit a cigarette, stepped on the gas and drove down the street, stopped for a tomboy in goalie pads to clear a hockey net from their path, dipped under a canopy of oaks, careened around an onion-domed Greek church, past used cars and garden hoses and hot-pink inflatable swimming pools, and merged onto the Blue Route.

The interesting thing about 15/16 time, Brain was thinking, *is that if you tap your foot in strict quarter notes along with it, defying the jerky pull inherent in the time signature, you find that once every four measures your foot lands on the downbeat and the sonic knot that seemed beyond your ability to unravel suddenly betrays an underlying pattern, a governing principle. Chaos yields to order, the situation is under control.*

Theo read Brain's mind and didn't approve: "Ya know, just because a pop song has only three chords in it doesn't mean the band members are retarded. Who gives a shit if you can play faster than Eddie Van Halen, or if one of your legs can do the dishes while the other does the laundry or whatever? At the end of the day, I'd rather hear hyenas tearing each other apart or like terminally ill people fucking or something like that. Ya know what I mean?"

"Can't say I do," Nick said.

"*Feeling.* I'm talking about feeling. I mean, if a song doesn't make you want to jerk off or bang your head against a wall, then what's the point, right?"

"You realize," Brain said, "if we do an about-face now, we automatically forfeit the fans we've already got."

"Tell me something, Brain. How many of our fans are hot chicks? One maybe? And do you really mind losing the fat dork contingent? Did you ever pay attention to how many of the people at our shows are wearing glasses? It's like fucking Mensa out there."

"Money's money," Nick said.

"And how much of that are we making?" Theo said. "Jesus, I wouldn't even mind the lack of money if we were making up for it in pussy."

Matt looked wounded. "Would you mind maybe not using the Lord's name that way in my presence?"

"Look, I just wish I could get you to think bigger is all. So what if we get reviews in obscure metal magazines and our website gets x hits a day? As far as I'm concerned we're at rock fucking bottom, and the only way to go is up."

Brain smoked cigarettes like they were going out of style, which according to *Maxim* they were. There was a note of autumn in the air, a whole minor-seventh arpeggio in fact, and despite the circumstances, his grimace was by and large affected—which got him wondering whether there wasn't some area hidden in the folds of his brain that did *not* loathe the idea of this tour, thrived a little even on the hope that something might exist out there to divert its attention away from itself. Was that why he'd let himself get talked into this thing in the first place?

But by the time they stopped for gas in Middlesex County and he watched in the rearview as the attendant inserted his nozzle into Volva, a pall had already descended on Brain's optimism. He wasn't even sure he wanted to be in this band anymore. It had all been so adrenalizing in the early days, but after three demos and a full-length album, his glands had all but dried up. He'd compromised too much. Like when Matt couldn't play that bass line and wondered could he play this easier, lamer one instead, or when Nick took it upon himself to unsyncopate that roll, or when Theo wrote lyrics about the "fudge tunnel of love," he should have put a stop to it. He should have said, "Do it right or don't do it at all." But instead he'd just swallowed each perversion like a spoonful of ipecac, and to this day Agenbite had yet to record a song he could listen to without his stomach churning.

For the rest of the drive, anxieties rained on Brain like so much interplanetary dust, viz. would he have to eat raw fish when he already found the cooked kind unpalatable enough? Would he catch a nice case of dysentery to go with his already irritable bowels? Would fans show? Would they speak English? Would they sing along even if they didn't? Would Nick's ludicrous business model actually pan out and turn them into a huge overnight success, and would that success then translate to America or would they be professionally obscure in their homeland forever? Would they be bound to Tokyo for long stretches at a time? Would Sarah Milliken, dropping her kids off at Saturday detention, never hear Brain's wailing guitar solos on the car radio and pound her sagging chest while she relived in her mind's eye the day she'd had a clear shot at being his girlfriend and botched it? (Miss Kane had seated her next to Brain one First Friday and he'd fairly throbbed as Sarah's left leg, the one with the freckle, drifted on the kneeler until it pressed against his and didn't retract but stayed there, *had its being* there, for so many agonizingly beautiful minutes that when they finally stood up for communion—a misnomer if ever there was one—that whole section of his calf went cold, and when he returned to the pew, Danny Spotto was furtively picking his nose where Sarah ought to have been, and Sarah herself had landed two rows back, sandwiched between Patrick Hewitt and Brian Lombardi, nice enough guys Brain suddenly wanted to disembowel, and yes Jesus was on his tongue, but Sarah's freckle was way over there, way *back* there, and some sickening clairvoyance told him it would never come within his compass again.)

When the time came, they exited the turnpike, parked at the park-n-ride, and shuttled over to the airport. It was Brain's first time in one, and it seemed to him to have all the warmth and good cheer of a slaughterhouse. "Ya know what I want to do?" Theo said while they stood in line at the security check. "I wanna get my face tattooed on my face, right on it, actual size, only maybe like an inch or two off to the left so you never know if I'm really here or if I'm really over there, ya know what I mean?" Nick and Matt egged him on. "And I think I might like to get like 'fragile' and 'this side up' on my internal organs and then donate my body to science, give some med student a real kick in the pants."

Any other day, Brain might have added to the conversation—it had occurred to him, for instance, that a well-drawn tattoo might create the illusion of the rock-solid abs the two hundred crunches a day of his recent self-improvement crusade didn't seem to want to impart to him—but at the moment he was of no mind to communicate.

Matt seized on his aloofness—"Everything all right?"—and Brain said, "I'm fine," and looked down at the belt conveying them towards their terminal, which word felt so right, and found himself, in point of fact, terrifically unfine. His tear ducts were dry-heaving and his hair hurt. It wasn't even just this damned tour. It was bigger than that, like all the myriad disappointments of his life had steadily accreted into a malignant, a *malevolent*, tumor inside of him and finally chosen this day to burst. He'd wanted to be dead before, but always in some slightly hypothetical way. But this new despondency was blacker, more immediate, unmitigated by self-pity or dreams of posthumous glory. He looked around for something sharp or a ten-story drop.

What he found instead was a reason to live.

Only a few yards away, wheeling a suitcase towards the Boeing 767 he hadn't wanted to board until now—not least because his father had very likely had a hand in designing the thing—was the most unhorrible creature he'd ever laid eyes on. And by all appearances she'd just smiled at him.

Theo noticed her too: "Dude, check that stewardess *out*! I think she digs you, Brain."

"Too skinny," Nick said.

But Brain was too palsied to defend this perfect cliché of porcelain and silk until she disappeared into the jetway, and even then all he could do was to shut his eyes, take a deep breath and steel himself for the resumption of life inside of time and his rangy body, but when he reopened his eyes and swept them across the gate, he made a preposterous discovery: Gate C121 was luxuriant with her. There was one of her right across from him even, peering into a hand-held mirror, outlining doe eyes in lilac. He stroked her with his eyes until she noticed him and met his gaze and a moment of profound awkwardness ensued before she resolved it with a smile and he requited with a fit of involuntary twitching.

"Asian chicks are horny as hell," Theo said. "I fucked around with this one chick for a while, she was Taiwanese or Malaysian or some shit, ridiculously hot, and I itch as much as the next guy, but sometimes I just wanna like sit around and smoke a bowl, watch a sitcom or whatever, but with this bitch it was always like whenever we weren't fucking she'd start getting all antsy and bored. At first I thought it was cool, ya know, but it got to be like, Jesus, will you chill out already?"

Brain flipped through his memorized yearbooks. Had he never seen a Japanese girl before? There'd been a Filipina in his grade school, Rosa Beltran. He'd been attracted to her for a few minutes once, at the ice rink. But then he'd gone to get a hot chocolate from the vending machine and spied her peeling off her socks and changing into new ones, and her toes were corpse gray and had brittle hairs curled on top of them like pubes on a toilet seat, and that had sufficed to slake his interest. She'd always been more the Latina than the Asian girl anyway.

"There are plenty of horny white girls too," Nick said. "Don't you think it's a little racist to say that just because you went out with one horny Asian girl, then all Asian girls must be sluts?"

To think that all those years he'd spent aching for Stephanie Cantor's calves in study hall, Jen Applebaum's budding breasts in her gym t-shirt, the nape of Katie Clemens' neck, Gwen Randazzo's ankleted ankles, Maureen O'Donnell's painted toenails on field day, Maria Bevilacqua's harelip, that pair of anonymous cheerleading bloomers on the floor of the cloakroom, the lingering eyelashes of that snobbish *Québécoise,* and those thousand other specters of love; to think that during all those abject hours his heart's truer objects had been quietly sitting here in Gate C121 of Newark International Airport: the notion at once seared him with regret and exonerated him of a whole history of blistering solitude. This Gate C121 was a purgatory of sorts, and if that were true, then Japan, contrary to all expectations, was shaping up to be paradise. He took care not to wear this hope on his face lest it seem to Nick that Brain's debt of gratitude had increased yet again.

"Who said sluts?" Theo said. "I said horny. Sluts aren't horny."

"What's that supposed to mean?" Nick asked.

"Sluts are just sad. Straight-up horny chicks are different, more like guys. Maybe they have extra testosterone or whatever, I don't know, but they fuck around because they like to come, not because some dude dressed up as Santa Claus used to finger-fuck them or whatever."

Did women get horny the way Brain got horny? Couldn't, or civilization would never have developed as far as it had because everyone would just be out fucking in the woods until the alpha male gnawed all the competition's genitals off. Anyway, horniness dried you out, made you haggard and ugly. These Japanese girls weren't that. They were so *pure*. Look at that one over there. The beauty queen with the fucked-up teeth. Even in four-inch designer heels, she was so *barefoot*.

Soon they were all funneling into the same plane. Two stewardesses ministered to Agenbite's section of economy class. One was a sort of walrussy blonde, but the other was one of *them*. She had jet-black hair and pigeon toes and a way of assuaging Brain's fear of flying completely. He reeled a little at his first sip of green tea, which tasted something like the essence of a gym sock, but it was she who was doling it out while the Walrus manned the coffee pot, so when she came back around for refills, he eagerly held out his cup, and as she bent at the waist to pour and her face came close enough to his that he could smell her makeup, he made an ardent attempt at telepathy: *Don't you recognize me, my sweet? It's me. The one you've been waiting for all these years. Maybe you've built up a wall around you, but you can let it crumble now, for I will do you no harm. For years I've driven around in the moonlight pining for you, I've composed a thousand melodies in your name* (he read her name tag: "Kyoko"), *and I'll admit, even today I was beginning to lose my faith in you, to write you off as a fantasy, something I'd conjured up to buoy me in this drowning world, but now here we are together at last, in spirit and body both, and I feel the fool and I swear to you, if you'll have me, I'll live every day for the rest of my life happily in your thrall.* He could have no idea whether she'd received the transmission or not, but she smiled and bowed her head, and Brain's heart boomed like a timpani.

"Did I show you guys the Dogsbody review yet?" Nick asked.

"Let me see that," Theo said, snatching the printout from Nick's hands. Brain pretended his sense of well-being didn't hang on what the world thought of him. He played piano on his lap while Theo read. Several eternities passed.

"Not terrible," Theo said when he was finally through. "Except the part where he calls you a schizo, Brain, but it's cool, we love every last one of you."

"Give me that," Brain said.

The ProgNosticator
Agenbite, *Inwit*

Reviewed by: Dogsbody

I first heard Agenbite a few years back at a shadowy, prog-friendly cabaret in Center City Philadelphia called The Far East. At the time I thought they were a little wet behind the ears, but when Ben Steinbrenner's New Jersey-based label Gypsyweed released Agenbite's first full-length EP, *Inwit*, last month, I immediately sat rapt through two listenings. That is, once I got past the cover art, which would seem to depict a space-dwelling dragon wearing a leather vest and vomiting fire towards a planetoid inhabited by every major pop star of the last twenty-five years.

The band has undergone a fortuitous change in lineup. Matt Hamilton, formerly the band's Cookie Monster vocalist, has replaced Ish Barban on bass, and on vocals we have the welcome addition of Theo McCall. Whereas most prog vocalists tend to rely heavily on their upper registers, McCall tends to hover around the middle, and when he does occasionally unleash a scream, it seems to owe as much to

Screamin' Jay Hawkins as to any prog vocalist. You get the feeling he'd be just as at home, maybe more so, in a straight-ahead rock band.

To be sure, Agenbite is about as progressive as rock can get without leaving the genre altogether. From the bulerias of "String Theory" (track 2) to the minimalism of "Crab Nebula" (track 6) to the all-out thrash of "Divertimento" (track 9) to McCall's largely successful attempt at Inuit throat-singing on the title track (note the pun), *Inwit* draws on a boggling array of influences. The only conspicuously missing influences are jazz and other improv-based forms, which brings me to the question of whether or not Agenbite ever establishes its *own* sound on *Inwit*.

Everything on the album is in the way of parody or pastiche, and while this makes for some engaging listening, you have to wonder if Agenbite isn't so deadly faithful to the objects of their impersonation that their own identity gets lost in the shuffle. Is it enough to say that this lack of identity *is* in fact their identity? And if so, why does an album so playful in its method seem to take itself so seriously?

Take track 5 for instance, "The Fifth Column," which, musically, is one of the most boldly experimental, genre-busting pieces I've heard in years. Now here's the first verse, which is sung over a kind of Jobim-esque bossa nova: "Paranoid minds in parabolic times / hurling Molotov cocktails at the *New York Times* / In geodesic domes and catacombs / death breathes life into garden gnomes." The lyrics aren't terrible, but they're just so dark and cloak-and-dagger that they have the effect of casting a nullifying shadow on the aurora borealis of what the instruments are up to.

A look at the liner notes reveals that guitarist-and-sometimes-keyboardist Brain Tedesco does the bulk of the writing, lyrics and music both. I can't help wondering how someone so prodigiously talented can at the same time be so oddly schizophrenic?

In sum, I have no idea whether this band has come into its full musical maturity yet—we'll have to wait for the next album to see—but either way, it's frightening to think what they'll be doing a couple of years from now.

★ ★ ★ ½

Brain crumpled the review and stuffed it behind the duty free magazine. Un*friggin*believable. He'd taken Theo to be kidding as usual, but Dogsbody really had called him a schizo. What he meant of course was a sufferer of Dissociative Identity Disorder—not the same thing at all and one of the few psychological disorders Brain was pretty sure he didn't have to worry about. Still, a review like that might have made him eat his own liver were it not that Kyoko had just padded past and smiled at him, rendering music—and Dogsbody—somehow beside the point.

Matt sat in the window seat to Brain's left, alternately studying his phrasebook and an old paperback called *The Genesis Flood: The Biblical Record and Its Scientific Implications*. Now and then he squinted at the clouds. Across the aisle, Theo busied himself playing videogames on the personal entertainment system and taking the Lord's name in vain. Nick closed his eyes, pursed his lips and bobbed his head while listening to his iPod. Like a band, they all watched the romantic comedy, all had the chicken, all tried to sleep.

On top of his never being able to sleep face-up (attributable, he believed, to an atavistic fear of castration), Brain's seat wouldn't recline, and he'd had far too much tea and erogenous stimulation to allow for a general surrender of consciousness anyway, so for lack of anything better to do while Kyoko was out of eyeshot, he studied his bleak, asymmetrical mug on this week-old passport that still thought his name was "Brian." Brain's father, Brian Tedesco Sr., was the last person on the planet who called him that. Brain had worn the name comfortably enough until entering first grade to find himself but one of three who went by that name, and not even Brain himself could ever say for certain how much this newfound feeling of ordinariness had or had not motivated his re-christening himself atop a phonics test later that year; or how much, by contrast, that act had constituted a symbolic patricide—for already Brian Jr. and Brian Sr. had begun disapproving of one another's way of life; or how much, finally, it had been an honest mistake. In any case, the thick-calved Mrs. Harbold had teased him in red ink in the margin: "A wonderful paradox! Would a 'Brain' misspell his own name?" Brain hadn't actually understood that until the sixth grade when he encountered the word "paradox" in his vocabulary workbook. On the other hand, he had understood, to a fault, that Mrs. Harbold had penalized him ten points for the blunder and then gone on to announce it to the entire class. And even while the misspelling may not have been entirely accidental, he'd nevertheless blushed and welled up, and to this day he still found himself, from time to time, lost in the fantasy of sawing off Mrs. Harbold's head with the metallic edge of his ruler and impaling it on the flagpole in the school parking lot for all the township to see, especially the lovely Ashley Roselli, since it was sure to impress her and as yet his telepathic overtures had gone blatantly unrequited.

•

When it finally/already came time to disembark, Kyoko and her prototype from C121 stood by the door, smiling and bowing and thanking passengers in their dulcet Japanese and adorably mangled English. Brain suffered an afflictive ecstasy, a vertiginous blurring of masters. "Thank *you*," he said, too loudly, looking into each of their four eyes longer than the situation dictated, as if to say, "Come with me, save my life." But they just kept on smiling and bowing, and Matt nudged him along until he was out of the plane and in the jetway, dejected. But then a pair of achingly exotic housewives deplaned after him and strutted into the airport, and he followed their succulent butt cheeks like a convert to some magnificent new religion. He was so preoccupied with the women that for all he knew Narita Airport might have been a state-of-the-art spaceport or it might have been a blasted old tarmac with a customs agent, a currency exchange and some vending machines—and he only knew about the vending machines because Theo insisted on stopping at each one to see if they indeed vended soiled panties as someone back home had informed him (no such luck). In any case, this certainly was the promised land, which until now he'd thought of not as a place so much as a state of being, the repose that comes with dying, something like that. But no, he'd been wrong, it was a place.

They went through immigration, retrieved their bags and instruments from the carousel, bought train tickets from a bilingual vending machine and hefted their cargo over the turnstiles. The train arrived in exactly two minutes and forty-three seconds, per the digital timetable.

"What's up, Brain?" Matt said. "You seem distracted."

"I'm just tired," he said, though he was anything but that. He'd never seen fishnet stockings on living breathing legs in his life, only in the odd porno flick and on mannequins in South Street shop windows, but of the fifteen…sixteen…seventeen females in this train car, six were wearing them. Then a few more stations flipped past and this other breed of nymphet got on, two of her in fact. They wore vivid sundresses and platform shoes higher than they were long, and they had twiggy, chemically tanned legs that shone in the rising sun, and their hair was dyed this tinselly blonde, their faces buried in makeup so that they looked almost panda-like. Brain placed his backpack on his lap and stroked furtively at his glans with his index and middle fingers until, not half a minute later, feigning a spell of whooping cough, he pumped a hundred million hightailing sperm into his underwear.

"What the fuck are you doing?" Theo said.

"What do you mean? I'm not doing anything."

"You sound like you're gonna hack up a lung."

Usually clearing his balls meant clearing his mind as well, but not today. It was another three or four stations before he even thought to realize there were men on this train as well: teenagers riding low in their seats and thumbing cellphones; a bright red old-timer in a fishing vest tippling from a paper bag; businessmen in somber suits pretending to read manga and averting their gaze each time Brain turned their way. They looked like ... Asian guys. They were probably very good at math. But how they could possibly have fathered these women, Brain had no idea.

"Thank God these signs are in English too," Nick said, leading them through Shinjuku station to the Marunouchi line. It was getting on rush hour and the trains were taut with commuters, which was fine with Brain since he soon found himself pressed up against a ponytailed nymphet in a school uniform and a pixy-dusting of glitter. On the downside, the abortion in his pants was drying and all this stimulation was starting to hurt.

Finally they reached Nakano Shimbashi station, lugged their instruments up a steep flight of stairs and down two blocks, past a clutch of unicycling kids, to their apartment. "This is it," Nick said. "La Maison Blanche."

"Nice," Theo said. "A highway embankment with windows."

The realtor spotted them from his office and came out to meet them. "Nicku-san? My name is Junichiro Hamada." He handed them each his name card and directed them into his office to fill out some paperwork. When they were done, he escorted them up a rattletrap elevator to their fifth-floor apartment, gave them their keys and left them with a bow at the door.

"Don't forget to take off your shoes," Brain said as he bent down to untie his Doc Maartens. But by the time he'd finished saying it, Theo had already trod on the straw-mat floor with his obnoxiously red All Stars.

"What's with you?" Theo said, and while the rest of them respectfully divested themselves of their footwear, Theo ignored the custom outright, irritating Brain to a degree he himself could hardly make sense of.

Matt turned to Nick. "So this is your room then?"

"No more than it is yours," Nick said.

Heads shook. For one boarder this room was small, but for *four*? Brain knew Nick had spent days searching for something their producer/manager's meager allowance would afford, but this was really preposterous.

"Why's Ben gotta be such a fucking jewbag?" Theo said, grabbing one of the futons from the closet, unrolling it on the floor and flopping on top.

"If anything will teach you to count pennies, it's millennia of persecution," Matt said with what seemed to Brain like uncharacteristic relativism until he followed it up with, "And if anything will bring on millennia of persecution, it's nailing God to a tree."

No one indulged him. Brain stealthily tweezed a fresh pair of underwear out of his bag and went to the bathroom to change into them. When he got back, the lights were out, the blinds drawn, and his bandmates all laid out on their futons trying to sleep. Brain unrolled a futon of his own, lay on his stomach and closed his eyes, and for a few minutes he was thinking *You know, this isn't so bad*, but then Nick and Theo began their snoring solos, trading fours, calling and responding, and Brain had to get up and fetch his earplugs from his gigbag, but even with the earplugs he could still hear them, so he focused on running the Gypsy scale up and down in his mind in all twelve keys until the notes thickened and grew feet and strapped on heels, which they pressed into the base of his throat and the elephant flesh of his scrotum so that he could barely breathe, and he gazed up at the nimbus-ringed head to find it was she, God, and she looked like Kyoko and all the rest of her, and he didn't want to touch her so much as just lie there and venerate her, do her bidding, whatever it might be, and if it was to have his balls stood on, then he was honored to lay them out for her. She hocked a loogie on his face and pressed her stiletto into his neck till she'd punched a hole clean through and all he could do was to smile deliriously as his lifebreath came whistling out...

•

Brain awoke to Theo tugging on the hairs of his forearm.

"Dudes, what do you say we go hit a club? Get us some slanty poontang?"

"It's Sunday night," Nick yawned.

"So?"

"Where's Matt?" Brain asked.

"Went out. Said he had work to do."

"I was thinking about going for a walk," Brain said.

Theo sneered. "A *walk*? Since when do you go for *walks*?"

"What's wrong with walking?"

"Nothing, in principle. It's just I have this suspicion that you don't really want to go for a walk so much as you just *don't* want to go out and get laid. Or rather that you *do* want to get laid, but you're scared you'll get shot down again the way you did in Montreal. Maybe I'm wrong, but if I'm not, then you need to get over that shit real fast, Brain. I told you, my cousin used to be stationed over here and he says any half-decent-looking American can go to this place called *Rope*...something or other...I wrote it down, anyway there's a bunch of bars supposedly and all you have to do is like show up and smile a little and the next thing ya know you're gazing up some model's asshole."

"In that case, I think I'll definitely pass," Brain said, standing and making for the bathroom.

Theo followed him. "What the hell's that supposed to mean?"

"What? I'd rather go for a walk is all."

"Than gaze up a model's asshole? Are you gay?"

"No."

"'Cause I've been telling myself this story for some time now about how you're just shy and misunderstood, but if you're gay, Brain, that's cool. I've got plenty of gay friends. I'm cool with you guys. I used to do theater for Christ sakes."

"I'm. Not. Gay," Brain said.

"Then why in God's name do you not want to peer up a model's asshole? Explain it to me, please, because I really don't get it."

Brain found refuge in the bathroom and locked the door behind him. He slipped his feet into the designated toilet slippers and sat to pee.

"What do you want, Brain?" Theo asked from outside the door. "Love? 'Cause dude, if that's it, I'm down with love. What do you think I hold onto Mary for?"

Mary was a spring breeze gently wafting honeysuckle.

Brain didn't reply. Why he couldn't admit to Theo that more than anything in the world he wanted sex, or love (or sex? or love?), he had no idea. After all, it would be in his best interest to have Theo's feelers out for him. But Brain hated handouts—e.g. his job at Nick's dad's pharmacy—and despite numerous attempts to destroy it over the years, there persisted in him a strain of romantic fatalism that didn't know how to separate the two, sex and love. But he did want to gaze up a model's asshole, didn't he? Did it really matter whether he loved its owner-operator or not? Flipping through his yearbooks in the heat of his anguished euphoria between sessions at his keyboard, he sometimes found himself licking portraits of the dumbest girls in school, girls that revolted him with their vanity, girls he could surely never love. And yet there they were in his fantasies, randy and sweating, pleading with him to perform unspeakable acts. *Lick the fucking bottom of my feet, you asshole. Yeah, like that. Take my*

pretty fucking toes in your mouth and suck on 'em. Yeah. Lick 'em clean.
Now stick your fucking tongue up my asshole, swish it around and make
me come. Oh yeah. Just like that.

No sooner would he towel off his abdomen than he'd hate himself
anew and recant the professions of love that had flowed from him a
moment before like so much semen.

The pressure of all that green tea threatened to rupture Brain's
bladder, but as long as Theo kept standing there, talking, looming,
his big feet casting shadows under the door, the floodgates refused
to open.

Fortunately, Theo didn't wait long for a reply. "Whatever. Nick,
you wanna go or what?"

"I need a shower first," Nick said.

"Fuck that," Theo said. "It's ten o'clock already and I don't see
Brain coming out of the closet anytime soon. Put on some deodorant
and a fresh shirt and let's get outta here. I have Altoids."

While Nick readied himself, Theo's harangue transported Brain
back to another foreign toilet he'd loathed himself upon not a couple
of months ago. They'd chosen Montreal for their first international
"tour" for no other reason than that Nick wanted to check out the
Jazz Festival and they could crash with their old bassist, Ish, who after
kissing his first girl a couple years back had transformed overnight
into a kind of hippy intellectual and soon thereafter quit the band
to take up French translation at McGill. Ish's lack of faith had cut
the others deeply then, but it had also afforded them a chance to
take stock and regroup (Matt had been wanting to divorce himself
from his essentially satanic vocal stylings anyway and could already
hold his own on bass; to fill the void, they'd agreed to recruit Theo
McCall, whose versatile larynx easily outshined the rest of Mixed
Ape, the crappy emo band he'd been playing the local circuit with),
so any hard feelings they might have had towards Ish had softened
into negligibility.

The night before their show—more of a no-show, as it turned

out—Ish had taken them to a dance club, and though the thudding, lame-brained music had prefigured for Brain a ghastly evening, some undeniable part of him had leapt up. He'd sat on a couch and ogled all the jiggling women until a particularly nerve-wracking one sat down not ten feet away. As always, he thought about doing the thing he never did and trying to talk to her, but then her chubby friend plopped herself down next to her like a sack of pink potatoes, and he was sure he'd lost his chance. But they didn't desert him the way they usually did, and it was this very sense of watching a regret harden before his eyes, combined with a Molson Triple X and the anonymity of being in a foreign land, that finally compelled him to leave his safety zone.

"Hi. I'm Brain. Do you speak English?"

"Sure do," replied the Sack. The angelic one looked around distractedly.

"Cool," Brain said. "Cause I don't speak French. So that's good that you speak English because it means that we can talk." *What a stupid thing to say.* "What's your…uh…what are your names?"

"I'm Rebecca," said the Sack.

"Nathalie," said the beatific one, and she gave him a fleeting, eighth-hearted smile.

"All right. Nice to meet you. I'm Brain. Did I already say that? Maybe I already said that." *How can one human being be so stupid?* "So…uh…where are you from?"

"We're from here," said the Sack.

"Oh, all right. I like it here. Me and my friends are from Philly." *Damn it. Bad grammar.*

"Philadelphia?" the Sack said. "I was there once when I was a little girl."

Brain couldn't believe the Sack had ever been very little, but anyway she was friendly, unlike this elusive other, the object of his deepest yearnings, who looked like she had somewhere else to be.

"So what do you do?"

"We don't do anything," the Sack replied. "We graduated last year and we were planning to travel around and see the world and stuff, but then we figured out that you need money for that, and so now we're like stuck wondering if we should get jobs or…"

He shut her out and concentrated on the heavenly one. He heard an adagio. His chest had windows that opened out onto a vast sea. "I'm in a band," he said, by way of a last-ditch effort.

And abracadabra, she perked to life, sat up, exerted enough energy to look him directly in the face. "What kind of band?"

His upper lip twitched. What kind of band? Could he possibly say "prog rock" without mortifying himself? "It's kind of hard to describe."

"What do you play?"

"Guitar, and keyboard, and I write most of the music and half of the lyrics."

She was still with him. "Are you big down there?"

Brain shuddered. *Did she really just ask that?* "Excuse me?"

"Are you big? What's your name?"

"Oh, it's Brain…formerly Brian."

"No, your band. What's your band's name?"

"Oh right." *What a friggin idiot.* "It's Agenbite."

"Hmm. I might have heard of you. How big are you?"

"We're…uh…we're big in Japan."

"Oh," she said, sitting back again on the couch and taking up interest in her fingernails.

Just then Nick returned with their drinks. "Sorry, fellas. I just had a run-in with some womenfolk. Speak of the devil, how do you do, ladies? To what do I owe the pleasure?" Nick took the girls' hands in his, kissed them, handed them back. The girls giggled.

"Got to go to the bathroom," Brain said.

"Too much information," Nick said. And the girls went on giggling at Brain's expense.

•

Three waves of chills and one squelched fart later, Nick and Theo went out into the Tokyo night, and Brain's floodgates opened at last.

He took a quick shower, donned one of the new outfits he'd bought expressly for this trip, including the first pair of *blue* jeans he'd owned since puberty—he generally went for black—and slipped into a new pair of sandals. When the elevator reached the ground floor, he headed out to the main road and walked left towards some blinking skyscrapers off in the distance. It was humid and spitting rain and the streets were smeared with reflected signboards and vending machines. He passed a 7-11, which was oddly *un*-odd, and made a right and continued walking towards those blinking beacons, but except for a few new cars zipping by (Was there a single used car in this whole country?), a couple of slickered mopedists and the churning of the odd laundromat, the street was eerily inert. Then four silhouetted nymphs stepped out of the fog, school nymphs by the looks of it, and as they approached, he could make out the bleached-blonde hair and the socks bunched up around their ankles like leg warmers. He inhaled them as they shuffled past under their single umbrella, then he pivoted to keep them in view, but when they glanced back and subsequently quickened their pace, he got a kind of objective glimpse of his own creepiness and wrestled his attention to the pinkly blinking arcade they'd just come out of.

Back when Nintendo was the thing, Brain had played *The Legend of Zelda* until it frayed his nerves enough to make him blink compulsively, destroying his batting average. He hadn't played a videogame since, nor even wanted to until now. Arcades in the States were the sanctuaries of wayward adolescents and growth-stunted adults. But not in Japan. In Japan whole families gathered around these machines the way American families had once done around dinner tables. A couple of kids cheered on their grandmother who was scratching records like some dope turntablist. A sweat-drenched salaryman stood up on his mechanical horse for the homestretch. An androgynous infant reached over its mother's shoulder and tapped the head of a drum. A crane hooked a bloated frog. A curtain closed on a photo booth. There was even a guitar-playing game—"GuitarFreaks"—which Brain thought about playing but finally decided against, because the other thing this arcade had was girls, lots of them, and he wasn't about to mortgage whatever cool his foreignness might afford him. There was one girl especially, an awkwardly dazzling racecar driver with a face full of not-quite-humanizing pimples. Her friends cheered her on as she shifted into fifth, and while Brain was aware that she probably didn't speak English, he half-expected that she did, that everyone did. And so, drunk on his anonymity and flying in the face of reason, that heinous killjoy, he found himself anon peering into those amaretto eyes and saying, "You know you're really something," and she trembled, hid behind her hands and said, "No Engrish," but Brain stood his ground because he could see her reaction wasn't one of aversion but of fear, and for the first time ever he wasn't the weak one here. "It's okay," he said. "I don't bite," and she repeated, "No Engrish," and he said, "I saw you from across the room and I knew I couldn't leave here without talking to you," and she gave him her doe-in-headlights look while her friends, each attractive in her own right, formed a kind of emotional phalanx and drove him away.

Nevertheless, by the time he got back to the apartment, a triumphal march was still booming in his mind, if bone-scrapingly out of tune, because in overcoming his inhibitions, he'd stumbled onto this language problem, which was more of a doozy than he'd realized, and yet he knew that if only he'd had the proper words, she might have been his. And that decided it: first thing tomorrow he'd pick up a Japanese phrasebook all his own. He cradled Ibaneza and picked an unamplified falseta, but his burbling heart wasn't in it right now. It was still out there, at the arcade, in the misting rain, in *life*, and before he had a chance to resent himself, his shoes were back on and he was out the door, headed towards the train station, repeating under his breath, "*Rope*-something, *Rope*-something, *Rope*-something."

Roppongi. That had to be it. It was the only English name on the transit map that began with those three letters. He reached into his pocket and brought out a handful of change. Fifty-yen pieces had holes in their centers. One-yens weighed about as much as a breath or two. He bought a ticket at the English-speaking vending machine and boarded the train. It was twenty minutes to midnight.

When he arrived in Roppongi, he was primed for a vigorous nightlife. The smells and dimensions of city life were all new to him, and not uninvigorating in their own right, but Theo'd led him to believe this place would be crawling with ravenous women, and so far he found only a few stumbling drunks and an alley cat. He walked down what seemed like the main street, but it too was lifeless. Two blocks away a taxi ran over a manhole cover. Where was this enormous population Tokyo boasted of? But then it *was* Sunday night, and whether they celebrated the Sabbath or not, he supposed the Japanese still had to go to work Monday morning. He began to doubt whether this was the right place at all, even if it did seem to have a lot of vertically stacked, flamboyantly advertised bars and nightclub-type places. Then he spotted his first two Americans and knew this had to be it. They were coming out of a Starbucks. They wore civvies but had a military air about them. For a moment he felt a kind of affinity with them, the way a lion might for a zebra should they find themselves on Mars, but it didn't last more than a few seconds before turning to antipathy. These were the sorts of thick-necked All-Americans who'd have done just fine in Iowa or Texas or wherever the hell they'd come from. What did they have to come to Japan for? He knew these feelings of propriety for a country he'd been in just twelve hours were, on the surface, inappropriate, but they weren't on the surface, they ran deep. And so what if he'd only been here twelve hours? He'd been looking for this place all his life. And so what if those seeming compatriots turned out to be speaking German or something? He resented their being here all the same.

He reached the end of the street, crossed and doubled back. A blue-black club promoter in a khaki suit handed him a yellow flyer and said with what might have been a Jamaican accent, "You like Japanese girls? For Japanese is eight thousand yen, but for *gaijin* like you just four thousand. Best deal in Roppongi, guaranteed. You like titties? We've got all kinds of titties, big titties, little titties, any kind of titties you want. How about it? Four thousand yen."

"Will you take three thousand?" Brain asked, and the promoter said, "For you, okay," and Brain was just about to hand over the three bills when a souped-up SUV—spoked wheels, spoiler, simulated fish tank running floor to ceiling and visible through tinted windows— pulled up alongside the curb and a familiar voice cackled, "Holy fucking Christ, Brain strapped on some balls!"

Theo.

"We're blowing this pop stand. Get in."

Brain apologized to the promoter and squeezed in next to Nick in the back seat. At the wheel was some Japanese guy with meticulously ruffled hair and flipflops.

"Brain, meet Keith Tanaka. Keith, Brain."

"Hey, Brain," Keith said, without any trace of an accent.

"Keith grew up in Hawaii," Nick said. "He works for Raytheon." Keith looked about as much like a Raytheon employee as Nick ever had. "He's the guy I was telling you booked our gigs for us."

"He knows where we can get some cheap pussy," Theo said. "Are you wearing *sandals*?"

"So what?" Brain said.

Nick intervened: "Keith and I used to do teleconferences all the time back when I still had a job, but we never met face-to-face until five minutes ago."

"Probably never would have," Keith said, "if this guy could have kept his pen out of the company ink."

Nick chuckled, the smug bastard.

"Nick picked a good time to call," Keith said. "Today's the beginning of *Obon* so I don't have to go to work tomorrow. Do you know *Obon*?"

In their various ways, they signaled no.

"Big Japanese holiday. Everybody goes back to their hometowns for a week to greet the spirits of their ancestors."

"Which would explain why Tokyo's such a ghost town tonight?" Brain said.

"That and the fact that it's the middle of a Sunday night. But you'll see come tomorrow morning it'll still be pretty quiet."

"So in other words," Nick said, "Tomorrow night's about the worst possible timing for our gig?"

Keith sucked his teeth.

"Great," Nick said. "Ben will be thrilled."

"I'm really sorry about that. I'm Japanese *American*, you know. I've been living here a while, but I still think in terms of Labor Day and Memorial Day."

"We'll just think of this week as a warm-up for next week," Theo said.

"There you go," Keith said. "You guys wanna hear some Japanese hip-hop?" He pressed play without waiting for a reply.

Brain waited for the news about *Obon* to sink his disposition, but the promise of pussy was more than enough to buoy him. As far as songs went, he didn't like this one much. It was shamefully derivative, a sampled Smashing Pumpkins riff over the exhausted Canon in D chord progression, but the chorus was sung by a Japanese soprano in an English so broken his imagination had no qualms whatever about reconstructing it as a love song to himself.

They listened to another twenty or thirty minutes of this lovely garbage before anyone had the gall to comment. "Why do I keep hearing choruses in English?" Nick asked.

"Not English," Keith said. "Japanglish. Sense has nothing to do with it. Japanese just associate English with modernity. That's why a little girl can walk around in a t-shirt that says 'Crack Whore' or something and nobody bats an eye. Somebody's trying to pull something over on them, I guess, and they might get a few *gaijin* to snicker, but mostly they just end up showing how random language is, which pretty much defeats their whole purpose. It's like, everybody's getting Chinese character tattoos in the States these days—at least they were last time I was there—and they all think they're getting 'Strength' or 'Love' or 'Samurai,' but the tattoo artist could just as well be writing 'Contagious' or 'I Can't Read This' or something and nobody'd be the wiser. As far as they know, if it looks cool it is cool. And I'm not sure 'Crack Whore' looks any less cool than 'Ninja' or whatever."

"But a tattoo's just a picture though," Theo said. "A song *builds*. Like say I'm listening to a track by Wu-Tang and the Rza's dropping rhymes like a muthafucka over the verses and then the chorus comes along and suddenly this chick comes out of nowhere and starts singing in bad Japanese—not that I would know it was bad, but anyway—I'm gonna feel kind of robbed, ya know? The verse is supposed to get you hard so the chorus can suck you off. You leave me hanging like that, I'm gonna wanna go wreck shit."

"Yeah, I don't know," Keith said. "But while we're on the topic of sucking you off, welcome to Akebono-cho."

"What, here?" Brain said. This place was quieter than Roppongi even, a largely residential neighborhood by the looks of it, and not a stray cat to be found. Keith parked and they got out and he led them around the corner, and only now did Brain understand what type of establishment they were headed to. Neon signs buzzed, "NUDE GIRLS," and, "XXX."

"You're taking me to a strip club?" Brain said.

"Sort of," Theo said. "The interactive kind."

"What, a whorehouse?"

"Japanese call it 'fashion health,'" Keith said.

Brain exhaled through his nostrils. "I don't care what they call it."

"No need to worry," Keith said. "The girls are clean as a whistle and you're not allowed to have full-on intercourse with them anyway, just everything else."

"I thought we were going to a club?" Brain said.

"Think of it as a club minus the risk of rejection," Theo said.

"What about the risk of VD? Look, I don't want any part of this. You guys do whatever you want. There must be a train around here somewhere?"

"The station's a couple of blocks up that way," Keith said, and Brain began speed-walking in that direction until Keith continued, "but you missed the last train by an hour. Public transportation stops around midnight. Starts up again at five. You could take a taxi but you're probably better off just hanging out. Taxis over here are hella expensive."

"God damn it," Brain said.

"Look, why not join us?" Keith said. "Think of it as going for a massage. I felt a little weird about it myself at first. But it's really no big deal. It's a great tension-reliever. Japanese guys do it all the time. I'm here a couple times a month now."

"Brain," Theo said, "no one's gonna make you come with us if you don't want to, but I think it might be good for you, I really do." He looked to Nick for support, but Nick just gestured as if to say "leave me out of this."

Brain stood his ground, "I'm not interested." Even if he had been—and really he wasn't at all sure he wasn't—Theo's condescension would have barred him from admitting it.

"Well you can't say I didn't try," Theo said.

"We'll see you in exactly an hour then," Keith said, and he proceeded to lead Nick and Theo into what was presumably his favorite of these houses of ill repute. The sign read: "CLUB PINKY."

Brain lit a cigarette and circled the block. He tried not to imagine what was going on behind those wooden walls. Somehow the image of Keith defiling the natives didn't bother him so much. Keith had Japanese blood and a Japanese face, a Japanese mother and the Japanese tongue. But as far as Brains was concerned, what Nick and Theo were doing was a hair's-breadth from burning down villages and decapitating babies. Nevertheless, he soon found himself jerking off into a "Mr. Donut" napkin borrowed from the dash, and in the moments immediately preceding his ejaculation, he felt nothing so much as the sting of jealousy.

When he was done, he zipped up his jeans and went back outside to find a trash can, which took longer than one might reasonably expect. When he got back to the SUV, he reclined his seat, shut his eyes and thought—more rationally now—about Nick's enviable phallus, without which they most certainly would not be here.

One evening last month, Nick had shown up four cigarettes late for band practice and announced with a wobble that he wouldn't be staying. Brain had wanted to practice without him, but Theo and Matt had been all too willing to go lick Nick's wounds for him. "The hand's got a sore thumb," Matt said. "Let's go get a drink. We can practice tomorrow." Brain had very much wanted *not* to go with them, but the chance to see Nick in distress like this was too rare and precious a gift.

"All right," Nick began once they'd arrived at Maggie O'Shea's and drunk their first round. "So you remember me talking about my supervisor, right? Brooke? I know I told you about her."

Brain never forgot a woman's name. Nick had mentioned her exactly three times since taking the job at Raytheon a couple of years back.

"Well anyway, it's my very first day on the job and she invites me to lunch. We eat Italian and she toasts me aboard and I figure it's all in the normal course of things, right? But then the next day too, she goes and invites me to lunch again, and I'm all like, um…okay. But what am I gonna do, right? She's my supervisor. So we go and get

Chinese and talk more about the job. No big deal, right? But then Wednesday rolls along and one of my coworkers, this kid Sean, he asks me if I want to go get lunch with him, and I'm like yeah, right, because I do. But then wouldn't you know it, guess who comes by my cube at 11:30 and asks me out to lunch? So I'm like, o-*kay*, and I e-mail Sean and tell him maybe tomorrow. Think I had lunch with Sean the next day? Fat chance. So needless to say, I'm starting to find this a little odd, you know? I mean, other supervisors aren't taking *their* assistants out to lunch every day. I kept waiting for her to stop asking me, but one week rolled into two and two rolled into three, and by this point it was like completely taken for granted that we'd be going to lunch together. Naturally my coworkers, who I barely had a chance to get to know yet, were all like, 'What's going on with you and Brooke?' and I was always like, 'Nothing,' because as far as I knew nothing was. It wasn't like she was putting the moves on or anything. We ate lunch and talked about work mostly. What's more, she was constantly talking about her husband, Peter, who'd been her high school sweetheart and restored antique European dollhouses for a living. He even came out to lunch with us once and we got along fine."

Theo ordered some nachos.

"And it's not even like I was attracted to Brooke. She's kind of, you know, 'on the heavy side,' and she has absolutely nothing in the way of a chin. On the other hand, I must say, she's funny as hell. One time, I forget what she said, but we were in the middle of a crowded restaurant and she actually made Pepsi come shooting out my nose. And not only that, she's freaking smart too. She's the first girl I ever met that I don't feel I have to dumb down to in some way, you know? Did I tell you she was valedictorian of her class at Villanova? And that she knits most of her own clothing?

"So you know how the more you hang out with somebody, the less their looks matter in a way? Besides, it's not like Brooke's a dog. She's just not what I would call 'hot' exactly. I mean, I've always been into thinner girls, you know, but somehow Brooke exploded my prejudices or what have you and suddenly I found myself paying attention to the plus-size girls everywhere I went. And the sunken chin thing I got over pretty fast too. I've always been a boob man anyway, and there's nothing at all sunken about Brooke's D-cups.

"Meanwhile at lunch we were gradually starting to talk about non-work-related stuff. Politics and religion, haircare, that sort of stuff. Naturally we get to talking about music at one point and that's when Brooke came out with this amazing confession. Get this, the girl loves metal! Her favorite albums of all time? How about *Powerslave* and *Ride the Lightning*! I mean, come on, right? So after that it was like I really had to make an effort to keep reminding myself she was married. And to complicate things further, Peter and I were getting to be pretty good friends by this point. We got together for drinks sometimes and even went to see that Tool show together. But then back at lunch, Brooke was really starting to open up to me, saying how she wished she hadn't married so young, before she knew who she was and what she really wanted out of life. How she'd do anything to go back in time and do things differently. Then she actually ended up crying into her tortellini one day, and I was all like, 'Um … are you okay?' and I really didn't know what to do but it was killing me to see her cry like that so I just reached out and grabbed her hand and she sniffled a little and like magic her crying morphed into laughter. Then she went to fix her makeup in the bathroom and when she came back we had a couple of cappuccinos and she spilled her guts out to me even more, telling me what a parasite Peter had become over the years, how he worked as little as possible and blew hundreds of her dollars every month on beer and comic books, and how the only time she felt like herself anymore was when Peter went away to Austria or somewhere on one of his treasure expeditions, speaking of which, there was one coming up, and she'd never seen *The Godfather*, and did I have any plans for Saturday night?"

Matt stood them another round of hefeweizens, even as he drank only ginger ale.

"I knew I should say no," Nick continued, "but there was just so much hope in her voice when she asked it. A kind of cute nervousness too, like she'd had it on her mind for days and finally gotten up the courage to ask. So I did what most guys in my shoes would probably do. I told myself it was all perfectly innocent, that Brooke and I were just friends and friends did things like watch movies together on a Saturday night. And I went on telling myself that straight up till she showed at my door.

"She looked pretty hot, I'm not gonna lie. I was so used to seeing her in work clothes and contacts, but now she had on scrubs and a pair of glasses I'd never seen before. Neither of us was very hungry so I shook up some martinis and popped in the DVD, and we took our places on the couch and watched the movie for all of maybe two minutes before we ended up playing with each other's hair—mine's longer than hers, by the way—and then pretty soon we were good and soused and the rest I'll just leave to your imaginations."

Theo used the straight index finger of his right hand to fuck the curled one of his left. Matt adopted his they-know-not-what-they-do look. Brain felt sick to his stomach.

"But let me just say, and I'm not usually one to kiss and tell, but let me just tell you that I'd never done it with a married girl before, let alone an unhappily married girl, let alone an unhappily married *overweight* girl, but if you can forget about all the moral ramifications and whatnot, I'd recommend it to anyone. You become like an outlet for all their pent-up repression or what have you. I swear I've never seen a girl squirm the way Brooke did when I touched her. And moaning like some kind of beast in heat, and actually pleading with me to do this to her and that to her, very specific-like, and then before I knew it there she was, breasts jiggling and full-on slapping me across the face and biting my nipples and…well, you get the point.

"So the next morning I woke up feeling like shit. Okay, half like shit say. It was just so weird to look over and see my boss lying there all big and naked and married. I got dressed and left a note that I was running across the street for some coffee, and when I came back a few minutes later, there she was in the kitchen, dressed, and frying up some eggs for breakfast. We didn't say much as we ate and thank God she had a nail appointment or something because to tell the truth I couldn't wait for her to leave.

"Naturally things were all awkward at work Monday, but we had lunch together as usual. She kept apologizing for what happened, said she'd done a lot of thinking and decided that from now on we should just be friends, and I was like, 'Cool. Okay.' Truth is I'd been thinking the same thing anyway. So we kept our distance for a few days, I even had lunch with some other coworkers for once, and then Thursday, I think it was Thursday, I ended up staying late at the office, and Brooke did too, and inevitably, as everyone else left, a certain amount of tension developed in the air, a quiet-before-the-storm kind of thing, and sooner or later Brooke's head ended up in my lap and I was stroking her hair and one thing led to another and we went to her office and turned out the lights and broke our resolution and broke our resolution and broke our resolution some more. And that was pretty much the pattern we followed for the next year and change. Make a promise, then break it, over and over again, in the office, at my place, in a motel, and I'm not proud of this, but even in the marital bed once or a dozen times."

Brain's vision tunneled. Nick's voice came at him through a didgeridoo.

"Then, I don't know, we reached a kind of impasse. From the start I'd had reservations about getting involved with a married girl, let alone a married girl I worked under and whose husband I went to concerts with. I kept telling myself I had to be responsible and resist the temptation, but I don't know, I guess because we were seeing each other every day, nature just kept on taking its course, urging us to procreate or what have you. But then one day, I don't know why, maybe because things were getting too serious, I don't know, but I just sort of snapped out of it. It wasn't like I was about to steal Brooke away and marry her, so it got to be like what's the point, you know?

"Now you have to appreciate what a delicate situation I was in. I couldn't just stop seeing her. I worked under her for God sakes. If I broke the girl's heart, it was bound to backfire on me someday. So I decided that what I needed to do was to wean her so gradually and subtly that it would seem like she'd dumped me and not the other way around.

"The Monday after we got back from Montreal, Brooke and I went to the same Italian place where we'd gone on my first day at the company. She asked me about the trip and I made a point of playing up how much fun it was. I told her how great it was to see Ish again and how the jazz was so magnificent and reminded me why I'd taken up drums in the first place, and how I'd even lived up to my image for once and smoked a joint. Then after that I started ever-so-delicately turning her down for lunch, saying I'd found myself enmeshed in other people's plans. I also made a point of leaving the office right at five, saying we'd booked some studio time in August and were shifting into higher gear. When Peter left on the spur of the moment last Saturday for an auction in Budapest or somewhere, she called me up and tried to invite herself over, and this was really hard because she was obviously, you know, 'in the mood,' but I told her my brother Dan had come down from New Haven for the weekend and was staying on my couch. She kept asking, 'Is everything okay?' and I'd always be like, 'Yeah, yeah, everything's great. I've just been extremely busy lately.' I was even like patting myself on the back until yesterday morning when I came into work and there on my desk was an interoffice envelope with a note inside asking me to drop by Human Resources ASAP. There was no explanation as to why, but obviously it made me kind of nervous.

"So I went right up and was taken into an office by this disciplinarian, bulldog-type guy and he told me they were doing random polygraph tests and my number had come up. So I signed the consent form, as if I had a choice, and he hooked me up to this thing and started bombarding me with questions about drugs, and that's when I knew for sure the bitch had ratted me out.

"When he asked if I'd ever smoked marijuana, I said no of course and did all I could not to fidget or overblink or otherwise betray myself, and I think I might even have fooled the thing. But then, when he handed me a cup and asked me to fill it up to the line, I was stuck. I prayed that the THC had left my system, and I diluted my pee with water from the tap, but then this morning, the same guy came down to my cube and asked me to follow him. We went in his office and he told me he was sorry to announce that the results had come in positive and I was being excused from the company effective immediately. I had two hours to gather up my things and leave. I protested, saying what if it was a false positive, but he just said, 'Yeah, no, it wasn't one of those.' So I marched right into Brooke's office, but conveniently she was nowhere on the premises, which was a smart move because I was honestly ready to cut the bitch's tongue out. *You happy now that you've fucked me every which way?* That's what I was gonna say to her. But she was nowhere to be found, so all I could do was gather up my things and walk outta there and now here I am, unemployed."

Brain's jaw hung slack. Nicholas Benini—that selfsame chronic overachiever who'd profoundly influenced Brain's life by turning him onto music when they were in the ninth grade, who'd made the honor roll every year of high school *and* been the drum captain of the marching band, who'd won a full scholarship to Penn to study computer science and design his own video games while Brain was forced to take out unconscionable loans for four years at West Chester and a degree in psychology he didn't really want but which made his mom proud and was easy enough since he already had a working knowledge of most of the neuroses in his textbook, who'd graduated with a 4.0 and an unethically high-paying job at one of the nation's top defense contractors while Brain graduated with a 3.78 and no real career prospects beyond inheriting Nick's job at his father's drugstore, who in his two years at Raytheon had garnered not one or two but *five* departmental awards while Brain had garnered a quarter's raise, who'd shown up Brain in just about every area of his life while all the while looking cool *and* getting laid—that same Nicholas Benini had gotten fired! Brain took up his glass and hid a smile in the foam.

It wasn't a minute, however, before his joy began to putrefy. So what if Nick had lost his job? Big deal. Now he'd be able to do all the things he'd spent the last couple of years bitching about not having time for anymore. He could sleep in and read, catch up on movies and spend some of that ridiculous amount of money he'd saved up in so little time. What was the real tragedy here? Nick had traded his job for *over a year of sex*! Was that any reason to feel sorry for him? Since grade school Brain had nursed fantasies of sacrificing his life for a woman's love—Nick's deal sounded like a bargain.

Brain's own summer had been typically dull. He hadn't fucked anyone's wife at any rate. Rather he'd spent most of his time in the suffocating aisles of Good Guy Rx, shelving laxatives and enemas, hemorrhoid and arthritis creams, dandruff shampoos, petroleum jellies, finger cots, breast pumps and various other reminders of how frail and disgusting a human being is. One night he'd taken home a pack of rubbers just to see if they'd fit—they did, but by no means snugly.

At least he'd had band practice to look forward to—every Monday, Wednesday and Friday evening. Theo and Matt usually left after an hour or two to attend to their other lives, but Brain and Nick went on steering the music from crisis to crisis for hours until a kind of tonal aphasia set in, and for Brain there was an undeniable religiosity to those evenings such as he hadn't felt since swinging the incense as an altar boy back when he'd believed in all that. The music opened up a kind of interdimensional hallowed space right there between the PVC and the reels of heavy wire, and it was precisely these sessions of evensong, coupled with a heavy regimen of masturbation, that enabled Brain to bear up under the rest of life. But this new knowledge that Nick had been plugging his married supervisor all that time—*and* keeping it to himself—had the effect of profaning every last one of them.

"You know, Nick?" Matt said as they walked through Maggie O'Shea's parking lot back to the Range Rover. "Maybe instead of seeing this as a bad thing, you can try to see it as an invitation. Like maybe instead of building weapons, you'll find you really enjoy working with kids or, I don't know, fighting fires, or who knows what?"

"A missile defense shield is the exact opposite of a weapon," Nick said.

The very next afternoon, however, Nick called up Brain at the pharmacy to say he thought Matt had a point. "He's dead right," Nick said. "This time off is the perfect opportunity for me to reevaluate what I'm doing with my life."

"*Dead right*?" Brain said. "Can you say that?"

"So I've reached a decision. For the foreseeable future I'm gonna invest all my time and energy in this band. It's all I've ever really wanted to do anyway."

"*Dead wrong*, yeah, but *dead right*?"

"The first thing I propose is that we up the ante on rehearsals. I'm thinking four or five times a week from now on. Are you listening to me?"

"I've been saying we should go five times a week for years," Brain said.

"And you might think this is crazy, I know you're not real fond of traveling and what have you, but I've already talked to Theo and he's on board, so just promise me you'll think about it."

"How can I promise if I don't know what it is?"

"You know we sell the majority of our records in Japan, right?"

"I've heard that."

"And we get reviews left and right over there?"

"Uh oh."

"Will you just hear me out please? All we'd need is a month, two max. We have a name over there already."

"No."

"You haven't even thought about it."

"I don't have to."

"You aren't interested in expanding our market?"

"Just think how many people around here have never heard of us."

"Unfortunately, Brain, the kind of music you write has an audience over there that it'll never have here. We could play the local circuit from now until doomsday and we're never gonna be a household name. You *know* that."

"And I'm supposed to what, quit my job?"

"They can get along without you for a month. My dad won't care."

"And who do you suppose is gonna pay for this thing?"

"Ben."

"You're kidding me?"

"Do I sound like I'm kidding?"

"You've asked him about it?"

"It'll benefit him as much as us."

"You really think he's gonna spend a penny more on us than he has to? Remember how he took it when we told him we didn't love the cover art?"

"Think how many sales we could generate. We'd be doing him a favor. Besides, it's not like we'll be staying at the Four Seasons and eating blowfish every day. We'll camp out and eat baked beans if we have to."

"And what about Matt?"

"Matt's the sticking point. We'll ask him. If he says no, we'll get Ish to fill in. Can you imagine Ish turning down a chance to go to the

Land of the Rising Sun?"

Brain heard Mr. Benini's tasseled wingtips stuttering up the cellar stairs. "I gotta go do some work."

"All right, but just promise me you'll think about it, okay?"

Brain hung up. Mr. Benini topped the stairs looking like the stereotype of a mad scientist—white lab coat, bloodshot eyes, tousled salt-and-pepper hair. He'd always been nice enough to Brain, but like all fathers, he also scared the crap out of him. "How's showbiz?" he asked as he asked every morning before leaving exactly no space for Brain to answer. "You about set for a delivery run? Only three today. The Pointer Sisters." He meant the Hanover sisters, identical triplets, spinsters all, who lived in three separate row-homes all within a block of each other. Mr. Benini handed Brain three double-ply shopping bags filled with drugs, chocolate bars and adult diapers. "You play your cards right," he said, "you might get to poke one of those old gals one of these days. Course you'd have to scrape the cobwebs off first. Ha!"

An hour later, after escaping the arthritic clutches of Gert and Betty Hanover, Brain had found himself enclosed in the porch of Pauline, learning more than he ever cared to know about the 1973 Oil Shortage. When his cellphone rang, he seized the opportunity to take his leave, but poor old Pauline Hanover just nodded her steely blue eyes and went on talking to ghosts.

"Green light," Nick said.

"What?"

"It took some finessing, but I finally got Ben to agree. He's not gonna give us a *lot* of money, but more than enough to live on."

Brain reeled. He'd been sure Ben would find Nick's idea as asinine as he had.

"Seems he had the same idea himself a while back but decided the profits probably wouldn't justify the outlay. So I asked how he was able to estimate the profits with no experience to base it on, and he admitted that he couldn't with any degree of accuracy. So I got him to think long-term. Because even if this tour doesn't spike sales for this record—and I'm sure it will, how could it not?—but even if it doesn't, it'll still get our name out there, and word of mouth's the best kind of publicity there is so who knows what it'll do for our next record. Sowing seeds and what have you. I told him we don't expect much at all re compensation, just somewhere to sleep and something to eat. Think of us as your guinea pigs, I told him. All five of his bands do better over there than they do here, so if there's money to be made touring, I figure it behooves him to know. I said I'd even pay for some of it myself if I have to. He told me to let him think about it, but then not two minutes later he called back and was like, 'What the hey. You're on.'"

Brain felt a tingle of enthusiasm in his hindbrain and rejected it like so much charity. "How many times do I have to tell you no?" The tally was somewhere in the mid teens when Nick finally exhausted his plea.

The next morning, Brain had been lying on his Soloflex, inventorying his tiny store of knowledge about Japan (Nintendo, Sony, Yamaha, Loudness, *Ghost in the Shell*, Concerto Moon, Godzilla…) when Matt called to make his own crazy bid.

"Frankly," Matt said. "I thought Nick was off his rocker. Karen's six months pregnant. Lisa's barely a year old. How could he possibly expect me to just drop everything?"

"That's what I tried telling him," Brain said.

"But then last night I had this dream. Picture this. I'm standing at the lip of hell, only it doesn't look like hell, it looks like Center City, but I know in that dream-logical way that it's also hell. You know that city block Disney bought and dug up and didn't do anything with for years?"

"Sure." Brain had no idea what Matt was talking about.

"Well I look in there and instead of a regular old trench, it's this kind of sulphurous pit all roiling and smoking like a cauldron, and then I notice some movement between the flames and my dream eye zooms in and suddenly I realize that what I'm looking at is actually millions upon millions of cockroaches all burning up and squirming and struggling to climb on top of each other and out of the pit, but then every time they start scaling the sides they get hurled back and land on their backs and just lie there flailing their legs and broiling till they burst and blood goes flying all over the place, which when I look down it's all over my hands. And the weirdest part is that while these cockroaches are wriggling and dying, they keep calling out my name in this reedy chant, saying over and over again, 'Save us, Brother Matthew, save us.'

"And bear in mind that I never have dreams. Or if I do, I never remember them. So why should last night have been any different? Well I got to thinking about that, and I don't know how you feel about these things, Brain, but I happen to believe, as C.S. Lewis did … or E.B. White? … whichever one didn't write *Charlotte's Web* … that science will never be able to account for God because He exists outside of the universe, not as some measly fact within it. Do you follow me? It's like an architect who designs a house. Well he can't simultaneously be the architect of the house and a part of the house, right? A stairwell or a fireplace? On the same token, I don't think God just sits out there on his hands all day either while we're down here working our butts off. He gets *involved*, and sometimes he even goes as far as to reveal himself to us, either through Jesus Christ, or Scripture, or, as with Jacob and the Pharaoh and Joseph and probably a whole buttload of other people throughout history, through dreams. It makes sense if you stop and think about it, because what is a dream really if not a kind porthole between worlds? A window if you will. Which brings us back to that house. Even if the architect of the house can't physically be seen in the house he designs, he can certainly take a stroll past the window, can't he? So that's what my dream felt like—like God was strolling past my window. That's the only way I can think to describe it."

In the last one minute Matt had divulged more about his personal creed than in the two years since he'd found whatever it was he'd found, and Brain could hardly believe how loopy it all sounded. He'd been a Christian himself once, a Catholic anyway, attending mass with his mom and kneeling at his bedside asking God for things. Then at some point he'd become an altar boy because his classmates decided that that was the cool thing to do, and then Brain graduated and went to public high school and learned about Darwin and Einstein and Freud and met heathens who didn't sup on baby flesh, and then, week by week, he began finding excuses for *not* accompanying his mother to mass and *not* kneeling at his bedside and gabbing with God, though he never quite gave up asking for things in those mealy minutes before sleep (Jen Applebaum, Katie Clemens, Gwen Randazzo...), if only in a to-himself kind of way. Brain had outgrown Jesus like the plush Mogwai that was the first thing he'd ever bought with his own money. That Matt could actually grow *into* religion was a mystery of the first degree, especially since he was no idiot—even if he had only gone to trade school.

"Do you know what percentage of the Japanese are Christians, Brain?"

"I'm sure I don't," Brain said.

"Well I didn't either until I went online this morning and looked. Would you believe it's less than one percent? One percent of a-hundred-and-twenty-some-odd million? And the vast majority of them still practice ancestor worship? Now as a Christian I find myself faced with a choice. Do I just turn my back and ignore all these lost souls crying out to me for help? Or do I step up and do my part in securing their eternal salvation?"

Brain wondered at the state of mind that could make the leap from dream-cockroaches to real live Japanese with such stupefying aplomb.

"So I called up Karen's dad and told him about all this, about Nick's idea and the dream and how I was thinking of asking him for a month's leave if he thought he could manage without me for that long. I was sure he was gonna say no because we're due to wire a 7-11 in a few weeks, but all he said was that my first duty was always to my conscience and that if I truly thought this was what the Almighty had in store for me, then who was he to stand in my way."

Brain closed his eyes. "So you're saying you want to go then?"

"It's not a matter of what *I* want."

"This is not a trick question, Matt."

"I guess I have to say..."

"I friggin knew it. You're on their side."

"I'm on none but the Lord's side, Brain."

"And you're gonna what, give out pamphlets all day?"

"Not *all* day. Not while we're playing."

"Karen's okay with this?"

"Karen will understand that my first obligation is always to my Creator. I'd expect her to do the same. Look, Brain, for me this has more to do with *being* an instrument than playing one. I hope you guys will decide to go, but I'm going either way."

Brain sighed. "I don't friggin believe this."

"So anyway," Matt went on, "if you could just let me know as soon as possible so I can go ahead and book my flight."

Brain was the first to show at the practice pad the next evening. Nick came a few minutes later, descended from his high-and-mighty Range Rover and said, "Looks like it's gonna start pouring any minute," which struck Brain as the smuggest thing he could possibly have said since (a) no it didn't, and (b) the real issue here was Japan and Nick knew it as well as he did so why couldn't he just come out with it, the prick? But when Matt pulled up in his ichthus-slathered Dodge, bowed at the waist and said, "*Ko-nichi-wa*, Nick-*san*. *Ko-nichi-wa* Brain-*san*," Brain found himself wrestling an urge to press his thumbnails into Nick's eyeballs, and when Theo climbed out of the window of his twice-totaled Trans-Am and said, "Brain, what the fuck are you so goddamned afraid of?" Brain wondered at how much getaway time one might have after dropping a lit match in a Range Rover's gas tank. But for the time being, he settled on shushing his bandmates with such unbridled intensity that sequins of spit went dancing through the air about his head, and continued dancing well after he'd put his finger down.

"Dude, you're an asshole," Theo said.

Brain took a moment to let his pulse slow a few bpm's. "Look, I'm not happy about it, but I'll go. And make no mistake, I'm only doing this for the band. I don't give a fuck about you as individuals. And I'm not helping pack and make arrangements and crap like that. Okay? You all happy now?"

Shit-eating grins in three cardinal directions.

"Now can we please fucking practice please?"

"You bet," Nick said. And it was just in time too, for no sooner had they entered the warehouse than it began to pour outside. Which was all Brain needed: one more defeat to add to the litany.

Now here they were just a few weeks later, and who knew but that Brain was secretly kind of happy about it.

Brain might have fallen asleep in the SUV were it not for the castration thing. He straightened his seat and smoked two more cigarettes before Keith, Nick and Theo rounded the corner and got back in the SUV with him. No one said a word about what had happened in there and Brain didn't ask. They drove past the train station en route to the main road, and Brain happened to glance up and catch its name (Kannai), which name he then happened to commit to memory, to test himself on every few minutes until they got back to La Maison Blanche, to jot down on the back of the realtor's name card and tuck deep inside the guts of his wallet. Like yesterday, he had trouble getting to sleep, but less because of the external sound this time than the internal lighting—the ghostly, incandescent hope that one of these days his life might change.

•

Matt prodded them awake. "What time is it?" Theo mumbled.

"Almost five."

Nick sprang up. "We're supposed to be there by seven-thirty!"

"That's plenty of time," Theo said. "I need something to eat."

"I picked up some pizzas at 7-11," Matt said. "I hope you don't mind corn, mayo and hotdogs for toppings. I don't eat pork but it was all they had."

"What the fuck?" Theo said.

Nick called first shower and took it. Theo chewed his pizza like a farm animal. Brain asked Matt how his work had gone yesterday.

"Not at all bad," Matt said, "except would you believe I forgot to request literature in Japanese. I don't know whether I just forgot or whether I unconsciously assumed that everybody in the world could read English. All Japanese have six years of English in school, you know? Doesn't seem to mean anything though. They're whizzes when it comes to math and science, but language isn't their strong suit. You should see the percentage of pamphlets that make their way into the nearest trash can—which is actually pretty far away. Did you notice that? All these people and so few trash cans. Anyway I wish they'd just give them back to me if they're not gonna be able to read them. I've only got twenty-five thousand of these things to last me. It would seem to me the decent thing to do."

"The Christian thing," Theo interjected.

"Exactly," Matt said, without a hint of irony.

•

Marz was a respectable venue, could probably hold a couple hundred people at capacity. There was a bar upstairs and a nice-sized stage, which they took at precisely nine o'clock, per the schedule. The first band had been an all-Japanese punk outfit called God Awful— which they were, but in an impressively marketable sort of way. They'd brought in a couple dozen fans of their own, but Brain knew the chances these fans would warm to Agenbite were roughly nill. Indeed, by the time he finished ushering in their set with his newish melodic-minor rag(a)time waltz, the audience had dwindled to exactly nine, seven of whom wore glasses, all of whom (so it seemed, at least) had dicks. Keith was among them, cowering sheepishly and mouthing "*Obon.*"

With his fingers on autopilot, Brain got to wondering whether some correlation didn't exist between the smegmal musk in the air and his own disinclination to bang his head, whip his hair around, lick Ibaneza's neck or otherwise fan his plumage. Would fairer pheromones improve his showmanship? Agenbite had occasionally had women in its audience, but never of a very feminine variety. Could it be that in spite of all his lofty notions of art and beauty, these songs themselves were really nothing but plumage? That even when he told himself the objective of his work was to demonstrate set theory or evoke Pandemonium, each song was really just an appeal to the opposite sex? That, like KY Jelly, the sublime existed solely for the sake of easing procreation, and if you regarded it as valuable in itself then you deserved your premature crowsfeet and irritable bowels? That, for all your brilliance as a composer, if your audience didn't have a poontang, then you were a perfect failure as a man?

He'd had such thoughts before, so often in fact that they were more like itching truisms than thoughts, and as soon as he went to scratch one, his ring finger flinched from the scored C to some microtone closer to C-sharp, and since the song they were playing— an alternating 6/8-7/8 trip-hop flamenco jig entitled "Neverafter"— was almost entirely in the key of A harmonic minor, a C-sharp was like a slice of onion in a bowl of ice cream, and he knew it would take weeks to forgive himself.

Or would it? Had this happened a week ago in Philly, he'd no doubt relive the failure a thousand times a day in his mind's eye and it would haunt him in his sleep like some wraith or boogeyman—

he'd never yet rated a succubus—but for once Brain sensed some space between himself and his discontents. In the course of his adulthood, hope had rarely lasted an hour, but this last rush was now a couple of days old and showing little sign of wear. Not even this pitiful gig could bring him down, for even if there weren't any in this particular "live house" at this particular moment, women the likes of which he'd never seen swarmed the megalopolis beyond the door.

•

The next morning, he dropped by a bookstore for a phrasebook, got back on the train, suffered the million little heartbreaks of beautiful girls bound for other places, and finally arrived in Kannai. Curiosity had racked him since the other night, but he couldn't very well show his hand and *ask* Nick and Theo about it. In any case, it was to healthy curiosity, and not soul-withering loneliness, that he ascribed his first visit to Club Pinky.

Behind the counter stood a youngish dude, nineteen or twenty at most, in an Armani suit and dark shades. Coiling from his scalp were these snakelike dreads that made Brain think right away of Cerberus, the three-headed, serpent-maned dog about whom he'd once written a—dreadful, in retrospect—song ("Fetching Styx").

"Umm...how much is it?" Brain asked, eyeing the curtain— white moon on blue background—that hung between him and whatever was back there.

Cerberus pulled out a laminated menu with an unfeasibly breasty silhouette reclining in its upper right-hand corner, the words "Enjoy hot times with excitement mentality," and a pricelist in Japanglish. Brain was in luck. Today being Tuesday, he was eligible for the "summer special fare" of ten thousand yen/hour—three thousand yen cheaper than the "always price" his bandmates had had to pay for their wee hours .

"I'll take one hour," Brain said.

Cerberus took out a photo album and handed it to Brain. Each page showed a girl in some beguiling stage of undress.

"What? I can pick any one of them?" Brain said, more to his incredulous self than to Cerberus. The girls were so unanimously desirable that he could barely tell them apart. At length, he opted for the one with the mole on her upper lip.

Cerberus helped Brain find the proper bill in his wallet. Ten thousand yen—about a hundred bucks. It didn't *feel* like a hundred bucks though. It wasn't even green. Brain handed it over and Cerberus deposited it in the cash drawer. Then Cerberus pulled back the moon and showed Brain inside. "Please wait," he said. Brain found himself in a longish corridor with rooms on either side, like a doctor's office but dimly lit and smelling of incense. By and by a form appeared at the end of the hall and floated towards him like an apparition.

"*Haro,*" she said.

"Hello to you," Brain said.

She extended an agile underhand. "America?"

"Yes."

"Can speak Japanese?"

Brain shook his head like some white-bread American who couldn't speak Japanese. "Can you speak English?" he asked.

She made the universal gesture for "a little bit," then said, "Please take off your clothes."

Brain balked. "Take off my…?"

"Must take shower."

So Brain unfastened his watch and put it in his pocket. Then he took off his shirt and felt scrawny and cold. She took the shirt and looked at him like *Come on already* and so finally he took a deep breath and undid his jeans—pausing, nodding his head, continuing—and as the waist of his boxers traversed the frontier, he could feel that he was already erect. He concealed himself with his hands, lamented that he could, and finally let go. It had occurred to him that some of these Japanese guys must have even smaller dicks than he did, and she'd be used to seeing them, so maybe he needn't worry. In any case, she didn't do a double take or vomit or anything. She led him over to the shower, pulled back the curtain and turned on the water, tested it with a long denuded foot. He drew back as the water scalded his hairless chest, but when she slipped off her robe and stepped in with him, he forgot all about what pain was. "First time?" she asked, and Brain shook his head *Of course not*, and she steadied it and massaged shampoo into his hair. "*Too* long," she said, and Brain blushed, decided to cut it ASAP. Her rosy nipple kissed his bicep and he had to remind himself that this was actually happening, right now, in the world outside of his head. He got to thinking there was almost something *un*erotic about living out your fantasy—because even in the throes of ecstasy, you still had to be boring old you—but then she squeezed some lotion onto a loofah and sudsed his cock and balls and her lithe brown-white skin shut off his mind entirely. Next thing he knew, she was handing him a towel.

She took him to a room just large enough for the bed she laid him down on. Dim lights glowed against russet walls. A mirror ball dangled from the ceiling. Music. She reached over to the nightstand and set a timer, and then, like it was the most natural thing in the world (Was it?), she mounted him, straddled his skinny thighs and asked, "Do like Japan?" and he mumbled something logoplegic. Without waiting to clarify, she kissed him, sans ceremony, not knowing that Brain had been waiting all his life for this, practicing on his fist and elbow pit. But now that the time had come, it felt so natural, like drinking water from a fountain. *This is happening*, he reminded himself again as her tongue wrote runes on his neck and his body deliriously trembled. She took his cock in her hand and began to jerk him off and her hands were narrow and long and he rejoiced to see the tip of his dick extend past her fingers because he'd worried that it wouldn't. She jerked at his root and massaged the head with her thumb, and Brain remarked to himself that of course she couldn't do it as well as he could, he'd been at it for fifteen years, but then she proceeded to do something he couldn't do. She enveloped his testes in her mouth, one at a time, sucked on them like hard candy, and something began to well up in him, cum certainly, but something else too. And then, at long last, in Brain's twenty-fourth year, a girl inserted his penis in her mouth, and in spite of Brain's most earnest protestations (*Come on, man, anything but that*), he began to sob. She spit out his dick and asked, "Okay?" And he said, "Yes," and she checked the timer and turned herself around and hung her pussy just over his nose and Brain began to sob even harder, tears streaming down his face, his whole body heaving. *There is a beautiful blossoming pussy not two inches in front of my face.* He breathed it in and it was so *there.* He touched a finger to it, unrepelled, then raised his head off the futon and put his tongue to it, sampled her God honey, and she made a little whimpering sound, and he cried an adolescence-worth of tears, lapping hard and fast at this Oriental dam while all the while mouthing, autonomically, *I love you I love you I love you,* hands gripping the soft soles of her feet, and she paused to brush the hair out of her face, then went back to bobbing her head on Brain's life-force until she'd taken him past the point of no return and he felt the backward sensations along his shaft, his toes curling, his scalp bristling, and he quaked with crying as her tongue pumped the pain out of him.

After Brain's ninth strikeout in a row, he'd agreed to see his mother's optometrist. Leaving the office with his first pair of corrective lenses suctioned to his eyeballs, he'd marveled at the oak tree slouched over his mother's Buick. It was just a plain old oak, nothing out of the ordinary, but it had been months, maybe years, since Brain had seen a tree as anything more than a single gauzy entity, and these magical lenses revealed anew the complexity of the tree, the wormholed leaves, the woody acorns, the variegated bark—worlds within worlds within worlds. Leaving Club Pinky felt something like that. Shadows had lifted. Shapes had shifted.

Things are going to be different from now on, he told himself. They already were.

•

The gig that night saw a slightly higher turnout, if only because Budweiser Carnival was foremost a restaurant. Couples shouted sweet nothings over pitchers of beer, fried or skewered meat-looking things and an hour and a half of balls-to-the-wall prog while micro-skirted waitresses flitted about the room taking orders and heralding newcomers in unison. Theo was chronically off-key, Nick tied his kit in knots, Matt's frets buzzed, but Brain was in top form. He'd stood stock still for the first verse-chorus of "Jizmopolis" (lyrics by Theo), but when it came time for his solo, his body had surprised him by stepping into it like a tennis player. *Where'd that come from?* He certainly hadn't planned it. And it didn't seem to have anything to do with the audience's poontang either. Indeed it was with no discernible motivation that he then began to rock from the ball of his right foot to the ball of his left and back. And there didn't seem to be any accounting either for his trading in his hard-won efficiency-picking technique for a reckless go at windmilling. He'd never tried it before, not a single guitarist he admired did it, and yet here he was whipping his arm around and gaining momentum, slamming his knuckles into strings and drawing blood. He hit any number of wrong notes, but he wrung the blue life out of them until they had no choice but to be right. His bandmates looked alternately bemused and annoyed, but the set continued and Brain's drunkenness intensified despite his single Bud Lite. He licked Ibaneza's neck, dropped to his knees, chugged the rest of that single beer and took the sweaty bottle to the strings and made them weep. And the funny thing, the ironic thing, was that the louder his instrument wept, the less *he* wanted to, the higher his risibles rose until soon he'd laughed his consciousness right up into the smoke that swirled around the stage lights.

"What the fuck came over you?" Theo asked after the show.

Brain shrugged.

"We've been playing music together how long, Brain?" Nick asked. "Ten years? And I've never seen you so much as smile on stage before."

"Don't get me wrong," Theo said. "I'm actually kinda proud of you for once."

"You were slain in the spirit," Matt said. "I don't mean that literally. At least I think I don't. But there was definitely an element of rapture to what you were doing up there."

Brain considered confessing the real nature of his inspiration but knew that to fall in love with the first girl who ever sucked you off was an indefensible folly—at least as far as Nick, Theo and the old heathen Matt were concerned. In the abstract, Brain didn't love the idea either, but then there was nothing abstract about this girl—one of her concrete silken pubes was caught in his throat right now.

•

Brain slept soundly and rose with the sun. He tiptoed past his sleeping bandmates—he'd even beaten Matt to consciousness for once—flipped through Nick's guidebook on the kitchen table, quietly got himself ready and went out into Tokyo.

After a few wrong turns, as many cigarettes, a rice ball and a can of coffee from a convenience store, Brain arrived at Citibank. He withdrew three hundred dollars worth of yen from the ATM, which, including Ben's paltry stipend, was about half his life's savings.

He studied his phrasebook in the train, going over long strings of romanized small talk, straining to make some of it stick. Cerberus was working the counter again. Brain requested an hour, and it was only when Cerberus handed him the photo album that Brain remembered he had a choice in the matter of whose vagina he sucked on. It amazed him now, flipping through the pages, that just yesterday he'd found these girls so interchangeable. They were lovely all, but like so many strangers in a train station while he waited for a loved one. He dodged and elbowed his way through to the fifth page, and as soon as he spotted her, a hot liquid flooded his extremities. He handed over a large bill.

"*Haro*," she said. Brain leaned in to kiss her, in the fully clothed, European way, but she retracted her head, coyly, and so he stripped like someone who'd been coming here for years, and she led him hand in hand to the shower.

"How are you?" Brain asked while she ran her fingers through his too-long hair.

"I am fine. How are you?"

"*Onamae wa nan desuka?*" Brain asked.

"Oooh. You can speak Japanese. My name is Miho."

"Mi-ho," Brain repeated to himself, thinking *What a lovely name*, knowing it could just as well have been Herpes or Chlamydia and he'd have found it no less lovely. "My name is Brain," he said.

She pointed to her head, and Brain said, "Yes, like that kind of brain. It's a long story. I'll tell it to you sometime." He hoped he would.

She handed him his towel and led him into their room. Little talking followed, and even that was muffled and incidental. Brain had meant to save a few minutes at the end of their session, but after ejaculating in Miho's mouth, he'd plunged his tongue headlong into her asshole, that holy asterisk, lapping at it like a dog at a fresh wound, and Miho shuddered a little, did nothing to discourage him, and then as soon as he felt himself growing hard again, the damned buzzer sounded on the night table and she stood up like a businesswoman late for a meeting and said, "Shower." There was little talking in the shower too because Brain was so preoccupied with frotting himself against Miho's thigh—it came as instinctively as kissing had—aiming for her seam, though she steadfastly crossed her forearms and said, "*Da-me*," which, he later learned from his phrasebook, meant what it sounded like: "useless, hopeless, no good."

At the Imperial Palace and the sumo match, over yakitori on a park bench and ales at the Outback Steakhouse, Brain had to gulp back the good news about his penis. He jerked off to Miho in two public restrooms, but each time, as soon as he spilled his seed in the general direction of those porcelain troughs that sometimes passed for toilets in this country, visions of Miho's trembling haunches yielded to imaginings of the broken home she must have grown up in, the abusive father, the suicidal mother, the poverty. He couldn't even begin to imagine all the factors that might drive a beautiful young woman like Miho to do the kind of work she did.

The next morning he made a point of coming quickly (no trouble there—he usually exerted his energies in trying *not* to come). "You must hate doing this kind of work," he said.

Miho tilted her head.

"This work. This … umm … *shigoto*."

She nodded comprehension. "*Mm-mm-mm*," she hummed. It was three notes—B, G, A, falling and then rising—but whether it meant yes or no, Brain hadn't a clue.

"You can't … err … do you like it?"

She nodded once, unequivocally.

"I mean, not work in general but this particular job."

She tilted her head again.

Brain kept consoling himself that she must not understand the question, but when he asked whether it wasn't disgusting to service some of the older clientele with their wrinkly dicks and B.O., she seemed to take offense and insisted that "*Old mens is very nice*," and finally he was forced to give up his illusions. Miho did this job because it paid well and was more "fun" (her word) than the part-time jobs most of her friends had. By the end of his session, through cognates, simple utterances and all manner of gesticulation, Brain had gathered that Miho was just two years out of high school and that she told her parents she worked at a clothing store in Harajuku, a youthful section of town where they were sure never to visit.

He kissed the top of her head goodbye.

•

"Where'd you go?" Nick asked when Brain got back to La Maison Blanche.

"Walk."

"What is it with you and all this walking shit all of a sudden?" Theo asked.

"I don't have a car. If I had a car, I'd be driving."

"Yeah, I bet you were out there paying to get your little pee-pee drained."

Brain might have flinched—he wasn't sure—but either way, Theo's wager was enough to compel him to take a couple of days off from Club Pinky. Besides, he wasn't in an especially healthy financial situation, which was why he'd have to get up the nerve to ask Miho out sooner rather than later. He'd spent the train ride wincing at her admission that she'd chosen her line of work of her own free will. But more troubling still was that rather than to sully Brain's opinion of her, this fact only seemed to heighten her mystery quotient, her essential otherness, and he wanted her now in a way that was more than just physical, and not merely "mental" or "spiritual," but cannibalistically entire.

•

Agenbite played the last of their *Obon* gigs at a place called Earthdom. They made sure to keep their expectations in check, and though the turnout was the saddest yet, they did manage to put on a good show. Brain acted out his inner life again, but in a muted way, taking care not to upstage the rest of the band like last time.

In their time off, they sang through the annals of hard rock in karaoke booths and explored the indigenous music via listening stations at the big, endangered record stores. Most Japanese rock music was plainly derivative, if backdated by fifteen to twenty years, which, to its credit, meant that guitar solos wailed their way into even the most accessible of pop tunes. They ate their meals at Denny's and TGIFridays mostly. When Brain suggested they try a conveyor-belt sushi restaurant, they all reeled in surprise.

"*You* want to eat sushi?" Nick said.

"What's so weird about that?" Brain said.

"Nothing," Nick said. "It's just remarkably normal for you."

Brain knew what he was getting at. Back in Montreal he'd felt a little out of his element, and when Ish and Nick had tried force-feeding him a local delicacy called *poutine*, he'd lashed out and discus-ed the plate across the pizzeria, where it shattered on the floor, hushing the dining room and making the day of someone's seeing-eye dog. And *poutine* was just glorified cheese fries. As a rule, Brain didn't think much of fish even when it had been cooked, but what with Miho's absence, the idea of chewing on some raw pink animal flesh didn't seem so unappetizing all of a sudden.

•

Sure enough, the unapologetic fishness of certain sushi did trigger Brain's gag reflex, but he managed to swallow everything except the sea urchin, *uni*, which Nick and Theo liked just fine, but which Matt spit into the wet towel they gave you to wipe your hands with, and which Brain himself insisted on calling *uhu* after the brand of glue stick he'd once sampled in grade school (on a dare, Anne Lacewell looking on), though Keith informed him that *uhu* was already the Hawaiian name for Parrot Fish. It took Nick a full two hours to buy a digital camera in one of the superstores of the electronics district because they'd gotten so caught up in testing out different types of stereos and watching Japanese girls leverage chopsticks between their g-strings and buttocks and snap them in two on dozens of cutting-edge TVs. Matt resisted Nick's suggestion that they go check out some Buddhist temples and Shinto shrines, so they waited until he went out proselytizing before visiting some of the don't-misses and must-sees. Nick read to them from his guidebook: "The bell is rung one hundred and eight times at the new year, representing the number of worldly desires the bell is said to push away... Sacred objects of worship that represent Shinto gods, or *kami*, are stored in the inner sanctum where they cannot be seen by anybody." They then went to the Tokyo National Museum, which was as boring as any museum, except for the handscroll paintings of the hungry ghosts. According to the signs, these hungry ghosts, or *gaki*, were denizens of one of the Buddhist hell realms. They had mountainous bellies and needle-thin necks that made it physiologically impossible for them ever to sate their hunger. In each of the scrolls, the ghosts—humanoid if distinctly ratlike, with knobby knees, jutting ribs, and more often than not, long hair—could be found squatting in latrines, trying and failing to gorge themselves on human waste.

At Theo's request they went to a porn shop, another attraction Matt had refused to visit. Unbelievably, though it boasted actual sections for bestiality, uro- and copro-philia, and what at least seemed like pedophilia—though you could never tell with these Japanese women, who aged so bewilderingly well—all the naughty bits were scrambled. Despite Brain's objection to the lovelessness of it all, his loins raged. If he squinted enough he could glimpse shades of his inamorata in every one of these spread-eagled starlets, and seeing her with all these faceless, better-hung pornstars confirmed for Brain what he'd long suspected: that there was a natural comorbidity between sexual appetite and sexual jealousy, between the desire to fuck and the desire to kill.

•

The next morning, he withdrew the last of his cash and pestled his angst in the mortar of Miho's adorable, snaggle-toothed mouth. After coming, he engaged her in ever deeper conversation, finally mustering the balls to ask, in his embryonic Japanese, whether she would care to have dinner with him sometime. But Miho just crossed her arms in an X and said, "*Da-me*," as she'd done when he tried to ball her in the shower. With her head she indicated the corner of the room and only then did Brain notice the tiny square cut out of the mirror ball and the point of red light peering out like a bat from its cave. The idea that Brain's entire sexual history had been captured on video didn't bother him as much as it might have. He was glad at least to have a history to capture.

He saved the rest of his plea for the shower: "Look, Miho, I'm out of money. I can't possibly pay to see you anymore." He spoke slowly and she seemed to get his meaning. "Please, can I call you sometime?" he asked, holding his thumb and pinky to his face like an old-school telephone. But Miho just did her *da-me* routine, and in words he hadn't composed beforehand but which were bound to come out sooner or later, he pled, "Miho. I love you. I love you and I want to see more of you. Do you understand? I *love* you." She looked stunned and a little scared. Her eyes widened and her arms fell to her sides. She inhaled to get breath for her reply and opened her mouth and readied her tongue and said, "*Da-me*." She stepped into her bathrobe and padded down the hall, leaving Brain to rinse out the conditioner all by himself.

Slinking out of Club Pinky, Brain was intercepted by Cerberus. "Excuse me please," Cerberus said, steering Brain behind the counter into the back office where an older dude sat at the head of a conference table gutting a tangerine with a fishing knife. He had long silver hair, pockmarked cheeks, and muscles big enough to keep him from looking ridiculous in his skintight black t-shirt.

"Mr. Brain, my name is Matsuo Kenji. I am Club Pinky's owner."

"Nice to meet you," Brain said, tentatively. Matsuo made a gesture like he'd shake one of Brain's hands if his own weren't so sticky. Brain didn't have to ask how Matsuo knew his name. No doubt the mirror ball had ears too.

"Please, take a seat. Do you want to drink a coffee or a tea or something?"

"No thank you," Brain said, taking the only seat there was to take.

"Mr. Brain, you are guitarist, no?"

Brain nodded.

"I am guitarist also. Maybe thirty years ago I am starting to copy *Disraeri Gears*.

I learn everything from that record. How to play blues, how to speaking English. You are a fan of Slowhand?"

"Slow what?"

Matsuo screwed up his face. "You are pulling my leg, no? Slowhand is nickname of Eric Clapton. It seems you are not fan."

"Not much of one," Brain admitted, wondering, *Is this why he brought me back here? To talk about Eric Clapton?*

Matsuo inhaled a slice of tangerine from the tip of his knife. Juice ran down his chin and he didn't bother to wipe it. "I understand you are fond of our Miho-chan?" he said.

Ah, Brain thought, *now we're getting to the meat of it.* "Miho and I have become good friends," he replied.

"I see," Matsuo said. "It's good, no? First principle of business is customer is king, no? But, Mr. Brain, you understand also that we need money to survive, no?"

It wasn't hard to see where this was going. "Sir, with all due respect, I merely asked Miho to have dinner with me."

"Tell me, Mr. Brain, why you are so wanting to have dinner with Miho-chan? You are handsome guy, no? Do you know Roppongi? Many Japanese girls is looking for American boyfriend."

"I've been to Roppongi," Brain said. "It's not really my kind of place."

Matsuo ripped a tissue from a box of them and finally wiped his chin. "You believe you are falling in love to Miho-chan, no?"

Brain wriggled. "I suppose you might say that."

"Then you are planning to be married with her?"

What the—? "I hadn't thought that far ahead."

"Well, Mr. Brain, please tell me what is so special? Miho-chan is very beautiful girl. Not so hard to fall in love. Many men must be falling in love to her. This is how Club Pinky can survive, no? Love is kind of addiction, no? Imagine if tobacco company is giving cigarettes for free, how they are going to survive?"

"With all due respect, sir, I only asked her to have dinner with me. I don't think you offer a dinner service here, right? So where's the conflict?"

"Mr. Brain, Miho-chan is not slave. If she wants to change works or get married or something, she can do it. But while she is working for here, I am afraid she must be obeying Club Pinky's policies. If I make exception for her, I have to make for everybody, and then how we can survive? I sincerely hope you can understand." He held out a gleaming wedge of tangerine on the tip of his knife. Brain didn't especially want it, but he lacked the balls to decline.

•

Over the next few days, *Obon* came to an end, Tokyo filled out again, and Agenbite braced themselves for their first full-blown performance. For all Keith's failings, he couldn't have managed this one better: Friday night, 10 PM, at the O-Nest, right in the heart of Shibuya. How then could Agenbite explain, peeking through the curtain at five minutes to the hour, the presence of a mere eleven heads in the audience?

"This is just great," Nick said. "Ben's gonna just love this."

"Screw Ben," Theo said. "You've gotta stop worrying about Ben all the time."

"You wanna be the one to tell him how the show went?"

"Make something up."

"I'll embellish a little, but soon he's gonna look on Soundscan and wonder why we're not moving more product."

Throughout the set, Brain's body remained inert, but his mind was running numbers. If Ben was to be trusted, Agenbite's debut album, *Inwit*, had sold approximately seven thousand copies worldwide, with another couple thousand partial downloads on top of that. According to Ben's pie chart, Japan accounted for some sixty percent of those sales, while the other forty percent were split almost evenly between the U.S. and Germany. In other words, not counting the cheap bastards who'd pirated it, a bare minimum of 4,200 Japanese owned a complete copy of *Inwit*, and another twelve hundred or so owned at least one track. Why then were there only eleven people in the audience tonight? And all of them (or so it again seemed) wielding cocks? He hadn't expected them to fill a stadium necessarily, but he'd been sure Theo would get to do some crowd-surfing. Not that he wanted him to, but Theo did live for that kind of thing.

"Japan's a big place," Keith said. "Maybe your fans are concentrated more in Hokkaido, where it's always cold and people are trapped in their houses listening to music all day. Or maybe it was 4,200 U.S. servicemen down in Okinawa who bought the album?"

Not that a better turnout would have inverted Brain's depression. In fact, he rather liked that it seemed to bring the rest of the band down to his level. He'd been three days without Miho, and while he jonesed for her like any addict for the object of his addiction, he did believe he was making some progress. He'd willed himself into paying attention again to all the other magnificent sluts sashaying about this city, and he was even planning to jerk off at the next available opportunity to a certain kimono-clad temptress he'd glimpsed picking a pebble out from between her right foot and her wooden sandal. He rickshawed her in his mind until just after the show when Nick, brooding, made the suggestion that they go hit Club Pinky, and Miho reclaimed her seat.

"I'm in," Theo said.

"I was going to suggest it," Keith said.

"Why don't you guys try some other place?" Brain urged. "For variety's sake."

"You gonna join us?" Theo asked.

"I'm just saying."

"There's plenty of variety at Pinky," Keith said. "They've got like twelve girls to choose from on weekends."

Twelve girls to choose from, and only one of them was Miho. Still, one of them was Miho. Supposing each of them went for a girl they hadn't gone for last time—not a foregone conclusion, but probable—that would leave them each with eleven girls to choose from. The odds that any one of them would choose Miho then was about nine percent, which yielded a twenty-seven percent chance that she'd be chosen by any of them at all. Of course, there were variables, like the wait time, and the mole on Miho's upper lip, which set her apart from the rest of the girls in the album. And let's face it, the odds that Keith, an avowed patron, had employed Miho's services by now, were pretty good. But Brain could live with that. He already lived with the notion that she must fellate at least a few Japanese every day. On the other hand, he could not, really could not, live with the idea that Theo or, God forbid—*Please, God, forbid it*—Nick might make a cuckold of him. Eighteen percent. One in five-point-five repeating. Only slightly worse than a round of Russian roulette, and the stakes felt every bit as high.

Brain let them go, and in the agonizing hours that followed, a bold and possibly crazy notion took shape in his mind. Matsuo wouldn't permit Brain to see Miho outside of Pinky as long as he was just another client. But suppose he had said yes, that he *was* planning to marry her?

Brain had long been aware of certain contradictory aspects to his personality. He was reasonably consistent on most things, as consistent as any human, but when it came to the fairer sex, it often felt as if he had not one but two brains, the Romantic and the Hedonist, and they didn't often get along. Never before had the split felt so robust, however, as on the question of whether or not he might conceivably ask Miho to marry him. As soon as he came down on the side of one of these brains, the other gainsaid it, and more than any suffering imposed by either brain was that of vacillating between the two, the dayslong friction wearing down on his fundamental self, on *Brain*, until all that remained was this maddening debate:

THE HEDONIST: *Marriage? Who's thinking about that? She's your first girlfriend for Christ sakes. Look around. There's so much more where that came from.*

THE ROMANTIC: *But with Miho it's not just about the sex. Strictly speaking, you haven't even* had *sex yet. But there's this spiritual connection there you've been looking for all your life. You had to travel to the other side of the world to find this girl. Don't blow it.*

THE HEDONIST: *This is just a trap women pull. Emitting some opiate in their pheromones to get you to give them a baby a year while you're supposed to be out there making a hundred a day. Biologically speaking anyway—the last thing you need right now is a kid. Responsibility is something you take on if you absolutely must. You don't sign up for it. Besides, a woman doesn't love you after the kid's born anyway. All the cooing and the batting of eyelashes, the cooking and cleaning, it's all in the service of getting you to give them what they want. After that, you're only as good as your next paycheck. And you might as well forget about your dreams. The last thing a woman needs is for the father of her child to be out touring the world with his rock band, debauching groupies. Sounds good though, doesn't it?*

THE ROMANTIC: *How will you ever be able to act in this world if you don't learn to stop overanalyzing everything? The fact of the matter is that being with Miho feels good. Why not leave it at that? Embrace your humanity for once. You've been searching for this girl your whole life, and now that you've finally found her, are you really gonna pay heed to all this bullshit machismo? Do you really think you could go back to driving around at night believing there's something spiritually meaningful in your loneliness when you've already found your soul's true companion and let her go? So many people go their whole lives without finding what you've got right in front of you. Be honest with yourself. You're not some soulless playboy. Ask this girl to marry you. There's no guarantee she'll say yes, but at least you won't have any regrets.*

THE HEDONIST: *Now you're pissing me off. You drive around at night because you're addicted to nicotine. Take the long view. Do you really want to be imprisoned by one woman for the rest of your life the way your dad was? Look at him. Is he happy? Middle-aged and good as dead. And a gelding for how long? The promise of sex with a new woman is the thing that makes a man get up in the morning, its fulfillment his greatest joy. Do you really want to give that up? Martyr yourself for what? There are ways to love a woman without signing a contract and it's not like you're in a rush to procreate, so why rush into this thing? Slow down, mull it over and see if you can't eat some pussy in the meantime. At the very least sow your oats, damn it. Otherwise you'll never forgive yourself.*

THE ROMANTIC: *That's just your ego talking. If it's regret you're interested in, go ahead and let this one get away…*

And so on and so forth, ad nauseam and a whole brochure of other ills, viz. insomnia, dry mouth, heart palpitations, hyperventilation, dizziness, loss of appetite, indigestion, irritable bowels, chest pain, jaw ache, clenched fists and the possibly paranoid, certainly unsubstantiated, conviction that his best friend of over ten years had lately dipped his overachieving penis in some humid lagoon of his girlfriend's body.

•

It didn't help things when Nick got off the phone Sunday morning to inaugurate a countdown. "Well, looks like we might as well start packing our things."

"What?"

"Ben's pissed. I stretched the truth a little and told him there were about thirty people at the show, but he still went ballistic, saying what a waste of money this whole thing was turning out to be and how he was about ready to call the whole thing off. I narrowly convinced him to give us one more show, but if we don't get a decent turnout this time, he says he's gonna wash his hands of the whole thing. He'll fly us home but he's not gonna give us another penny to 'beat this dead horse with'—his words."

Agenbite's next gig was scheduled for Tuesday evening, which, unless they could somehow recruit legions of fans between now and then, left Brain less than three days to chart the course of his adult life.

Ben hadn't given them an advertising allowance, and publicity wasn't exactly forthcoming, so Nick designed some flyers on his laptop, took the disc to Kinko's—they had those over here too—and had ten thousand of them printed up.

They spent the next three days festooning the city, each taking his own route. Nick lit out for universities, phone booths and music stores; Theo for nightclubs, restaurants and bars. Matt folded his into the pamphlets he disseminated. And Brain took to the trains and subways, once going a molelike six hours without a UV ray and resurfacing in the garish late afternoon of Nakano Shimbashi feeling like his head might be glutted with someone else's feces. It so happened Matt was there braying scripture just outside the turnstiles.

"How'd it go?" Matt asked.

"I'm not feeling too great if you wanna know the truth," Brain said.

"Could be allergies. I know mine have been acting up. You'd think in a city with so few trees like this, there'd be nothing to worry about, but I guess there are other things like exhaust and whatnot. Dogs."

"It's not that."

Matt nodded knowingly. "Do you wanna talk about it?"

And for once Brain sort of did want to talk about it. "What happened to you, Matt? I mean really, what happened? I'm not judging you. I just really want to understand. What changed you overnight from being this like crazy hedonist to being married and religious and all?"

Matt really had been pretty crazy at one time. Everyone who'd gone to their high school still knew Matt as the guy who'd crocheted his pubes into Katie Leonard's sweater, who'd filled the showerheads in the girls' locker room with Sanka, and who'd sodomized Janey McGraw, the gothest girl on stage crew, in the eaves of the auditorium while their parents applauded the second act of *Fiddler* unfolding beneath them. Longtime fans of Agenbite—there were a few— remembered pre-Christian Matt as the bare-chested frontman who occasionally interrupted his demoniac vocals to fill his mouth with Coleman's Camping Fuel, light a lighter by his face, and blow like a hellhound till the flames licked the ceiling black.

Matt smiled. "I'm happy to talk about this, Brain. Let me just say that up front. I stop myself sometimes from bringing it up of my own account because I don't want you guys to think I'm preaching at you, but I really am happy to share."

"Cool," Brain said.

"You know what kind of a family I grew up in, Brain. My parents don't just not believe in God, they *believe* in not believing in God.

Devoutly. Did I ever tell you I used to spend my summers at atheist camp?"

"I don't think so."

"It was just like any ordinary summer camp, I guess. We hiked and went fishing. We ate smores. The only difference is we had to attend all these workshops on evolution, the scientific method, things like that. That's how they indoctrinated us. And what did we know? We were just kids. All we knew was we didn't have to go to church like other kids. Most of our parents still let us believe in Santa Claus at least, which is really messed up if you think about it. Anyway, I remember sitting around the campfire one night under a full moon listening to ghost stories, and can you imagine how much scarier the boogeyman is to a ten-year-old kid when he doesn't have God in his corner?

"I don't mean to say my parents aren't well-meaning people. You know them. They're nice enough, right? But they're just such intellectuals that sometimes they cut themselves off from the more spiritual side of things. It's like, for them, if they can't fit it together logically in their own minds, then it doesn't exist. I used to challenge them a lot. I'd ask like, 'Does electricity exist?' and of course they'd say it did and I'd say, 'How do you know if you can't see it?' and they'd say they could see its effects, and I thought who's to say we're not seeing God's effects all around us? Who's to say electricity's not one of God's effects? Not that I was moving to the other side yet, but if ever anyone encouraged me to ask questions it was them, and more and more I found their answers left me wanting. They used to give me all these Charlie Brown science books to help explain the things they couldn't, and I learned a lot from those books, but even they couldn't really answer my questions because behind each answer I always felt the niggling of some other question until finally I'd arrive at this like ultimate question which none of those books ever addressed. By the time I got to high school, atheism had been so drilled into me that I'd pretty much given up on finding the answers

I was looking for. Or more like I decided there weren't any answers, and I just took it for granted that religion was just some kind of politically motivated team sport. So what do you do in a case like that where you're barely a teenager and you already don't believe in anything? I'll tell you what you do. You turn to the one thing you do believe in, categorically, which is your senses. Because even if you do believe in God, it's always a matter of faith, you know, but your senses don't leave any room for doubt. They're right there. Sex feels good. No honest man can deny that. So that's what I sought out, any way I could. And I'd be lying if I said I didn't enjoy it. Of course I did. But the more I began to spiral out of control, the more I appreciated how complex a human being is. We're more than just our bodies. There's something else. Call it a spirit or a soul. Whatever it is, all the sex in the world wouldn't do a thing for it. It might even injure it.

"You probably had no idea how miserable I was back in those days. I put on a good show maybe, but I spent most of my time, really, on the brink of suicide. My parents picked up on it and took me to see all kinds of therapists and had me try all kinds of antidepressants and all, but none of them ever really worked because ultimately my problems weren't psychological, they were philosophical. My whole view of the universe was so cold and mechanistic. As far as I was concerned, men were just a bunch of monkeys trying to outwit each other in the race for power, and vaginas were the prize. The rest of a woman was just incidental, a kind of packaging is all. I'm sure you never knew how I used to drive over to Camden to pick up prostitutes? Well I did. It got so I knew most of them by name. They're not bad people, you know, just misdirected. Of course I was doubly so back then, and I lived that way for a long time, a lot longer than I'm even willing to admit. It got to the point where sex was practically the only thing I was living for, and I didn't even really enjoy it that much anymore."

"Anhedonia," Brain said. (Sophomore year of college, Abnormal Psychology.)

Matt nodded. "Then one day I was at work. This guy I work with, Dave, and I were wiring this fast-food place in North Philly. We were up on our respective ladders just shooting the breeze to make the time go by. But then I asked him some question and he didn't answer so I looked over to see what was the matter, and in no way was I prepared for what I saw. All the veins in Dave's neck were sticking out like tree roots and he was clenching his teeth and convulsing. His legs were anchored around the rungs of the ladder, so I thought everything was cool on that front, but he'd gotten stuck in this leaning-back position and next thing I knew his body weight started pulling the ladder off the building and he went sailing through the air, in slow motion it felt like, and then he landed—*Bam!*—with his back against the ladder rack on my truck and I swear you could hear the guy's vertebrae snap.

"Turned out it wasn't even his fault. The light fixture was incorrectly wired by the manufacturer so the polarity was reversed. Basically, when Dave touched the metal base of the fixture, the current used his body like a conductor and raced through him like lighting, into the ladder and down to the ground. He was mighty lucky though. Or mighty unlucky. I wasn't sure which. The doctors said he was going to live, but I thought what kind of life is it when eighty percent of your body's covered in third-degree burns and you're paralyzed from the waist down? As soon as they let me, I went to see him at the hospital and in the car on the way there I swear I felt like I was going to a funeral. I mean what do you say to a guy like that? Tough break? How do you offer the guy hope when you both know he's never gonna walk again or get married probably or have children or even sex for that matter? That would've been the big one for me back then. But then when I went into his hospital room I was surprised to see he was sitting up in a wheelchair watching *The Price is Right*, and as soon as he spotted me he said, 'Hey, look who it is! Matty, come on in,' and for the next hour or so we shot the breeze about this and that like it was just another day atop our ladders and we spent most of the hour not even mentioning the accident. But then finally I said something about how he seemed to be taking all this in stride, and do you know what he said to me? Get this. He said, 'Jesus's got my back,' and there might've been a funny kind of pun in there, but I could see he really meant it, and that's when I knew for sure my parents had been wrong all these years. Not about whether there was a God or not necessarily, but about believing that believing in one made you weak. No way. Dave was the living proof of it. If I'd been in his shoes, I'd have wanted to be put out of my misery. But Dave was strong. He wanted to live. And that's what made me decide to start checking out different religions and going to different services and things. I asked Dave which church he went to, and it turned out he was a Seventh-Day Adventist. Now I didn't know Seventh-Day Adventists from Jehovah's Witnesses from Tibetan Buddhists at the time, but I went down that next Saturday to check it out, and frankly I was a bit weirded out by how overzealously I was welcomed and I might have snuck out the back if it wasn't for the cantor, who was easily the most beautiful girl I'd ever seen in my life. She made the announcement at the end of the service that there'd be refreshments to follow on the lawn, so I had to stick it out. This is Karen I'm talking about of course. I poured her some lemonade and she started telling me about the year she'd just spent doing relief work in India, and I made sure to focus on what she had to say and not just what she looked like, and I can honestly say it was the first time in my life I ever fell in love with a person's mind. So we saw each other every Saturday after that, she got me reading the bible cover to cover, I got baptized, and a few months later we were married.

"And before you ask the question, let me just preempt you. Would I have stayed involved in the church if not for Karen? To tell you the truth, Brain, I don't know. I like to think I would have, of course, but the truth is I honestly don't know. All I can say for sure is if I had it to do all over again, I wouldn't change a thing. I mean I wish

Dave didn't have to get electrocuted, but since marrying Karen and having Lisa, I've known a kind of peace I never even thought existed before. I died to myself. It's something no amount of blowjobs will ever bring you, take it from me. Here, you might as well take one of these while I'm preaching at you." He handed Brain a pamphlet.

Brain folded the pamphlet into his pocket, thanked Matt for his candor, and, abandoning his napping plans, looped back around to the station's other entrance. He consulted the Tokyo map he'd pinched from Nick's guidebook and presently found himself in a section of town called Ginza, browsing for an engagement ring at Tiffany. He'd asked to see two solitaires up close before the Hedonist awoke from his slumber: *What the hell are you doing? (a) You don't have any money, and (b) Even if you did, this would not be the thing to spend it on. Look at that girl behind the counter who just handed you that ring. A Japanese chick with huge knockers who speaks roughly comprehensible English. Do you realize how rare that is? Open your eyes, damn it. She's smiling at you right now. Tell me you want to disappoint her?*

As God was his witness, Brain did not want to disappoint her, and were it not for this sudden rumbling in his bowels, he might have introduced himself. He handed her back the ring, waddled to the—mercifully—Western-style bathroom, dropped his bluejeans, and erupted with a vesuvian shiver. While waiting for the second wave, he took out the pamphlet Matt had given him and began to read.

DYING TO LIVE?

Are you tired of chasing after worldly pleasures only to find they leave you feeling empty inside? Have you given yourself over to drugs or lust only to discover that they rob you of the satisfaction you really crave?

The great King Solomon was disappointed in life too. Despite possessing great wealth and surrounding himself with all the pleasures of the flesh, he "hated life; because the work that is wrought under the sun is grievous unto me: for all is vanity and vexation of spirit." (Ecclesiastes 2:17)

[*And irritability of the bowels*, **Brain added through chattering teeth.**]

But ultimately Solomon found a deeper meaning to life. He concludes Ecclesiastes with this admonishment: "Fear God, and keep his commandments: for this is the whole duty of man."(Ecclesiastes 12:13) It was only when Solomon stopped "chasing the wind" that he was able to open himself up to God's love.

[**A bead of sweat rolled off Brain's forehead, burst on his knee.**]

God invites you, Dear Reader, to make this same leap. In dying to ourselves, we allow Christ to live through us, and it is only then that we can truly be said to be alive. As Saint Paul, another convert, writes: "I live; yet not I, but Christ liveth in me." (Galatians 2:20)

[*SHPLARGFT!* (*con fuoco*)]

Where the desires of this world rage, there can be no peace, but by dying to ourselves and "being born again, not of corruptible seed, but of incorruptible, by the word of God, which liveth and abideth for ever," (1 Peter 1:23) we can break free of the grasp of Satan and enter into the fullness of God's blessing. As Christ himself said, "Except you are born of water and of the Spirit, you cannot enter the kingdom of God." (John 3:5)

[*SHPFHHT. SPHGLT.*]

Dear Reader, God longs to give you the satisfaction that you so desperately desire. Will you not heed his call?

[*SHPLEUUUGGGHHFFFFF... (dolce, espirando)*]

"If any man be in Christ, he is a new creature: old things are passed away; behold, all things are become new." (2 Corinthians 5:17)

✝

Brain's apostasy was far enough along that no religious tract stood to undo it. He was not, however, unsusceptible to magniloquent language. His spirit *was* vexed. He *did* yearn to be born again of incorruptible seed—his dad's had to be about as corruptible as it came—and if that meant dying to himself so that this new creature might come into being, then that was what it meant. The Romantic welcomed all of this, of course, while the Hedonist went reeling Lucifer-like into a deep and pitch-dark abyss.

•

Back at the apartment, Brain picked up Martina and impersonated a bluesman. He'd gotten in two double-stops and a trill before bending the G string past its capacity to bend and snapping it down by the bridge. He unwound the string from its tuning peg and lay back on his futon, staring at the ceiling, pining. *If only I had more money*, he thought, and as always thoughts of money led to thoughts of Nick, who had so friggin much of it. More unconsciously than not, he began to stretch the string taut between his fingers, whitening his knuckles and yielding a makeshift garrote. A tussock of torn-out hairs made Nick's pillow a likely effigy and it was several times dead before Brain shifted his energies to the incubation of certain connections being made behind his forehead. Before long, he'd hatched a plan.

He scrubbed the string with a bar of soap and a washcloth, dried it with his towel, returned to the tatami room, took the wire cutters out of his guitar case and cut the string down to size, wrapped it around his little finger, held it in position between his thumb and forefinger so he could braid it on the third go-around, then snipped off the remainder, went back inside his case and took out a tube of Krazy Glue and applied a dab to the end of the string to keep it from coming unrung. It didn't look half bad. It wasn't Tiffany perhaps, but the phosphor bronze did shine a little if you held it in the light just so.

He prowled over to Nick's duffel bag and unzipped the pocket where he'd watched Nick deposit an envelope of exchanged currency the other day. He took off his socks and transferred them to his hands, tugged on the envelope just enough so that he could tweeze out a ten-thousand yen bill and tuck it right back the way it was. He rezipped the bag, artfully tousled the fabric, transferred his socks back to his feet and retired to the kitchen table to study his phrasebook—everything was now accounted for but the words. "I love you" was right there on the twelfth page, but he was still searching the appendix of his dictionary for the grammatical gluten that would adhere the words that only sort of meant "Will," "you," "marry," and "me," when his bandmates swung by to pick him up for dinner at a cheap Italian restaurant whose menu featured squid-ink spaghetti, no meatballs to speak of and an additional charge for bread.

•

A persistent twitch in Brain's left thigh kept him from sleeping that night, though rising with the sun, he felt anything but tired—anxious, a little religious, but not tired. He dressed himself in his finest, triple-checked that he had his ring and Nick's money and went out into the cool, quiet morning, the sun spotwarming his... *Fuck!* He'd been so preoccupied with getting everything else right, he'd forgotten all about his hair. No matter. There was plenty of time yet to locate a barber. On the other hand, he didn't have any money to spare. *Damn it, why didn't I take another bill?* Only one solution presented itself. He entered the 7-11 and made like he was comparing and contrasting fabric softeners while, with a guitarist's legerdemain, he pulled a pair of scissors off the hook and tucked them in his waistband. He would have made a pristine break too were it not that, when he stepped up into the "WC" in the corner of the store, the scissors jabbed him in the abdomen. No blood was drawn, but a yelp was, and the clerk's attention. Thinking on his feet, Brain yelped again and covered his nose and mouth like it was just some kind of weird American sneeze, and wouldn't you know the clerk went back to his listless nothing-doing.

In the WC, Brain looked at himself in the mirror. *Any way you cut it*, he thought—not intending the pun but recognizing it—*this is a big fucking deal*. Which explained why he'd kept this issue on the back burner of his consciousness for the past two weeks. Like all people, he'd had short hair once, but since meeting Nick in ninth-grade English all those years ago, he'd come to associate short hair on men with a kind of bourgeois conformity. Brain himself had entered high school an archetypal nerd, the sort who read fantasy novels in his newly finished basement after school. But Nick was a breed apart. A metalhead, but not of the downcast, inward-looking variety. People liked him. He was charismatic and crass—you knew without asking that he had older brothers—and while Brain went to great pains to keep folded into his armpit the insigniaed breast of his Batman jacket, Nick wore his denim one with the Cannibal Corpse patch ironed on the back without apology. And epitomizing this new sense of possibility—this new kind of *person*—that Nick represented to Brain, were the ink-black locks cascading down his spine. By November of that year Brain had accumulated enough allowance to buy a Korean-made Fender Strat and enough nerve to announce at the dinner table that he was forswearing haircuts indefinitely, to which his father replied, "What do you wanna look like a girl for? You going gay on us or what?" Brain chose not to dignify the question with an answer, excused himself from his mother's table and went down the basement to practice his power chords. In the ensuing weeks, months and years, Nick taught Brain which CDs to buy at the record store, which boots at the Army/ Navy. He lit Brain's first cigarette, uncapped his first beer, showed him his first porno (*The Speleologist*). And all the while Brain delivered himself up to the project wholeheartedly, saying in effect, *Make me more like you*, and growing his hair as a sign of his fealty, and even now it was impossible to say where Nick ended and Brain began—if indeed Brain began at all.

Why am I even hesitating? he thought, holding out a shank of hair and straddling it with the scissors, *I should be looking forward to this*, and in the spirit of a slave freeing himself from his bonds at last, he pressed his fingers and thumb together and heard the life-altering whoosh in his ear. A few whooshes more and he could feel naked air against the cleft of his neck for the first time in a decade. He didn't cut it all off, but to just above the brow and ears—a bowl cut that made him look either ten years younger or ten years older. He gathered up what hair he could and threw it in the trashcan, wiped the sink with toilet paper, slid over the ceramic slab atop the toilet, and hid the scissors in the tank. He alighted in the fluorescent store again and the clerk cocked his head like some inquisitive dog, but Brain just played it cool and used the last of his spare change to buy a melon bread and a can of coffee. He hoped the meal might settle his nerves, and for a time it seemed to. But after he arrived at Club Pinky and paid his admission and Miho billowed out of the curtain at the far end of the hall, her every graceful step in his direction intensified the twittering of his amygdala (again, Abnormal Psychology—a very useful course), the pounding of his heart, the rate of his breathing and the volume of blood squeaking through his asymmetrical ears.

She was upon him now, widening her eyes and forming her surprised face. "Cool!" she said, looking at his hair and giving him a double thumbs-up.

"You look stunning as always," he said.

She tilted her head. He stripped the phrase of its nuance: "You are beautiful."

At that, she pinked, took him by the hand and led him to the shower, and he felt an almost violent sort of tenderness towards her as she disrobed, like he wanted to eat her alive and lick his fingers after. When she'd finished scrubbing him, he offered to do the same for her—*and she let him!*—and every squeeze of the loofah had the effect of mollifying his inhibitions. But then, after the shower, she led him hand in hand down the hall and he noticed that they were bypassing their usual room.

"Is something wrong with that room?" he asked, indicating the closed door.

"Now is using," Miho said.

And so they went into another room, and even though it was nearly identical to their old room, something about it unnerved him. The air felt a degree or two cooler. Or maybe he was imagining it. But either way, something was out of joint, and by the time Miho had her tongue on his navel, he'd made up his mind what it must be: this was the room where Nick and Miho had enacted their treachery. The ghost of it lived in the air. Even if he was just imagining it, it made little difference, for now that the thought had hardened, it refused to deliquesce. The Hedonist threw himself against the walls of the abyss: "*Marry this fuck* (indecipherable) *your own best int* (indecipherable) *mother whore if you* (indecipherable) *best friend* (indecipherable) *troy us and you know it.*" But the Romantic held his ground, urging compassion, fortitude, self-surrender, and meanwhile Miho engulfed Brain's glans in her mouth and massaged it with her tongue and pivoted on it until her sex was in his face and he felt this thing welling up in him again, this visceral wad, and he knew for sure now it had to be Love, and *Fuck Nick,* he reached for the night table where Miho had folded his jeans and felt around in the pocket and there it was and he pulled it out and wondered *Okay, now what do I do?* because he'd never had the luxury of an older brother or a nurturing dad to teach him things like this, but he'd seen enough movies to know that the top thing you could do was to hide the ring somewhere and let her find it, and so, struck with this sudden inspiration and reasonably sure he was concealed from the camera's eye by Miho's burnished and heart-shaped buttocks, he speculumed her labia with his thumb and forefinger and pushed the ring inside with his other hand until it capped that ball-shaped thing back there. Then he returned his attention to her outards.

Sometimes as an artist you had a sudden intuition and you surrendered yourself to it, abandoning any preconceived plan you may have had. Oftentimes that inspired bit turned out to be the high point of the piece. Other times, you listened back to what had seemed like the work of divine afflatus to find it was only the product of your own stale breath. As soon as Brain returned to snarfing Miho's vagina he knew that his recent inspiration was a sham. *What were you thinking?* he thought, reaching back in. But just as his finger found the coveted band, the blasted buzzer went *Bzzlhhcrnkk!* and Miho bolted upright. He gazed down at her abdomen throughout the shower but she didn't seem to notice anything out of the ordinary and he wondered *Should I ask her to finger herself?* but that didn't strike him as a particularly charming prelude to a marriage proposal, and before he had time to come up with anything better, he found himself back out on the street again, solo.

He consulted his watch: eleven AM. Agenbite wasn't scheduled to take the stage until seven, so he looked at his map and decided to head north to the port area to think things over. When he got there, he took a seat on a bench and smoked a few cigarettes while he surveyed the sail-shaped skyscrapers, the lighthouse, the Ferris wheel, the golden retriever risking everything for a soggy tennis ball. *I'll go back tomorrow,* he decided. *I'll take one more bill out of Nick's bag and I'll just ask her right there in the shower. So what if I don't have a ring? I'll get her one down the road if she says yes.* He could only hope she'd pass the first ring without noticing. As time passed, however, Brain grew so firm in his plans that he lost the patience to stick to them. He started out at an easy clip but in no time found his feet gone hot with running, his hair bouncing in its own frenzied wind. He heard a triumphant score, the steady crescendo building to a climax that never quite came because, on rounding the last corner, he beheld Matsuo in the middle of the street gesticulating to a cop, and while he had little reason to suspect that he himself might be the topic of their conversation, he thought it best to begin gumshoeing his way back around the corner anyway. He'd almost regained his obscurity when Matsuo lifted his head, pointed his chin and shouted something abrupt in Japanese, and like a roach in falling shadow, Brain knew to take off running. He leapt over a trashcan, sprinted up one street and down the next. He heard the fusillade of footsteps behind him. His lungs gasped and wheezed. He looked over his shoulder, hurdled a curbed TV set, looked over his other shoulder. They were gaining on him, the cop in the lead brandishing his blackjack. *Well, a blackjack's better than a gun at least.* So Brain was thinking anyway when that same black

•

He woke to find himself not in the back of a patrol car or at the local precinct as he might have expected, but rather, naked and hog-tied to the conference table in the back office of Club Pinky, Matsuo peering down at him like a surgeon whose brother direly needed a kidney.

"I give you just one chance to answer," Matsuo said, scoring Brain's horripilated scrotum with the cold blade of his fishing knife. The cop stood at his side like assistant to the executioner. "Why you are trying to kill Miho-chan?"

"Why I am *what*?" Brain managed through chattering teeth. His heart seemed to be in the back of his head at the moment, and the throbbing hurt so bad he just about wished the damn thing would cease altogether.

Matsuo took a remote control out of his pocket and clicked on the TV. And there Brain was, *in flagrante delicto*, his chalky limbs poking out from under Miho's body, which from this angle looked especially animalian with its lean striae of muscle, its sinewy crouch and *that was him there doing that* and despite the atrocious headache, he soon found his visage all agrin until Matsuo elevated his balls a couple of centimeters with the point of his knife and he felt the sharp sting of it and the warm dribble of blood between his thighs.

"Here," Matsuo said, pointing at the screen with his free hand. And sure enough there it was, the incriminating evidence, Brain's waxy arm shooting out from behind Miho's ankle, feeling around in the pocket of his jeans and pulling out the ring—though from the camera's point of view it might have been any object small enough to fit in Brain's hand.

Matsuo pulled out Brain's indrawn penis and put his knife to its narrow base. "Final answer, Mr. Brain. Why you are trying to kill Miho-chan?"

And now, at the last possible second, Brain finally understood the absurdity of Matsuo's premise. "What, you thought it was a weapon or something? This is all a big misunderstanding!"

Matuo eased off the pressure. "Please explain," he said.

So Brain explained, about his feelings and his shortage of money and the makeshift ring and his not-so-bright idea of stuffing it inside Miho's body, and as soon as he finished, Matsuo immediately put down his knife and set to untying him. "I am very sorry," he said, swabbing Jack Daniels on the undercarriage of Brain's scrotum and applying a bandage. "I am misunderstand." He helped Brain on with his clothes and tossed the cop a change of clothes too, apparently asking him to man the brothel for a time, about which the cop didn't seem to have any scruples. He then got Brain an ice pack for the chin–sized bump at the back of his skull.

"Come," Matsuo said, leading Brain outside to his Mercedes.

"Where are we going?"

"Visit Miho-chan."

"Where is she?"

"Hospital."

"Hospital?"

"You can ask doctor."

The hospital was only a few blocks away. They found Cerberus in the ER waiting room. He couldn't seem to decide whether he ought to greet Brain or not and settled on a kind of shifty nod. They took their seats on either side of him, and Matsuo and Cerberus talked in what sounded like grave Japanese. Then Matsuo stood and walked away, leaving Brain and Cerberus palpably uncomfortable until he came back some minutes later with a doctor in tow.

"Mr. Brain, this is Doctor Wang."

"*Hajimemashite*," Brain said—nice to meet you. It was one of the few phrases he'd managed to make stick.

"I am not Japanese," Doctor Wang said. "I am Chinese but I grew up in Singapore so you can speak to me in English." Brain wasn't sure about the algebra of that equation, but while he was drowning in guilt for whatever horrible thing he'd done to Miho, it amounted to a gulp of oxygen to be around voluble English again, even this vaguely British variety.

"I was just explaining to Matsuo-san. Miho-san is doing fine, though it's a good thing they brought her in when they did because she was losing quite a lot of blood."

Brain felt lightheaded. "Can you … can you back up a little please? Matsuo hasn't told me a thing."

"Actually I was hoping you could help shed some light on what happened here. Can you tell me exactly what happened during your 'visit' with Miho-san?"

And so, once again, Brain explained about his feelings and his shortage of money and the makeshift ring and his not-so-bright idea of stuffing it inside Miho's body. Each word stung like bile on its way up.

"Did it occur to you that it might be *dangerous* to leave a length of steel string inside Miho's body?"

"I thought she would urinate it out," Brain said. This was the truest thing he could think to say. He had considered that there might be some health risks associated with leaving the ring in there, but he'd been so caught up in the romantico-sexual side of the problem that he'd inadvertently banished these health concerns to the outer edges of his consciousness.

"You haven't much experience of the female anatomy, have you, Mr. Brain?"

Brain balked.

"She could bring you up on criminal charges, you know?"

"And I would certainly deserve it. But look, this isn't about..."

"Attempted homicide maybe," Wang said.

Brain paused a moment, then started his sentence over again: "This isn't about me right now. It's about Miho. No one's told me a damned thing about what happened to her except that she's lost a lot of blood, which frankly scares the crap out of me."

Wang assumed his doctor persona. "Miho's suffering from a lacerated uterus. Unfortunately your 'ring' did not remain one for long. What I ended up removing from her cavity was a sixty-centimeter length of steel string. I didn't realize it was a *guitar* string until you told me a minute ago. Evidently your Krazy Glue didn't hold. So naturally the string expanded inside of Miho and lodged itself in there, and then when her next client began having intercourse with her, the string began scraping against the walls of her uterus and tore her up like a rag doll. I wouldn't be at all surprised if the client got pretty well minced himself."

"Jesus," Brain said, thinking *Did he say 'intercourse'?* and immediately burying the possibility.

"She was hemorrhaging so profusely I feared for the worst.

I thought we might have to do a hysterectomy, which is always heartbreaking to do on a young person since it means she'll never be able to have children. But it seems now her wounds are all superficial enough we may be able to get by with sutures. We'll have to keep a close eye on her until the tissue heals over."

"Can we see her?" Brain asked.

"She's still in the O.R., though it looks like she should be in Recovery within the next couple of hours. The most important thing is that she get a lot of rest, so the last thing we want to do is rile her up. It goes without saying that if it were up to me, I wouldn't let you within a square mile of her, Mr. Brain, but I'll leave that for Matsuo-san to decide."

Brain's first instinct was to retaliate, but his guilt overruled his ire and all he got out was a simple "thank you."

Two full hours passed before they were allowed in to see her. "Please let me go in with you," Brain had begged, but Matsuo didn't need any convincing. "Is better you tell her what happen, no? Must be very confuse, no?"

Miho lay in a beam of sunlight, motes of dust swirling about her baby-blue gown and folded hands. She smiled at the sight of Matsuo and Cerberus, though cowered a little when Brain crossed the threshold. *She hates me*, Brain thought. The three Japanese conversed in their language, and Brain just stood there with his hands in his pockets, the guilt rising all around him. At length Matsuo turned to him and said, "Please explain Miho-chan what happen."

"I'm not sure she'll understand…"

"I will translate," Matsuo assured him.

So Brain took a deep breath and closed his eyes a moment. He hadn't felt this kind of stage fright since Agenbite's first talent show a decade ago. She hated him, and she had every reason to, and he didn't even have the advantage of linguistic nuance to try and court her back. He would have to paint in broad strokes.

"Miho…" he began. "I love you. I have always loved you. Ever since I was a child I harbored dreams of..."

Matsuo extended his hand to cut Brain off and did the translation. Brain twiddled his psychological thumbs until Matsuo said, "Please continue."

But already Brain's train of thought had switched tracks and disappeared into the fog. He set off on a different course: "The guitar string they found in you was a ring that I made and put inside you because I wanted to ask you to marry me and I thought if you found it in there you'd be... I don't know..."

Matsuo cut Brain off again and conveyed the translation, which somehow resulted in a five-volley exchange between Miho and Matsuo.

"What did she say?" Brain asked, but Matsuo waved his hand dismissively and said, "Is nothing. Please continue."

"So what it all comes down to, I guess, is every day I'm not with you is a kind of torment. I never thought I'd want to get married. I always thought marriage was for shortsighted fools, but now I get it. After having known what life is like with you, there's just no way I can go back to... there'd be no meaning in it..."

Matsuo extended his brake hand. This time the translation turned into a full-blown conversation that lasted five or six times as long as the original, which raised concerns in Brain's mind about whether Matsuo was qualified for this. He hoped it wasn't becoming an interlingual game of Telephone.

"Please continue," Matsuo said.

"So that's really it. I love you and if you're willing... I know we'll face many challenges because of our cultural differences and all, but I'll learn Japanese and you'll learn English and our love will get us through everything... I really believe it will. So, Miho,"—he got down on one knee—"I guess what I want to say is... and I'll completely understand if you think I'm crazy, but, well, *will you marry me?*"

Miho seemed to have captured the meaning of this last bit for she looked to Matsuo only for confirmation. Matsuo nodded and right on cue tears welled up in each of her eyes. She wiped them away with the flat of her hand and sniffled, nodded timorously but resolutely, and said "*Mm*."

"Yes? Is that a yes?" *It is, isn't it? The legato one is no, the staccato one yes?*

"*Mm*," she said, "yes."

Brain began to laugh. He didn't mean to, nothing was funny, but he laughed like he hadn't ever laughed before and soon he too had hot, fat, mirthful tears dripping down his cheeks onto his forearms. Matsuo shook Brain's hand, and Cerberus did too, if a touch less firmly, then Brain bent down and hugged Miho's head and kissed the top of it, and she was manifestly discomfited by it because Japanese didn't hug, least of all in front of other people, but he couldn't care less at the moment, she'd have to deal with it, because like it or not he was American and he was happy and this was what Americans did when they were happy.

Then Wang came back in the room to piss on things. "Miho-san should probably be getting some rest now," he said. They nodded their assent and said their goodbyes. Miho wrote down her cell number for Brain at last and Matsuo offered to drive Brain back to the station. Riding shotgun in Matsuo's Mercedes, Brain couldn't have suppressed his smile if he tried. He tried. Nope, couldn't do it. *What'd you have to go and get self-conscious about it for?* he thought, waiting for the joyride to end, waiting for it to end, still waiting for it to end… He pondered what he might have done so right. It had taken Miho's saying yes to make him realize how much he'd expected her to say no. He'd been *conditioned* thus. But now he felt as if he'd surmounted some great mountain, Fuji call it, and he looked out from the top and the horizon had leapt so quantumly far off he couldn't even be sure if it existed anymore. There was only space, all around him, infinite space brimming with white light.

Then Matsuo said, "I little bit change your sayings."

"You what?" Brain said.

"Mr. Brain, I know Japanese girl. Your sayings is very romantic, but need to be saying about babies or not so interesting, no? So I told about babies something."

"You told Miho I want babies?"

"Something. She is exciting because Doctor Wang is saying before maybe she cannot have."

"That's fucked up. Why'd you tell her that? I've never even thought about having babies. I mean, someday maybe, sure, but it's *way* too early for that."

"Mr. Brain, don't worry. Is just words, no?"

"No! I mean yes, it's just words, but *so is everything.*"

"Say again?" Matsuo said. But by this point they'd already pulled up in front of the station and anyway Brain wasn't exactly sure what he meant. "Forget it," he said, addressing himself as much as Matsuo. But Brain couldn't forget it. Why couldn't Matsuo have just translated as faithfully as he knew how instead of introducing an element of fraud into this purest of relationships? *Babies?* Who the hell was thinking about babies? Miho was barely out of high school. Surely she had some *ambition?* Didn't she want to *do* anything with her life before being crippled with responsibility? What was the point of perpetuating the species if nobody ever *did* anything?

But this was a conversation he ought to be having with Miho, not himself. He wondered how long such a conversation would take, despaired a little at his hypothesis, and took his phrasebook out of his pocket to study. The first phrase of the day was "*Nanji desuka?*"— what time is it?—and this led him to look casually at his watch and this in turn to suffer a panic attack: it was twenty minutes to seven.

•

By the time he found the Manhole, Brain was out of breath again. He was even later than he'd expected, in part because he'd underestimated how much time it would take to drop by La Maison Blanche and change into proper prog-rock regalia—Doc Maartens, black jeans, leather vest—and in part because he didn't have an exact address for the place and, once in Ikebukuro, had had to stop three young couples on the street before one of the boyfriends knew the Manhole and sufficient English to direct him there. When he finally found the place, Brain announced himself to the doorman, who briefly left his post to shoulder Brain through an impossibly packed crowd (cocks galore) to backstage. Brain was relieved to find Ibaneza leaning against the house amp on stage, her mirrored pickguard rebounding beams of pink and blue spotlight—he'd worried he'd be stuck having to borrow some beater from one of the other bands. Matt's bass lay face-up in its case. Nick's pedals looked anxious.

"Where the fuck were you?" Theo said.

"You still have maybe ten minutes if you want to play one song?" the doorman announced, taking his leave.

"And what the fuck happened to your hair?" Theo said. "You look like a fucking dork."

Nick, who was seated on a black leather couch smoking a cigarette, head in hands, eyes on floor, didn't bother to look up at this mention of Brain's new haircut. He was pretending not to care, though Brain knew that more than any arsenal of words he might have deployed, this outward sign of his perfidy would cut Nick to the quick. It was like saying to him, *I have a new master now. You'll have to go and find some other vulnerable kid to lick your boots for you.*

"My bad. I had some things to take care of. They'll let us run over, don't you think?" In the States, the show time advertised on the bill was generally a well-intended fiction.

Matt looked up from the book he was reading. "Didn't you hear the guy? We've got ten minutes left. They run a tight ship over here."

"What the fuck things did you have to take care of?" Theo said. "That doesn't even make sense. We haven't seen you all fucking day.

Don't tell us you went for a fucking walk either."

"Well..." Brain began. He was going to give them the truth this time. For once he felt he owed it to them, and besides *he'd gotten engaged!* It was kind of a big deal, and if ever there were extenuating circumstances for showing up late to a gig, this was surely it.

But before he had a chance to find the right words, Nick had charged him like a pitbull, knocked him to the floor, and set to pounding the wits out of him with a pair of gnarled drumsticks. "You...fucking...self-absorbed...bastard," Nick grunted through gritted teeth. Matt tried peeling him off, but Nick sidekicked him into the drywall.

The ridge of Nick's cranium had struck Brain square in the solar plexus, making his diaphragm spasm, rendering it impossible to breathe, and focusing Brain's energies not on deflecting these invisibly quick flares off his cheekbones but on the more pressing matter of recovering his lungs, and for the time being it was all he could do to watch with a queer sort of lucidity as his humors went sailing through the air above him, as Matt rubbed his coccyx, as Theo just sat there.

Then Brain got his breath back, and the difference of those thousands of seemingly ineffectual recent bench presses between them permitted Brain to capture Nick's fists in his own, to dig his thumbs into Nick's wrists and steer the situation into reverse. He pinned Nick to the floor and straddled him. He wiped the blood from his brow on his upper sleeves and only now did he begin to notice how his whole head felt like a giant bee sting. He splayed Nick's hands to the side, trapped them under his knees and concentrated his whole body weight onto them, made a fist and thrust it into Nick's schnoz. Blood trickled down Nick's upper lip into his mouth and bubbled pink like vodka sauce. "Fuck you," Nick said, and Brain reeled back and clocked him again in the same spot. Nick moaned and there was a pleasing—*Pop!*—this time and blood percolated over Nick's chin. Brain pulled back his fist and slammed it into Nick's face a third time, and Nick's nose didn't have much fight left in it but just sort of hung there, an undifferentiated mash of skin and snot, blood and bone. Brain stood up. Nick rolled over onto his stomach and cupped the blood in the bowl of his hands. Brain was impressed at how little compassion he felt for this erstwhile best friend of his threshing on the floor. He had no intention of punishing him further—already the experience had proven profoundly cathartic—but then Nick, struggling to his feet, made the mistake of muttering, "Fuck you," again, not quite under his breath, and Brain was left with little choice but to hop, skip and steel-toed boot Nick's right temple, and Nicholas Benini—that selfsame chronic overachiever who'd shown up Brain in blah and blah and blah—spilled onto the floor and pissed his pleather pants.

"I quit," Brain announced to Matt and Theo, who were eyeing him like the madman he suddenly wasn't so sure he wasn't. "Give me an hour to pack up my shit and I'll be out of your lives forever."

"Do you want to talk about it?" Matt asked.

"I won't be needing my ticket home. I'm getting married."

"You what…?" Theo said, but by this time Brain was already pushing his way through the crowd. He retraced his path to the station and it was only when he'd paid his fare and climbed the stairs to the platform that he realized he'd left Ibaneza behind, shimmering in the stage lights. He pivoted ninety degrees on the balls of his feet, but his heels didn't alight until he'd pivoted back. How could he go back now? His exit had been so final. Anyway, he still had what's her name… Martina. He walked over to the bench. There was only one open seat and it had a magazine on it. He picked it up and took his seat and began flipping through. It was a fashion magazine of sorts. He couldn't read much beyond the title—*Egg*—and the odd stroke of Japanglish, but like most things Japanese, the experience was heavily visual: one sexy freak after another, made-up and hair-dyed, sun-dressed and impractically shod. Not that he had eyes for them anymore. He had a girl now. And she was prettier than any of them, all of them put together. By and by there was a stirring, the gathering up of bags, a sport's page tumbling across the platform. Brain stood to take his place in line and tossed the magazine back onto the bench, and the remarkable thing about that—and he realized this only some days later in a postcoital review of his life's narrative arc— was that he paid no attention whatever to how it landed.

Brain and Miho were wed in a preternaturally white, secular little chapel that would have reminded any of Brain's friends, had they been invited, of the one Slash plays his first guitar solo in front of in the "November Rain" video. A bilingual Brooklyn Jew in a priest costume presided. Miho's family acted as witness. Brain had invited his mother, of course, and his father by extension, but he'd known well enough even before calling that his aviophobia had a prohibitive genetic component. "I'm so happy for you, honey," his mom had said, "but you know how I am about airplanes. I'd look into taking a boat if we had a little more time. Hey, why *don't* we have more time? Your little China Doll hasn't got a cake in the oven by any chance?"

"Miho's *Japa*nese, Mom. And she hasn't got anything in any oven."

"Well I'm sure she must be just delightful. When do we get to meet her?"

"That's the thing, Mom. It's expensive to be flying back and forth all the time. First thing I need to do is find a job."

"Oh, hon, that's not…"

"What?"

"I thought I heard your throat catch was all."

"Must be the connection."

It wasn't the connection. Marriage seemed to be a normal enough part of the life cycle, but Brain couldn't help feeling that in marrying someone so unlike his mother, he might be enacting some sort of betrayal. "I'm sorry, Mom," he said, rubbing his paranoia against the touchstone of the external world.

"Don't be silly, hon," she said. "I'm thrilled for you."

And while it had troubled him that she'd understood his

apology even enough to dismiss it, he'd decided to take her at her word. Besides, it wasn't like he was trading her in. She was the one American woman he was still in love with, and his heart had more than enough room for her and Miho both.

So while Brain didn't have the mixed pleasure of seeing his own people through the joy-tears that clouded his vision while Miho shuffled up the virgin road, Miho's people were there in abundance: her well-preserved mother dabbing at her cheeks while her husband gave their eldest daughter away, her grandfather looking solemnly on like the war hero he'd likely have been had the Japanese won, her two little sisters blushing at their new white idiot brother-in-law and the public display of an emotion they were only now on the cusp of beginning not to understand (Rina was thirteen, Akemi eleven) and a whole host of aunts, uncles and cousins Brain had yet to meet. A few of Miho's friends were in attendance as well, each nubile enough in her own right, though Miho was nonpareil. And standing at his side, double-breasted, bearing rings he himself had tried to front the money for—though Miho's family had ultimately picked up the bill—was the one guest Brain had insisted on inviting: his best man, Matsuo-san.

Not a few hours after quitting the band, Brain had found himself already on the far side of elation, lugging an acoustic guitar and a wheel-less suitcase to God-knew-where until finally, by force of habit, he'd washed up at Club Pinky. He'd had no reason to expect anything from Matsuo. He'd just stolen one of the man's star employees away after all—there was no question of Miho's continuing to work at Pinky now that they were engaged—but Matsuo, perhaps atoning for the Florida-shaped scab on the underside of Brain's scrotum, took Brain in and fed him, gave him a cubicle to sleep in and some ointment and band-aids for the cuts all over his head, even lent him some money and an old word processor to help him get on his feet and land a teaching job, which was the only kind of job to be had by Americans in this country, unless you'd gone to Harvard or someplace. And of all the things he bestowed on Brain, not the least of them was advice, for Brain's chief anxiety since extricating himself from Agenbite was the problem of still having to endear himself to the girl he was already engaged to marry. So far so good, he supposed, but in truth she barely knew him yet. She was okay with the diminutive cock apparently, but what if as her English improved she were to find his personality wanting?

It had taken him three attempts at dialing and fifteen minutes of anxious Japanglish to set up their first rendezvous—if anything made you appreciate the utility of hand gestures and facial expressions, it was talking on the phone—but by conversation's end they'd each repeated no less than seven times the words "Yokohama Station, Kentucky Fried Chicken, one o'clock PM." Brain hadn't a clue where to take her after that, but Matsuo came to the rescue: "Why not you are taking her to Disneyland?"

There might have been a time in Brain's life when he'd have been excited about that, but if there was, he couldn't remember it. As far back as he could recall, he'd resented Mickey & Co. since he was seemingly the only kid in the world who'd never been to Disney World (the farthest his own parents had ever taken him was Wildwood, New Jersey). But seeing as how Matsuo seemed so confident in his suggestion, Brain decided to overcome his reservations. Besides, the worst-case scenario wasn't that bad: Miho would laugh down the suggestion, he'd blame it on Matsuo, and they'd find someplace else to go. The ball was kind of in her court anyway, wasn't it? She couldn't possibly expect him to know her city as well as she did.

As it turned out, she welcomed the suggestion. "I love very much," she said, though Brain was too mesmerized by how she looked in clothes to feel anything like relief. For the first hour of their date, his nerves threatened to sabotage the whole affair. He tripped on words and his own feet and even one of her feet once, but then they got in the train and Miho flattened her green crepe skirt against her thighs and went to take a seat and he heard an unmistakable little explosion from her hindquarters. For her sake Brain tried to play it off like nothing had happened, but Miho covered her mouth with her hand and said, "*Hazukashii*," which he knew meant she was embarrassed and was tantamount to a confession, so he threw an arm over her shoulder to comfort her in her mortification, and while he was vaguely sad at the disillusionment—for it was nothing less—he soon found himself talking volubly, if not exactly fluently, drawing on every one of the hundred or so Japanese words he'd memorized to date, recombining them, sometimes ingeniously, more often not, so that even if he didn't know the word for "librarian," he could say, "bookstore-at-works-person"—not the same, but close—or if he didn't know the word for "aerospace engineer," he could simplify: "airplane-makes-person." In turn, he understood maybe a third of what Miho attempted to say in English, though he didn't see this as a bad thing necessarily, for imprecision was always a part of any two people's attempts at communication. In their own case, the disjunctions were simply laid bare, and no doubt maintaining a certain critical distance from one another's words would spare them heaps of the misconstrual that might otherwise threaten their union. Words were overrated anyway. On the handful of occasions he'd managed to strike them up with American girls, he'd always felt acutely aware of a tacit imperative to keep them rolling lest he betray himself as uninteresting. But silence didn't seem to bother Miho in the least. *He* felt a touch ill at ease with it at first, but gradually Miho's example served to tranquilize him until he'd gotten the knack of talking only when the inchoate be-bop of thinking had composed itself into thought, e.g. "I wonder why they don't give Mickey Asian features over here?" or "So why didn't you go to college?"

As for Mickey's features, Miho had her own ideas. "Looks Japanese," she said. "Black hair. Big eyes. Like manga."

"Well that's not really hair though, is it?" Brain said. "It's ears."

It was only after he'd put forth the argument that he realized how inane it was. Certainly the nubs were ears, but what was all that black in between? And how come that felt like a question no one had ever thought to ask before? Finally he conceded that she must be right. It had to be hair, even if fur was general on mice, but the head of hair must have been a stroke of anthropomorphism to distinguish Mickey and his girlfriend from the rest of their verminous breed. And though counterintuitive at first, she was right about the other thing too. Mickey did look more Japanese than not. Mickey was quintessentially cute, and by all accounts the cult of cuteness had its headquarters in Japan. Everything in this country was cute—*kawaii* was the word—from that ubiquitous kitty to the golden, smiley-faced poop charms dangling off cellphones, and of course, to a loin-maddening degree, the girls. You looked at the cover of an American magazine, *Maxim* say, and what you got was some imperious temptress, some large lithe cat who (if you didn't know her better) seemed bent on gnawing the meat from your bones. But if you looked at the cover of a Japanese magazine, what you got instead was some *kawaii* teenager (or maybe she was older, but looking like a teenager was part of what made her so *kawaii*), a bunny rabbit of a girl, and she was either smiling or pouting, framing her face with her fingers maybe, or leaping in the air, or just standing there, belly out, pigtailed, pastel-clad, or in a sailor suit maybe, head down a little but peering up at you with those sparkling, vulnerable eyes that made you want to protect the hell out of her while you jammed your cock down her esophagus. Which was not to say, as one line of reasoning might have it, that Brain fantasized about Mickey Mouse. On the other hand, if forced to have relations with a cartoon character, Minnie might not have been his last choice.

On the college question, Miho had only this to say: "I am not so interesting."

"What are you talking about? You're plenty interesting," Brain assured her, and she thanked him, even if it turned out what she'd meant was "interested," not "interesting."

"Wasn't there anything you wanted to be?" Brain asked.

"Always I am dreaming to be housewife," she said, prompting Brain to shudder and recall Matsuo's act of Cyranoesque ventriloquism. It wasn't that he didn't want to make her a housewife *eventually*. Hell, he'd make her anything she wanted. He just wasn't there yet. She was his first girlfriend for Christ sakes! Not that it mattered. It didn't, did it? Of course it didn't. Love was the great leveler. Or was that death? Death made more sense. Anyway, same difference. Eros and Thanatos. The life instinct and the death instinct. They weren't so different when you thought about it, for what was love if not a spot of quietude amidst the life struggle, and what was suicide if not a desperate plea for love?

"Just to be clear," Brain said. "Because I don't think it would be fair for me to marry you unless I come clean about this first..."

It was the first time since their engagement that either of them had mentioned marriage, and Brain began to blink hyperactively, but in the interest of full disclosure he pressed on. "I know Matsuo told you I want to have a family, and I do I guess, just not as soon as he might have suggested. I don't know when I'll be ready exactly, but I feel I've got some things to do first. I don't know what exactly. It's all very vague at this point. But there's some *Thing* I have to do. Am I making any sense? I mean, I'm still in my twenties. And look at you, you're not *even* in your twenties. Isn't there anything you want to do with your life before you get saddled with all that responsibility?"

Miho didn't understand a word of that, so Brain went back and spoonfed it to her a phrase at a time, and the end happened to coincide exactly with the end of whatever line they were in, making Brain feel even more vulnerable than usual as he climbed into their buggy, awaiting some judgment that never came. Miho simply said, "*Arigatou* for your true feeling," and as they careered into the darkness and the ether coughed up witches and ghouls, Miho clung to his arm, free of charge, and when he leaned over to kiss the top of her head, she turned to him and kissed back with a technique that was familiar but a conviction that was entirely new.

Leading up to today, Brain had been so worried about Miho's getting to know him better that he'd forgotten all about how little he knew her as yet. It hadn't taken long for him to be besotted with all that he imagined her to be, but over the course of several hours in Disneyland, he thought he'd begun to fall for who she really was as well. Inside Club Pinky, she'd been paid to be submissive, but out here in the world she had a girlish willfulness about her. When she wanted to go on It's A Small World, she simply set off towards it, confident he would follow. And when in the food court at lunch she fancied the squid-ink spaghetti despite knowing it would blacken her mouth for the rest of the afternoon, she went ahead and ordered it, and if, however illogically, blowing strangers for a living struck her as a sensible way of working towards her dream of becoming a housewife, then to hell with what anyone else thought. With his own penchant for infinitely regressive self-doubt, Brain admired this quality of hers as much as he resented it.

While he self-consciously paid mind to reminding himself not to get self-conscious about it, all outward signs seemed to indicate that Miho was having a good time, and all inward signs, that his own good time was feeding off of hers in such a way that they were like symbiotic animals, or it was as if they were feeling through a single effects pedal, their two signals merging into a greater, inextricable whole. Even as he retched into a plastic bag outside of Space Mountain, *her* feelings seemed to have *him* smiling. Theo had asked him once whether he thought someone who desperately had to piss would feel some measure of relief if shot point-blank in the bladder. Brain had argued on the side of unmitigated pain, but now, between heaves, he seemed to understand that pain and pleasure weren't mutually exclusive at all, that they were necessary counterparts in fact, like love and death, the one inhering in the other.

Once Brain had cleaned himself up in the bathroom and gargled some hand soap, they decided to head back home. They held hands in the train. Her fingers were long and thin and he told her she ought to play piano and she told him she had as a little girl. Her stop came first, but she didn't get up. Evidently she took it for granted that she was invited back to Club Pinky, which of course she was, though he hadn't wanted to presume. And so it was that in his austere cubicle at Club Pinky, among the various grunts and ululations of the sex trade, Brain finally penetrated the physical and symbolic barrier that had so long held his manhood at bay.

It ought to have been perfect, and the initial plunge into her body was, but whereas he'd expected the rest of it to come as naturally as kissing had, he found he had to struggle to keep from slipping out, and this in turn made him so excellently self-conscious that his essential animal, the part of him that might have enjoyed the act, was rendered numb. Only in subsequent attempts, on that night and others, did Brain come to enjoy the delirious groingrind and sackslap of it all. Miho, for her part, just lay there, closing her eyes and producing only the most inadvertent vocalizations. When he asked how he was doing, she'd assure him that she was enjoying herself (*"Kimochi ii,"* she'd say—"feels good"), but her general passivity unnerved him, seemed to accuse him of underperformance, so inevitably he'd switch into overdrive, doing his level best to overperform, pumping harder and angrier until sooner or later, usually sooner, the well ran dry.

"I love you," he'd say.

"I love you," she'd say.

During his refractory periods (she had no such thing), they went to the movies, ate, played skee ball, took photos and had them taken, all the while spawning a third entity between them, a mystical offspring made of memories and feelings, with a life all its own and a potential for death that was increasingly unbearable to think of—and which resurrected some of the old anxiety in Brain. He developed a verbal tic: "It's not that I don't want to have a family," he'd say. "Because I do. I can't stand the thought of growing old alone. It's just, I guess I always thought I'd be older when I got married. I just feel that there are certain experiences I'm supposed to have before I settle down, do you know what I mean?" It always seemed to surface at the happiest of moments, when she was so close to him that his individuality seemed threatened with annihilation.

"Marriage is happy meaning," Miho would say. "If not happy meaning, please not marry." And invariably her air of non-attachment would bring out the Romantic in him. It was evolutionary probably, like babies being cute to survive. "No. Mi, please don't misunderstand me. I'm just talking aloud. The truth is, I don't know how I'd live without you. You're the whole *meaning* in my life. Before I met you, I had nothing. I was so empty inside. But since meeting you I feel so... *alive*. Please, Mi, let's grow old together. I beg you, Mi. Please."

She'd squint, skeptically, and he'd have to go on rhapsodizing until he'd won back her faith, then finally she'd say something like, "Are sure?" and he'd say, "I've never been so sure about anything in my life," and then it was like nothing had happened and he'd turn effusively apologetic and in the back of his mind he'd be thinking *What the hell's the matter with you, Brain? It's like you've got a friggin dissociative disorder or something.*

Indeed, with the fall of the Hedonist, the Romantic had thought the battle won, but suddenly it found itself faced with a whole welter of new dissenters, a resurrected Hedonist among them:

THE PRAGMATIST: *You have no job.*

THE SON: *Your own mother, who suckled you at her breast and who is the best friend you'll ever have, is seven thousand miles away and probably crying.*

THE LAW-ABIDER: *You won't be allowed to live in this country for more than another six weeks unless you find a sponsor or bite the bullet and marry the strumpet.*

THE PRAGMATIST: *It takes fifteen minutes to express a simple idea to your fiancée.*

117

THE PURITAN: *Who incidentally was a WHORE not three weeks ago.*

THE CRITIC: *Going home now would constitute a failure, particularly to your friends, who in all likelihood are not your friends anymore.*

THE NOSTALGIC: *Marrying Miho means not marrying Ashley Roselli, Sarah Milliken, Stephanie Cantor, Gwen Randazzo, Maria Bevilacqua, Maureen O'Donnell, et al.*

THE PARANOIAC: *You have yet to meet your would-be in-laws and they're bound to hate your Caucasian guts.*

THE SNOB: *Miho doesn't have an ambition in the world besides making babies, which is something you've always faulted chicks for and don't pretend you haven't.*

THE BACHELOR: *You don't even know if you ever want to have a baby, let alone soon.*

THE PURITAN: *Miho's had her lips on how many penises before yours? And what was that Wang said about "intercourse"?*

THE BACHELOR: *Isn't it generally ill advised to marry the first girl you stick it to?*

THE CRITIC: *Your dick's miniscule.*

THE PARANOIAC: *Duress figured into your engagement and still does, which might mean you're not choosing this so much as it's choosing you.*

THE BACHELOR: *Theoretically, marriage is a lifetime commitment, which means it's not over until you're dead. There's always divorce, but you're way too much of a pussy to survive that.*

THE EVOLUTIONARY BIOLOGIST: *Marriage can only be construed as an admission of weakness. That is to say, you couldn't have a harem so you settled for a single mate.*

THE SNOB: *Miho owns a Backstreet Boys CD.*

THE HEDONIST: *If she hadn't made you quit, you'd be smoking a cigarette right now. And you'd have so many fuck-dates lined up you wouldn't have the time to torment yourself over any one pussy.*

THE ATHEIST: *You don't believe in God anymore, which leaves you precisely no one to talk to about all of this.*

Sometimes Brain would manage to slice through the Gordian knot of his various complexes and look Miho in the eyes and feel the warmth circulating through him and think *Oh yeah, I'm in love, that's why I got myself into all this.* Then for a sublime moment or two, he'd hear no voice but hers until inevitably she'd use it to rouse them all up again, by, for instance, inviting him to dinner at her house so that they could finally have that dreaded meeting with her parents.

•

At some Skinnerian level of consciousness, Brain had taken it for granted that beneath all of Miho's apparent volition, there had to be some environmental factor underpinning her lifestyle choices, making it inevitable that she'd favor peddling her wares over going to college. He was therefore quite beside himself when, come zero hour, Miho led him through the privately patrolled streets of a bosky neighborhood called something-or-other Plaza, punched a series of numbers into a keypad on a wrought-iron gate and ushered him up a wooden elevator into a solarium where her grandfather was practicing his butterfly against the jets of an Endless pool. She called out to him several times before giving up and tapping him on the scapula with an indoor putter. He stopped swimming and doffed his cap and goggles and reached up and shook Brain's hand with his pruney fingers. *Hajimemashite*, Brain told him—nice to meet you—and the old man bassoed something unintelligible, climbed out of the pool, and went over to the liquor cabinet and began doling out the whiskey, which Miho took as her cue to go over to the intercom and summon the rest of the family, while Brain meanwhile stared down from the bay window at the little saffron bridge and the pond teeming with koi and thought, *I don't fucking believe this.* Because as long as he'd been able to construe her as a victim of circumstance, he'd managed, more or less, to reconcile himself to her past, but now this really threw a wrench into things. Yet as the rabble began to rise, all it took was a single glimpse of her guileless smile to quell it.

Her two little sisters emerged first, Rina and Akemi, shy little counterfeit Mihos with the odd indent or slipped mole here and there. Then came her mother, a graceful gazelle in her own right, and then, ineluctably, the father.

Miho introduced them: "Brain, he is my father. My father, he is Brain."

"Pleased to meet you." He handed Brain a business card of which Brain could make out only one word: "TOTO." The rest was all hieroglyphs.

"Please call me Joji," he said.

"George?" Brain said.

"Yes. Joji."

Miho elucidated the situation.

"Miho didn't tell me you spoke English," Brain said, and her father waved his hand and said, "No, no, I don't," which struck Brain as a contradiction until it turned out to be mostly true. So for lack of a better candidate, Miho served as interpreter, which was like having a purblind tour guide for your safari, though it had a definite upside, for as long as Brain could convey the drift of his words to her, she could then edit them into shape before relaying them, and he welcomed any buffer he could get.

They finished their drinks and retired to a cherrywood dining room where Miho's mother had set out a feast: sushi and sashimi, pumpkin and sweet potato tempura, boiled tofu, some semblance of chicken cordon bleu—and, for Brain, the silverware to eat it with. Mercifully, mealtime turned out not to be the interrogation Brain had feared, if only thanks to the communication barrier. Miho's mother plied him with food and praised his chopstick technique while grandpa topped off Brain's glass—of beer now—every time he took a sip. The alcohol had slackened Brain's nerves some, but his taciturnity still distressed him and in order to break an especially long spell of it he asked Miho to ask her father what he did for a living. George replied in English, "I am *en-ji-ni-ya*," and Brain said, "Oh? What kind?" and George got up and went rummaging around in various junk drawers until he'd managed to locate a certain English-language pamphlet with a photo of some kind of modernist furn... no, it was a toilet. Some toilet though. Brain read: "Experience the pinnacle of personal hygiene with the TOTO Washlet. The essential component for complete personal cleansing, the Washlet provides an invigorating and revitalizing bathroom experience..." He rather liked having this new prop to manipulate, but Miho's mother, thinking of him no doubt, issued what could only have been a reprimand, and George in turn said, "Is okay," then swept his hand over the banquet and said, "Please."

So Brain went back to putting things in his mouth and saying everything was "*oishii*," which meant delicious, and which he was pretty sure it all was, though he was rather too on his guard to savor anything.

After they'd all finished eating, the girls got up and removed the dirty dishes—the men didn't budge—then Miho's mother served green tea and some kind of ice cream dumplings. Rina and Akemi played *Canon in D* as a duet on the Bosendorfer, and Miho's grandfather told Brain stories, which Miho couldn't possibly keep up with translation-wise, but which she informed him were about the war, and which Brain, smart with liquor, fancied he understood the emotional content of, if not the actual words. As a young man this guy had fought tooth and nail against the Allies, and now an eventful half-century later, here was the enemy in his dining room, making eyes at his granddaughter and drinking his booze. *How things change,*

Brain was thinking he was probably thinking, though in the event that the old man should get caught up in the spirit of reminiscence and point a bayonet at Brain's jugular, he might yet wriggle out of the way, for while both of Brain's lines had held U.S. passports before 1941, his blood was pure Axis: his mother's maiden name was Strauss; Tedesco was Italian for "German." There was some Irish back there too, but that was okay: Ireland was neutral.

Meanwhile, George had tuned in a baseball game on the huge-screen TV. "You like baseball?" he asked, and Brain did that "so-so" gesture with his hand and Miho's mother invited him to go sit on the couch, which he did, though not without quietly forcing Miho to sit between them as a kind of DMZ. Grandpa took a seat on the massage chair and passed out with his eyes open. The girls got up one at a time to take their baths and go to bed. Brain sat on the edge of the couch with his elbows on his knees and his chin in his hands, feigning interest in the game in an effort to keep from being talked to. Of course, in the posterior, undrunk part of his mind, he knew he'd have to face up sooner or later to the reason he was here to begin with. It wasn't like his strategy was working anyway. Miho's mother wouldn't shut up. She kept relaying questions about how he liked Japan and what was he doing here and what was it like where he was from and what kinds of Japanese food did he like, etc. Eventually she came around to the question she'd no doubt been holding back all evening.

"She asking how we are becoming friends," Miho said.

Brain straightened up, closed his eyes for a second, and seized the opening.

"Mr. and Mrs. Tanigaki, I realize this is only the first time we've met, but there's something I'd like to ask you."

Miho looked at him with some mixture of pity and admiration before interpreting. George muted the game.

"Miho and I have become very close over the past few weeks. So close that I can no longer imagine what life would be like without her."

Miho tilted her head and Brain gave it to her slow. She blushed. Her parents inched forward on the couch.

I've lost my mind, Brain thought. "So what I'm trying to say is ..."

They bowed their heads in anticipation.

"I'd like your permission to marry your daughter."

There.

Miho didn't have to translate. They'd gotten his meaning. George's nostrils flared.

Brain continued, "And don't worry, it's not like I intend to take your daughter away or anything. We'll live nearby. And you'll have to bear with me for a while, but I'll do my best to learn Japanese." Matsuo had advised him to stress these two points. Few Japanese fathers would welcome the thought of *gaijin* marrying their daughters, but at least he could minimize the damages.

Miho translated and Brain steeled himself for the unexpected, though what came was doubly so: George wept. Not cried, but really wept, tears flooding his eyes so that his irises appeared dilated. Brain wasn't at all sure how to interpret this. Finally, after a really long, really uncomfortable time, a full minute perhaps, George stood up, put an arm on Brain's shoulder and said, "Congraturations! It's wonderful news!" Miho's mother stood too and thanked him and nudged grandpa awake and went to wake the girls and tell them the good news. The girls giggled and congraturated him, and grandpa went and fetched the good *sake*, and Miho explained to her parents that they wanted to do it within the next few weeks so that Brain would be rid of his visa problems, and the family was not only amenable to that but set to making the wedding plans right away.

Only some days later did Brain understand what they'd been so happy about. Matsuo explained it to him. Miho's parents had never believed Miho would find herself a good match. She'd told him as much. "Miho is very beautiful girl," he said. "But too strong for Japanese mans. Okay for sexing, but for marrying, Japanese mans are wanting softer womens, womens who always are walking three steps behind. Miho-chan is walking behind nobody."

That was true enough. Even walking down the aisle two weeks hence as man and wife, grains of white rice pelting them in the face, Miho was a half-pace ahead of him, and he often wondered, during the unsustainably happy period that was the early part of their marriage, whether there was anything wrong with Miho's penchant for leadership, whether he ought to object in some way to her picking out all their furniture, making whatever she wanted for their dinner, washing whatever articles of his clothing were balled up in the corner of the room, all without consulting him first. But really he couldn't see what was so bad about it.

Indeed nothing was very bad of late. As if the deal had needed sweetening, Miho's grandfather had surprised them on the way home from the wedding by directing the chauffeur to a newly built 1LDK (one bedroom, living, dining, kitchen) in the upscalish neighborhood of Aobadai and handing Brain the key. Moreover, Miho had gotten him to quit smoking. His lungs were already feeling pinker and his wallet a little heavier. And not least of all, the act of marrying itself had mooted most of Brain's misgivings about the institution, brought the whole chorus inside of him into accord, freeing him to enjoy some of the simpler pleasures of life, like having his visa come through and scoring a gig teaching English to would-be nurses at a nearby vocational school. It was only six hours a week, but it paid well enough that he could stop leeching off his in-laws while he looked for something more permanent. Miho, for her part, had taken a part-time job at a women's shoe store in the Landmark Tower and was studying English the rest of the week at the AEON conversation school in the train station. And every evening, they'd reconvene in their new apartment, eat dinner, watch some TV maybe—there was a Japanese lesson for *gaijin* every night at eight and Miho had picked up a CNN habit—and take to their queen-sized Beautyrest several hours before actually going to bed.

Not that they limited themselves to the bedroom. They did it all over the place—up against the kitchen table, the mini washing machine, the balcony railing—and really it ought not to have mattered to Brain where they did it, for his attention was always fixed down on the nexus of it all. The sheer *sexness* of the sex astounded him, what with this really being his penis really jammed up Miho's real vagina. Still, he liked the feeling of marking his territory and imprinting new memories on the not-so-blank slate of Miho's mind. They did it so often he bought rubbers in bulk from the Condomania in Harajuku. She tried getting him to desist, but he was adamant about safety. It wasn't disease he was concerned about so much as pregnancy. Brain's one gripe against Miho's family, who otherwise treated him like an honored diplomat, was their continual insinuations that a baby ought to be on the way. In the absence of the band, Brain had no real concrete goals anymore, but that didn't mean his will was for hire either. He had lots to do yet, whatever those things—that *Thing*—might turn out to be. The way he saw it, you had kids when you were ready to pass the torch and live out the rest of your life vicariously. Ambitious people didn't have babies at twenty-four, let alone eighteen. They used to maybe, but not anymore, what with the life expectancy rising and all.

In lonelier days, Brain had been fond of deconstructing the very idea of happiness. "Are you happy?" his mom might ask, and he'd say, "Well that depends what you mean by 'happy.' Nobody's happy all the time. How can you even know what happiness is unless you've suffered?" He'd been absolutely convinced of the integrity of his argument back then, but now he was beginning to wonder. On the surface at least, he seemed to want for nothing these days beyond the creature comforts of food, sleep and sex—all of which he was getting in abundance. Once in a while, walking back from the station at night, a chill wind or the hum of a streetlamp might feather in him a ghost itch of that thrilling, gushing, quasi-mystical anguish that had sustained him through all the endless nights and days of his prolonged adolescence. But for the better part of a year, he was content to ignore it.

•

It wasn't until a halcyon Tuesday afternoon in early spring that life got the better of him again. He'd been on inter-semester vacation these past few weeks and had fallen into the habit of spending a great deal of his free time in the bathroom, which in this country was always separate from the room with the bath in it—a cultural difference Brain embraced since he'd long recoiled at the thought that other people should be defecating in the vicinity of his toothbrush. The room itself wasn't much to look at, but the state-of-the-art Washlet that Miho's parents had given them for their wedding gift was far and away the coziest piece of furniture in the apartment. Truly a toilet for the Swiss Army, it boasted a heated, self-cleaning seat; smart lid; temperature-and-pressure-adjustable bidet w/ blow-dryer; ozone deodorant system; automatic flush; and best of all—since Brain had no greater concern about cohabiting with Miho than how to keep her from hearing him eliminate—running water sound effects.

Brain lowered his pants, took a seat, sighed and reached over into the magazine rack and pulled out the latest issue of *Metropolis*, which he'd picked up the other day at the bookstore adjacent to where Miho worked. The magazine was mostly ads, but it *was* free and in English, and all the imported magazines cost at least twice what they cost in the States. He skimmed his horoscope, which informed him that "Things really take off when the heartfelt Sun joins Uranus. Speak up and you'll find you get what you desire." He read an article about the growing popularity of the cellphone novel, as well as a rhapsodic review of a first novel dealing, a little uncannily, with an American musician in Tokyo who gets married to a prostitute.

Then he turned to page thirty-three.

And his urine flow came to a halt.

He held the magazine up to his face. Sure enough, staring right out at him with unctuously unaffected grins, in 2"x 2" black-and-white, were his former bandmates. Theo stood in the middle with his arms out to either side. A miniature Matt was perched on his right hand, a mini Nick on his left. It didn't take a genius to see that they were actually standing twenty or thirty yards *behind* Theo—an insultingly low-tech illusion in the age of Photoshop. He shook his head while he finished peeing, without an iota of pleasure, before finally bringing himself to confront the block of text that lay in wait beneath the photo.

Agenbite, *Nitwit* (Virgin Records)

Rock music in recent years has suffered not only from the embattled commercial interests surrounding it, but from a certain generational malaise as well, a Prozac-flavored complacency that has resulted in the endless rehashing of old formulae and a dearth of anything even remotely new. Fortunately, with their major-label debut, *Nitwit*, Philadelphia-based trio Agenbite serves to remind those of us who were losing our faith in the form of just how exhilarating rock music can be when it's done with sufficient creativity, swagger and outrage.

The polycephal grandchild of Pink Floyd, Jeff Buckley, Primus, and Faith No More, Agenbite has something to offer rock fans of all stripes. Don't be put off by their being a three-piece. Theo McCall's freakishly dynamic voice could almost carry the record alone, and the dada lyrics are something of a bonus (see "Fecal Antimatter" or "Hitler's Testy"), recalling nothing so much as the best work of Captain Beefheart. Nick Benini on drums and Matt Hamilton on bass lay down insanely catching grooves while McCall, who doubles on guitar, sprays aural graffiti all over them in the form of minimalist single-note melodies and heavily effected sheets of noise that at times recall My Bloody Valentine. More than usual even, I find myself struggling to do them justice in so few words. In short, you need to hear this. We all do. We waited so very long.

★ ★ ★ ★ ★

As soon as Brain got to the end of the review, an invisible strappado drew taut. He struggled to breathe and set to cursing the great dead schadenfreude in the sky the way he used to as a kid when he couldn't put a speedball inside the strike zone he'd taped to the garage. He crumpled up the magazine and bashed it against the wall until it scuffed up the paint and tatters of newsprint snowed over his slippers. After a spell of blinding self-pity, he gathered up the news and flushed it with the rest of his excrement down the greatest toilet in the world.

He went to the living room, sat on the couch, turned on the TV and watched a talk show he didn't understand and wouldn't have understood even if it were in plain English since his attention was already so impacted. *It's got to be garbage*, he was thinking. *How can you write and record a decent album in a mere six months?* This was all in the way of denial of course. Many great records had been recorded in less time than that. *Thick as a Brick*—the only Tull album worth listening to, as far as he was concerned—had taken all of a month or something. Brain himself had often sought to be more prolific, but his inveterate perfectionism was like a kind of inhibitor gene. In the absence of Nick's nagging—*"Ben wants to hear something ASAP"*—he might never have finished anything. In a certain way he felt he never actually *had* finished anything; he'd only finished *with* things. Perhaps that was why he hadn't really missed composing this last half year or so. To be an artist was to have failure as your constant bedfellow, and his new bedfellow was much more becoming.

Miho came home shortly thereafter and he greeted her as best he could, given the circumstances. *"Daijoubu?"* she asked—Are you okay?—and he said he was, though really he wasn't at all sure as yet. He flipped the channel in an effort to stem the words pullulating inside his head. Two old besuited men were playing the ancient game of *Go*. He tried figuring out the rules, and, failing that, was about to change the channel when the camera panned out from the board to reveal the referee, who was a woman, kind of on the frumpy side, but with a marvelously streamlined body. He pulled out his dick—alarmingly adamant already—tugged on it a few times, and got up and went into the kitchen, where Miho was at the counter slicing radishes. She was wearing his favorite fishnets, the wide mesh ones that smacked of bondage. He snuck up on her and kissed her throat, cupped her bell-shaped breasts in his hands, licked her neck and slid his tongue down her salty back until he had her skirt around her pink feet and she was doubled as far as possible over the cutting board and he stuck his face right up in her crotch and felt around with his tongue and found what he was looking for and lapped and flicked at it and he could feel it swelling up and hear her voice off in the distance coyly protesting and he depantsed himself with one hand and said, "Wait!" and ran into the room with the bath in it to get a rubber out of the medicine cabinet and, donning the rubber, ran back and resumed working on her when he was stricken with a painful thought—*I'll bet anything Theo's using Ibaneza*—and that thought naturally sparked other thoughts, setting back into motion the machinery of self-doubt, and in six seconds flat the death instinct had prevailed over the life one. His hard-on became a parody at best, a soft-on or a hard-off, and for the first time to date the *sexness* of the sex seemed to be not such a good thing after all. His nose was halfway up Miho's ass and much as he wanted it to smell like flowers, it just didn't. It smelled like *ass*, and he wondered whether a man's ass would smell any different and decided it probably wouldn't, especially his own since they followed pretty much the same diet. His tongue grew tired so he gave it a rest and tremolo-picked her with his fingers, and he was thinking *Probably the only thing worse than an enemy's success is a friend's and these guys are sorta both.* He was scouring her like baked-on grease now. *I wonder how much they're getting paid? No doubt Nick brokered them the best deal possible.*

Carpal tunnel syndrome was of no small concern. *How long's it been since you picked up Martina anyway? When's the last time you even listened to any music beyond Miho's crappy J-Pop?* He was right on the verge of calling it quits when at last Miho's thighs began to tremble, her neck craned, and the essence of Girl came oozing down her thigh. He handed her a box of tissues, kissed her on the crown of the head, and went out to get some fresh air. She assured him dinner would be ready in a few minutes.

•

The next morning, as soon as Brain awoke, he went out and caught a train to the HMV in Yokohama. Not having visited a record store in months, he was anxious to see what he'd missed. He'd let himself get waylaid for a bit, but he was still a musician, and if Agenbite could make it without him, well then he could sure as hell make it without them. He'd find some new music to get excited about, go home and woodshed with Martina, regain his chops, regrow his hair, write some tunes, find a band, get a deal, go on tour, outsell Agenbite. As he entered the store, he knew there was some risk he might stumble across their record—if reviews were getting printed all the way over here, then they must be getting decent distribution—but in no way was he prepared for what he found. As soon as he crossed the threshold, Theo's eyes fixed him in their arctic blue gaze. It was the same asinine photo the magazine had run, but in full color and poster-sized now, and the place was festooned with them. Brain was determined to try and ignore it until, digging through the bargain bin, he made out some of the lyrics to the rock song he'd been inadvertently tapping his foot to: "*So go and throw your shitfit, my lonely little nitwit…*"

He instructed himself not to get paranoid, even as he felt reasonably certain this song was about him. As soon as he could move, he fled the store as if it were on fire and returned to the sanctuary of home, the chorus of what had to be Agenbite's title track playing like tinnitus in his head. The worst part of it was: it was catchy as hell.

•

That night, the eve of the new semester, Brain couldn't get to sleep for the clamor in his head. Agenbite's apparent success had dredged up a miasma in him. He remembered now what depression felt like, that withering necrosis of the spirit, and regretted having romanticized it for even a second. He tried counting his blessings like sheep, but his old bandmates kept impaling them on pickets and devouring them like kebabs. Of course, the band alone wasn't to blame. If it were just the band, he could have punched a hole in a wall and gotten on with his life, but evidently jealousy was communicative, for when he tried telling himself that at least he still had Miho, that she was his one success they couldn't overshadow, he found himself wondering why it felt like a purely intellectual line of defense, why the thought alone didn't sway his soul to peace. He wished the question were merely rhetorical, but sure enough it had an answer. He knew because he'd sealed it away in Pandora's box half a year ago and might never have looked on it again had that scabrous review not gnashed through the lid and loosed this world of ills.

"Mi," he said, nudging her awake. The clock read 3:42.

"*Nani?*"

"I need to ask you something."

She rolled onto her back.

"Remember when you were in the hospital last year?"

"Yeah."

"Well there's something I still don't understand about what happened back then. About how you got injured?"

Wang's explanation was still branded on the underside of his mind. Indeed, the only dreams to molest his sleep of late were horrible enactments of it.

"Can we talking about this tomorrow?" Miho said.

"No, Mi. I'm afraid I need to know tonight. Just answer this one question for me. Whatever the answer is, I need to know. I won't be mad, I swear."

She grumbled something in Japanese. She had this habit of reverting to her native tongue at the faintest sign of conflict.

"Did you ever have intercourse with any of your customers?"

She grumbled again.

"Did you?"

No reply, which was as good as an affirmative one, and a little bit worse.

"I fucking knew it. Jesus friggin Christ. Why didn't you ever tell me? Don't you think I have a right to know something like that?"

"I didn't want to hurt you."

"So you admit it! Jesus, did you ever think that maybe if you didn't want to hurt me then you shouldn't be letting other guys shove their cocks in you? Did that never occur to you? It's not even like it was a different day. It was the same friggin day!"

"Just business," she said.

"Well if it was just business then how come you let him fuck you and not me? What's that all about? Is it 'cause I'm a *gaijin* or what?"

"He was regular customer. Sometime regular customer pay tip for bonus."

"Bonus? How come nobody told me about any 'bonus'! How much did this 'bonus' cost?"

"Maybe ten thousand yen or something. Just business," she said.

"Jesus, do you not see anything remotely wrong with that?"

"Wrong?"

"Do you not think sex is *sacred* at all?"

"Sacred?" Was it just the words she didn't understand? He was beginning to think it was the concepts.

"I don't believe this. I kept telling myself you were just some

132

kind of thoroughgoing masseuse is all, but you were a card-carrying whore after all. It's not even like you grew up poor or something. You could have been anything."

She sighed and rolled back onto her side, away from him. He sighed crosswise and tried to get to sleep for a while, but he kept forgetting to breathe. He nudged her awake again. "So how many men do you think you slept with? I won't be mad, I swear."

"Why not sleep?" she suggested, but his mind was beset by streaming images of his wife the whore, sucking all variety of cock—white, black, red, brown, yellow, all bigger than his no doubt, one after another, and their fat tongues rummaging around in her cleft, *his* cleft, slurping at the ramen of her, sucking on her toes maybe while they rammed themselves inside of her and coaxed those same shivers and moans.

"Mi, I want to be reasonable about this. I know it was the past and I have no right to even ask this maybe, but I *need* to know. To settle my mind. I won't be mad, I promise."

"I didn't count," she grumbled. The first pastels of sunlight were just gloaming through the curtains.

"Please, Mi. Jesus, I have a right to know, don't I? I'm your husband for Christ sakes. Please. It's the last question, I swear. Then we can move on with our lives."

"Are sure?"

"Of course I'm sure. What do you mean am I sure?"

"I am working in Club Pinky maybe *ichi nen han*"—a year and a half.

"And how many times a day did you perform fellatio, on average?"
No reply.

"Twenty?" Brain offered.

"No," Miho said.

"Ten?"

"*Mm*. Maybe."

"Okay, so ten dicks a day. And how many of those got the

'bonus'?"

She grumbled again.

"Five?"

"No way."

"Three?"

Again no.

"Two?"

"*Mm*," she said. "Maybe."

"So two bonuses a day? On average?"

She nodded.

Brain's heart slipped into his duodenum.

"And how many days a week did you work?"

"Four."

"Four?"

"Sometimes five."

"So you sucked between forty and fifty dicks a week for a year and a half?"

"But we have many regular customer," she pointed out.

"Okay, so maybe twenty-five dicks a week then?"

"Maybe."

"For a year and a half. That's what, about seventy-five weeks? Seventy-five times twenty-five, that's..."

Miho rolled onto her back and began calculating on her hand with the index finger of her other hand, but Brain stayed in the game *carry the two five times seven is thirty-five plus two zero carry the one fourteen fifteen fifteen-hundred plus three-seventy-five is* , "One thousand eight hundred and seventy-five!"

Miho finished her own calculation near the base of her pinky. "*Mm*," she said by way of confirmation.

Now here was an epistemological crisis. Not only had Brain's Japanese wife been a card-carrying whore for a year and a half, but now he'd beaten her at a math problem. He no longer knew anything.

"So you figure you fucked maybe twenty percent?"

"Twenty percent of regular customer maybe."

"So you had roughly four hundred cocks in you maybe?"

"I don't know. Maybe."

"You have any other secrets for me while we're at it? Any of them fuck you in the ass?" He'd broached the topic of anal sex before. She wasn't interested—at least not with him.

She bristled at that. "Of course not." As if he'd been out of line to ask.

It sounded even worse when you did the math. His wife had sucked one thousand eight hundred and seventy-five cocks and ushered four hundred of them into her innermost sanctum. There was the fact, cold and hideous and hard like some modernist sculpture of the holocaust, and now all he had to do was to stare at it, refuse to avert his gaze until he'd mastered it. But what anguished him really wasn't so much that she'd had so many dicks in her as that he'd had his dick in so few of her, one in fact, and he felt the imbalance like a sledgehammer in the gut. She was so much more *worldly* than he was. She *knew* so much more. A Japanese woman no less! Even if she hadn't known him yet—and she had, for at least one of those clients she had—couldn't she at least have dreamed of him in some far-off way? He'd been dreaming of her sure enough. He'd been in his basement writing love songs. And now his band, *his* band, had gone on to great things while he'd stayed behind to marry a common whore. That was the long and short of it, and you could not edit life. You either accepted it, or you went on lying to yourself. She was snoring now. He tried again to get to sleep but his mind raged. Finally he got up and went into the kitchen and looked for something to throw and settled on the rice cooker and a stack of Miho's beauty magazines—a tantrum, in short. Then he showered and drank a pot of coffee and left a little early for the nursing school. He made a point of *not* kissing Miho goodbye and of leaving his wedding ring right where it was on the dresser.

•

It had hardly escaped Brain's notice the previous semester that his job was a playboy's paradise. Forty-five students, all but two of them women, all between the ages of seventeen and thirty-five. At the time, he'd been so happy with his new station in life that his libido had remained in check, but the events of the past couple of days had armed it, Miho's confession had pulled the linchpin, and now he could feel its white-hot ardor in every cell of his body. The newly arrived springtime didn't exactly help/hurt either, what with all the girls suddenly wearing skimpy shoes and short skirts.

He took roll. Forty-*seven* students this time. Same age group as last time. And not a dude to speak of. By the end of the hour-long session he'd picked out his favorites:

Ishida, Akiko – bratty, misbehaving type, eighteen or so, with feline eyes, a spill of inky hair and an ass he fancied wearing on his face.

Tanaka, Kaori – drowsy-looking housewife type with (an exceedingly rare thing in this country) tits like golden watermelons.

Maruno, Kyoko – quiet, classical beauty with calligraphic eyes and legs so delicately muscled, lustrous and smooth, they literally made his salivary glands shoot.

There was of course no shortage of alternates—there were forty-four of them in fact.

Over the next couple of achingly virile weeks, Brain pondered how he might go about baiting one of them. Clearly he'd have to begin by singling them out in some way, calling on them often or never, marking their papers in different-colored ink perhaps, stroking their shoulders while he moseyed about the classroom checking their progress and hiding his enthusiasm with a folder. But was it possible to single them all out at once? Or would he have to go one at a time? Probably one at a time made more sense, evolutionarily speaking, but then who should he go after first?

Chance relieved him of the decision after his third week of class. He'd just gained the platform when the Stradivariusly bowed legs of the auspiciously named Kyoko leapt out at him from halfway down the track.

"*Sensei*," she said when he alighted in the seat directly beside her.

"Well hello. What a coincidence."

"My name is Kyoko," she said.

"I know that. Of course I know that. Second row, last seat."

That geminate smile.

"You're headed home?"

She cocked her head the way Miho did when she didn't understand his English. "Where do you live?" he asked.

"I … live … Nagatsuda."

"Oh yeah? I live not too far from there myself. In Aobadai?"

"It's very close," she said. That part of it really was a coincidence.

A nearly vacant train arrived and they boarded it. He sat first and patted the seat next to him and she bowed her head and joined him, and for the duration of the fifteen-minute ride they attempted, with mixed results, to converse. Between Brain's two hundred or so words of Japanese—almost all of which were nouns—and Kyoko's requisite six years of English, they managed to fend off the dead air, for the most part. "What are your hobbies?" he asked, and she said, "Ballet?" and he thought *Well that explains the legs*. When a lull came along, she asked him, predictably enough, which types of Japanese food he liked, and he said he liked tempura and sushi and just about everything really except *uni*, which tasted like glue stick, and she asked, "Can you eat *natto*?" and he said he didn't know—he had yet to try the fermented soybeans he'd heard so much about—and she said, "I love *natto*," and he seized the opportunity and said, "Well then maybe we can eat it together sometime?" and she looked at her watch and said, "I am okay," and so it was by virtue of this minor misunderstanding that they ended up that very afternoon at a sushi place not a few blocks from his apartment.

Kyoko said the *natto* on the conveyor belt looked dry (to Brain it looked plenty wet enough—not unlike vomit) so she special-ordered more from the chef. When it came, she said, "*Itadakimasu*"—the Japanese equivalent of grace before meals—and she caressed the pad of rice with her chopsticks, inserted the whole shebang into her mouth in a way that was positively NC-17, and covered her mouth with her free hand while she chewed. "*Oishii!*" she said—delicious. Then it was his turn. He picked up the block of rice covered in viscous slop and dumped it on his taste buds. The nut-buttery consistency repelled him at first, but after a few more bites he got a feel for what it was possibly supposed to taste like. "It's kind of like coffee or something," he said, lacking a better analogy, and she laughed. They were sitting on stools and she had one leg crossed over the other and he couldn't keep from looking down at them and he was sure she'd caught him any number of times but all she did was smile and bat her eyelashes and shift her gaze elsewhere like the bashful adolescent she'd have been just a few years ago. How could simple legs have such a powerful effect on him? They were just legs after all, a couple shafts of muscle and bone that evolution had thrown together so her womb would have a means of transport. Even still, he could feel his salivary glands shooting off again and this made him wonder whether there wasn't something cannibalistic about his feelings for this pair of legs. He'd have given his right little finger to suck on them for a while. Why not take a bite while he was at it? Gnaw on them like drumsticks (the chicken kind)? Those eyes too. He wanted to do something to them but he wasn't sure what exactly. Lick them? What would they taste like? Candied almonds? Werther's Originals perhaps? And what about those adorable wisps of hair by her ears? You couldn't even really do anything with them. Floss your teeth maybe? How cruel desire was. He felt hollowed, scooped out. Indeed there was nothing figurative about heartsickness, he realized, for this kind of longing really did cause you pain right there in your cardiac organ. And there was no cure, for much as he wanted to fuck her—a long shot, but within the realm of human possibility at least—he knew he wanted more than that as well. He couldn't possibly behold this kind of beauty without wanting to become one with it somehow, to assimilate it, to have his Kyoko and eat her too.

They split the bill and Kyoko led him to a little wooded park off one of the side streets. A steep flight of granite stairs, each too deep for one step and too shallow for two, delivered them to a Shinto shrine. Kyoko poured cold water over each of their hands in the stone basin, gave him a five-yen piece to throw between the wooden slats of the collection box and directed him in the proper etiquette of Shinto worship. First you pulled the rope and rang the bell overhead, then you clapped your hands twice, bowed, closed your eyes and prayed (Brain winked open his left eye to find Kyoko unironically at prayer, so he prayed too, to these anonymous gods, for a spell inside her orbit). When that was through, they took a seat on the top step and gazed down at the amphitheater of the park where an audience of evergreens swayed in the whistling wind and children swung from swings and slid down slides. Kyoko's leg was touching his in two places. He visualized putting his arm around her (the way he used to envision hitting homers while he swung his donut-laden bat on-deck) and then he actually did it. And she smiled at him! And his arm felt like a log. What should he do now? Should he caress her shoulder? He caressed her shoulder. She purred. That was a good sign. They sat like that for a long time, the wind whistling through the treetops, the sun sinking behind a duplex. There was only one way this could end. Fuck the band, he hadn't a splotch of jealousy in him at this moment, for this was the kind of elemental encounter he'd dreamt of his whole life. The sickness in his heart went into remission and, having visualized it several dozen times in minute detail, Brain leaned over and affixed his trembling lips to the cold rouge of Kyoko's cheek.

But Kyoko didn't turn to him the way she was supposed to. She didn't murmur or offer up her milky neck. Instead she pulled away and said, "*Chotto kaze o hiiteimasu*"—I have a cold—which didn't seem to be true, for he hadn't heard her sniffle or cough once all day. Then she said, "*Ikimashou ka?*" which meant "Shall we go?" and it seemed to him significant somehow that she should now be speaking her own language instead of trying to speak his more universal one, and soon they were back at the station saying a rushed, perfunctory goodbye. He kicked a wall, limped back home and set to purging the bitch from his memory, but later that evening, in the dark of the marital bed, it was unmistakably Kyoko whose body he pulled all the way into him and pushed all the way away (it wasn't that far), Kyoko whose lips he kissed, Kyoko whose hair he pulled on like reins. But then in the aftermath, when the maelstrom had spun itself out, it was unmistakably Miho whose hair he buried his face in, Miho to whom he beseeched, "I love you. Promise you'll never leave me," and it was Miho, his unimpeachable, longsuffering bride, who promised she never would.

What a nitwi…what an *idiot* he'd been these past couple of weeks, getting all hung up on her past the way he had, cowering at the specter of all those stabbing dicks while the woman his wife was now, the only version of her that ought to have mattered, was as chaste and pure-of-heart as the Madonna herself. Come the ringing of his alarm, he'd already vowed to wear his ring to work by way of atonement, as a symbol—as the celebrant had put it—of their everlasting love. Of course, it didn't escape him that he may have had an ulterior motive as well.

The instant Kyoko spotted the ring, she looked seasick. All the other pupils eyed it as well, though only Akiko the Brat had moxie enough to say anything: "Mr. Brain, you are married?"

Brain looked right at Kyoko. "Yes I am," he said. "Very happily."

"Your wife is Japanese?" Akiko asked.

"She is," Brain said, and the classroom swelled with ohs and ehs, the Japanese equivalents of oohs and aahs.

He continued with the lesson. "So I'd like to look at some pronunciation drills today. Let's see, who wants to go first? Any volunteers? Kyoko, how about you?"

She stared weapons into him. He continued, "Repeat after me. *Rollerblader*."

She balked.

"Come on now. We don't have all day."

She gave it her best shot: "*Lollabrada*."

"Sorry, Kyoko. That's just not gonna work. Let's try a different one. *Laura's really leery of the liver river*."

Water was welling up in the corners of her eyes. He could see it from all the way up here.

"Come on. It's simple. *Laura's... really... leery... of... the... liver... river*."

"*Raura's leary reely obu ribel libel*."

"Yeah, now see, Kyoko, that's pretty terrible, if I'm being honest."

The whole class hung on tenterhooks.

"Try this one. *Cannibal carnivals cater to carnivores*."

But by the time he'd finished uttering the phrase, Kyoko's pretty legs had already shuffled her out of the classroom. He called after her: "*Sumo wrestler, small restaurant!*"

Fifty-five minutes later, he found her waiting outside the teacher's lounge for him, sniffling. "*Nande uso tsuita no?*"

She looked ravishing in her distemper. "Say again?" Brain said.

Kyoko took her electronic dictionary out of her bookbag, tapped out something, and showed him the screen: "to lie, to deceive." "Why?" she said.

"I didn't lie."

"You never saying you have wife."

"I don't recall you asking."

She leered.

"Look, Kyoko. You're right. I should have told you I was married. I guess I just didn't want to tell you because I think you're so incredibly beautiful."

Then, according to plan—an inchoate thing at best and more ingenious than he ever could have imagined—her scowl fell away like an ice shelf into the sea to be replaced by beams of iridescent light. "Are hungry?" she asked, and he thought *Was it always this easy?* He'd always been so eager. The trick was to make yourself unavailable.

They went to Chez Chez, a Sino-French restaurant not a few blocks from the school, where they sampled among other things the *foie gras*, which almost made Brain mention the liver river, though he quickly thought better of it. Kyoko insisted on paying and as they were leaving she asked, "Are busy now?" and he said, "No," so they returned to the same park from yesterday and to the very same seated position with her leg touching his in two places. But this time Brain let Kyoko do the universe-disturbing and soon she'd leaned in and phermonically requisitioned a kiss and Brain obliged and they sat there like that for maybe an hour. Kyoko's tongue was different from Miho's, slenderer, more probing. To be sure, he loved Miho's tongue, but it was softer, more nurturing. Kyoko's tongue was *erect*. He started groping around her groin area, rubbing the pads of his fingers against her dewy stockings, and with liquid eyes and glowing skin she told him, "Come." So he followed her around the way to a karaoke place and she got them a room on the sixth floor and Brain was thinking *She wants to sing?* but then she took hold of his hand and showed him her modest come-hither eyes, and when the waiter came to take their order they pointed out a couple of cobalt cocktails on the menu and while they waited for them to be delivered they kissed some more on the couch and watched some black kids breakdance in Central Park on the TV, and when the drinks were set down they sipped them precipitously through straws, then Brain pushed Kyoko back against the couch, lifted her skirt and lowered her stockings, pushed aside her pink-and-blue striped thong panties and sucked on the slick anemone between her thighs, and she trembled and raised her legs, toes *à pointe*, and he shoved a finger up her ass for good measure, and this went on for a few songs, then he lowered his own pants and thrust his naked cock into her, and her external genitalia were more pronounced than Miho's and felt like a pair of tongues lapping at him, and he interrupted himself only at the last possible nanosecond, spilling legions of heirs into her belly button. He felt like a god, less the Christian one than some lusty agrarian, a Pan or a Kokopelli. Kyoko reached over to her bag and pulled out one of those little packets of tissues advertisers were so fond of giving out over here, and she took one for herself and handed the rest to Brain, and they wiped themselves down and threw the briny tissues in the trashcan and fixed their clothing and finished their drinks and cuddled on the couch while some white couple gallivanted along the banks of the Seine on the TV. Kyoko held his hand as they walked past all the other rooms where people were actually singing, some in English ("Take On Me," "Dancing Queen," "The Final Countdown," Avril what's-her-face). He dropped by the men's room on his way out and scrubbed the shine off his genitals, an exalted chore if ever there was one.

It was dark by the time he got home. Miho lay on the couch watching the evening news.

"Sorry I'm home so late," he said. "One of the other teachers was sick, so they had me teach another class. I should have called but I didn't get a free second." Brain was the only English teacher at the school, but he didn't think Miho knew that. He kicked off his shoes.

"You can heat your dinner is on stove," she said. She didn't seem angry, just preoccupied. And if he needed further proof that she wasn't angry, she gave it to him later by going down under the bedsheets and coddling him with her nurturing tongue. It felt wonderful and Brain thought *I love Japan* and then he wondered if maybe this was a tactic women used to find out where you'd been, a kind of microchip in your head, and he hoped he'd scrubbed off Kyoko thoroughly enough—he'd even walked home the long way to try and build up a sweat. Anyway, if she detected anything, she didn't let on.

Mired in Kyoko, he had briefly, very briefly, considered that he might feel some remorse later on. He *was* a married man now, and even if he hadn't felt entirely ready at the time of the ceremony, he *had* taken his vows quite seriously. Would a transgression besmirch the whole thing? It might—he was a perfectionist after all. But then was an actual transgression any worse, morally speaking, than an imaginary one, of which he'd been guilty so many times already? By this point, of course, the question was merely academic, so he fairly swished the words away, and lying in bed with his wife that night, he went untouched by guilt. What he felt instead was buoyant, helium-filled, as if, were he to let go of Miho's hand, he might go sailing off into the ether.

He didn't feel particularly guilty two days later either when Kyoko took him to a Venice-themed love hotel with a mirrored ceiling and a gondola-shaped bed, nor for that matter in the aftermath of a half-dozen other assignations. It was only well into their fourth week as lovers that he began to sense the full weight of what he'd done. Kyoko wouldn't stop smiling at him in class and, while that was nice and all, there was a kind of tyranny in it as well, for he no longer felt free under that watchful gaze to spread his attentions around, which, however much affection he might feel for Kyoko, he seemed to be wired to do. When she seized him after class that Friday and asked where he wanted to eat, he told her, "I think I'll be heading straight home today actually," and she gave him a look like she'd been lashed across the back with a cat o'nine tails. As he got off at his stop, he shook her hand, and someone lashed her across the back again and he felt like total shit and thought how amazing it was that you could be fucking two beautiful women and still feel like total shit, that in fact you could feel like total shit *because* you were fucking two beautiful women. Much as he had wanted to ignore it, there was a moral dimension to his quandary. He was fucking around not just with bodies but with souls as well, his own not least of all. He'd felt, and continued to feel, this insatiable hunger inside of him, born of insecurity perhaps, or of an overweening mother, an immoderate all-consuming hunger for a woman's love so great it would suffuse him with light, fill his chest with blazing empyrean and leave no corner dark. His mother had done it for him when he was a boy, but she could not do it anymore. Nor could any woman, not even his beloved Miho. So he'd followed his common sense and sought to illumine the dark patches with another woman's love, but that arithmetic had proven faulty, for rather than redouble the beams of love coming in, it only seemed to halve them, leaving him bleaker inside than ever, a tenebrous cavern of dank stinking air and dripping stalactites. And the worst part, he knew, was that he was taking others there with him. He tried riding out his guilt alone, but come Saturday afternoon, the desire to unburden himself had grown so great that he found himself calling up the one real confidante he'd ever had in this country besides Miho. He hadn't seen Matsuo since the wedding and he was only banking on a few minutes of his time. It was Matsuo who suggested the fishing trip.

●

Brain had never been lake fishing before. His uncle Pete had chartered a fishing boat in Wildwood one summer when he was a kid, but Brain had spent the entire time in steerage turning greener by the minute and losing his guts in a bucket of squid. This lake was all looking-glass, however, reflecting the ancient face of Mt. Fuji with disorienting fidelity. It had taken them two hours to get there, but Matsuo had insisted Lake Kawaguchi was worth the drive. And was it ever. The weather was splendid, the sky cloudless and lazuline. On the north bank of the lake, the cherry blossoms were mostly in bloom. Several other rowboats were scattered here and there, but they were far enough away that it was as if the two of them had the lake to themselves.

Matsuo weighted Brain's line for him and hooked a night crawler and taught him how to cast, and they sat enjoying the cool morning for a good long while before Brain got the first bite of the day. His rod bent and he leaned back and reeled until at last a nice-sized bass emerged from Fuji's coruscating crater. The poor dumb creature was wearing the hook right through his upper lip. Matsuo said, "It's good one," and gripped the fish around the gills and pulled the hook out with a pair of pliers and threw the fish in a cage and tied the cage to the back of the boat. Then he opened the cooler and got out a couple of Kirin beers to celebrate. It was only eight in the morning, but it felt appropriate somehow. They clinked cans and drank, rowed to a new spot, cast again, drank, sighed. Brain lifted the cage up from time to time to make sure the fish was still there, and he kept thinking *You stupid fish, we've been pulling that same trick on you for millennia, why can't you ever learn?* But if part of him felt compelled to set the suffering animal free, another part of him knew that this was a rite of initiation he was going through here, years too late, and with the wrong dude perhaps, but nevertheless, and if he was to do it right, then that fish could have no destiny independent of his own guts.

Throwing back a scrawny pickerel, Matsuo said, "So what you are wanting to talk about?"

Brain stirred. He lifted the question cautiously out of its matrix. "Have you ever been in love, Matsuo-san? I mean in all the time I've known you, I don't think I've ever heard you say anything about having a girlfriend or anything like that."

"For nine years I am married," Matsuo said.

"You're married?"

"Used to be. My wife is died. Do you know reukemia?"

"Shit. I'm sorry," Brain said.

Matsuo nodded. A fat gull dive-bombed the lake, caught a minnow in its beak and soared off.

Matsuo segued for them: "You are having problems with

Miho-chan?"

Brain welcomed the change in gravitas. "No…I mean, I don't know…not problems exactly…"

He'd never opened up to any man about matters of the heart before, least of all a man old enough to be his father. What's more, Matsuo had known Miho far longer, and far better, than he'd known Brain. Was the unremarkable fact of their common manhood really grounds enough for Brain to expect his sympathies? It wasn't lost on Brain that the fishing knife in Matsuo's belt had a familiar gleam about it—and then there was the gleaming handgun he'd discovered in the Mercedes' glove compartment while Matsuo had gotten out to pump gas. He thought of spinning some smaller tale of conjugal strife, but Matsuo was too shrewd the physiognomist. "You are trying *uwaki*?" he guessed.

"*Uwaki*?"

"You are watching your wife and your outside women too?"

"Umm…"

"You are playing with girls?"

Brain hooked his apprehensions and cast them into the gentle northeasterly breeze. "I cheated on Miho, if that's what you mean. It was wrong. I never should have done it. But I did it and now I'm reaping what I sowed in guilt." He sucked in a breath and pushed it out his nose.

"She is Japanese?" Matsuo asked.

Brain nodded. "A nurse."

Matsuo grinned. "White angel, *ne*. You are in love to her?"

"I don't know…I mean, no, I'm not in love, but I have feelings for her. Tender feelings. I don't want to hurt her."

"Miho knows about her?"

"That's the thing. I'm honestly not sure. She hasn't said anything, but I've been coming home later and later. It used to be she wanted me to call her when I didn't need dinner. Now she wants me to call when I do."

"I see," Matsuo said. "Miho is smart girl. Must be knows, no?"

"You don't think she would have said something?"

"*So da ne.* I don't think so. Miho is *yamato nadeshiko.* Do you know?"

Brain shook his head.

"Means traditional Japanese woman. My wife is same way. You are lucky man, no?"

"I thought you told me before that Miho was the opposite of all that?"

"Must means she is very in love to you, no?"

Was that what it meant? Brain had no idea. Did Miho love him so much that she'd overridden her own nature to accommodate his vanity? It didn't compute. What was so lovable about him? From his own point of view, he was little more than an accomplished failure. Until lately he'd held up his marriage as a rare success, but now he'd gone and botched that too, and he couldn't shake the presentiment that one of these days she'd wake up, see how unworthy he was and pack her bags. Part of him sought to ignore the possibility, the other part just wanted to be ready when it came.

"Right now," Matsuo continued, "you are having *ryoute ni hana.* Do you know? Means flower in both hands. It's natural thing. You are man, *deshou*? But need to be very clear what is your true feelings. Don't confuse. You have your wife for *kokoro*"—here he tapped his heart—"and you have girlfriend for *chin chin*"—and here he tapped his groin. "Very important you are always keeping clear what is purpose. We Japanese have saying, '*Nitou ou mono wa ittou mo ezu.*' Means if you chase two rabbits, you are getting no rabbits. Means always need to be clear what is purpose. When my wife is still alive, I am very much enjoying to play with girls. But always my wife is number one."

"Of course Miho's number one for me too."

"So where is problem?"

"Well I can't bring myself to tell her about it for one thing. I want to, but then every time I go to say something, I end up swallowing my words."

"Why you are wanting to tell her?"

"I don't know. To clear the air, I guess. Keep things honest."

"It's very Christian idea, I think. Japanese are not thinking this way. You are Christian, Brain-san?"

"No," Brain said, with perhaps undue solemnity.

"Then why you are telling to Miho painful stuffs? For Japanese I think it's very... how do you say... *wagamama*?"

"Selfish," Brain said.

"*So.*"

Brain had never heard adultery espoused like that before, but it made an invigorating kind of sense. If he'd truly dispensed with God, poked out those all-seeing eyes, then what business did he have clinging to any absolute morality? Matsuo was right. What good could come of telling Miho he'd been fucking someone else? Wouldn't he just be heaping one selfishness on top of another, alternately stroking his cock and his conscience? Yes, from now on he would live in a world of people. The notion that morality should be based on how well you manage your misdeeds struck him as vaguely sophistical, but that was just the altar boy in him falling back on his default programming again. How liberating it would be to think like Matsuo, never having to rack yourself over your every harmless indulgence. His only real failing then would be in letting Miho detect anything. He'd gotten carried away with Kyoko; he saw that now. He'd muddled his allegiances, partitioned his *kokoro* and given her a share. He'd brought her perfumed shadow into Miho's home, and he was buckling now from the horizontal shame of it, even as he managed to slough off any guilt from above.

Matsuo got out a couple more beers and made a toast. "Maybe you don't know because I am looks like *yakuza* monster, but inside I am very sensitive man. Romantic man. Why else I am okay about you marry Miho-chan? Because you are truly in love to her, no? I can understand in your eyes. It's very rare thing, no? You have chance to be happy. Still I am loving my wife every day, even she is died five years ago."

Brain raised his can and toasted: "To your wife."

"To your *wife*," Matsuo said—he stressed the wrong word, but Brain knew what he meant. "If sometimes you are needing help about something," he continued, "*enryo shinaide ne.* Don't be shy."

"*Arigatou*," Brain said.

•

When he returned home that evening, Miho's smiling lips seemed to levitate off her face, slip through a porous pimple on his chest, and caress the dendrites of his heart. He felt like Odysseus returned to the hearth after years at sea. He kissed her on her mole and handed her a plastic bag filled with eight filleted bass. She donned her apron and painted a couple of the fish with miso paste and broiled them inside a small window on the range made for just that purpose. With his first bite still flaking and deliquescing on his tongue, he said, "This is so delicious I could cry."

"*Gomen ne.* I wish I can become more skillful."

"Oh I see. So not only did I marry the sweetest girl in the world, but she's the most modest too." He ate a few clumps of rice, then put his chopsticks down and gripped his temples like a football. When he'd said he could cry a few seconds ago, he'd meant it strictly by way of hyperbole, but now there was this sudden tickle in his sinuses that didn't seem to have anything to do with a sneeze.

"Are you okay?" she said, tilting her head on its axis.

"I'm sorry," he said.

"For what?" Miho asked.

"For hurting you." Matsuo was right of course. A confession of this sort was onanistic at best, cruel at worst, but he couldn't help it. He could aspire to Matsuo's insouciance in the future, but he was going to have to work up to it. For now at least this nonspecific act of contrition might scour a portion of the stain from his soul.

Tears plummeted from his cheeks. Miho wiped them away with the side of her hand and said, "You never hurt me," and much as he revered truth, he felt just how lucky he was to have married so magnanimous a liar.

The following day, after a penitential class, Kyoko took him to an Indian restaurant on the second floor of a shopping arcade in downtown Yokohama. Brain told her about the fishing part of yesterday's fishing trip. She smiled and made her *kawaii*-est faces to date. She had on a pink blouse with lace sleeves that showed snippets of her fresh-shaven armpits and the deltas of her breasts. When they'd finished eating, she said, "Shall we go?" but he suggested they have some chai first, for digestion. He couldn't decide whether his heartburn was foremost literal or figurative, for he regretted what he was about to do, the pain he was about to inflict, even as he felt how necessary it was. On the other hand, he *had* ordered the vindaloo. They finished their chai and she got up and he reached out and grabbed her by the arm and sat her back down and said, "Look, Kyoko, there's something I need to talk to you about."

Her eyes widened.

"So you know I like spending time with you, right?"

"I hope so."

"But you know also that I have a wife and that I love her very much."

"*Mm.*" She nodded.

"And so I guess what I wanna say... what I'm driving at is... I don't think we should continue seeing each other like this..." Already he was suffering the spiritual equivalent of blue balls.

"*Ii yo,*" she said.

"I mean, if you can separate yourself from your emotions for a minute, I think you'll see that nothing good can... wait, what did you just say?"

"*Ii yo*. I am fine."

"Did you understand what I just said?"

"I understand. You want to *wakareru, deshou*?"

"Break up. Yes." Her lips were so…pink. It took every ohm of his will to hold the line. "You're not upset about it?"

"Upset?"

"Sad."

"I am not sad," she said.

"You don't think you'll be, I don't know, lonely?"

"*Mm-mm-mm*. I don't think so."

His toehold gave way. "I mean, I don't know if we have to stop seeing each other completely. Maybe we can still get together once in a while. Like once a week or something?"

"No. It's good idea. Let's break out."

"Break up. Okay, but let's not go to extremes. I don't see any harm in meeting for coffee once a month, do you?"

She took a pinch of anise and fennel seeds from the check tray and placed it on her tongue. "In August I will marry."

Brain foundered. "What did you just say?"

She was busy chewing.

"What the *fuck* did you just say?"

She reached into her Prada clutch and pulled out her Louis Vuitton wallet and showed him a photo of herself with some probably very handsome Japanese dude making peace signs by the Trevi fountain. They looked very happy together, probably.

He sucked down the discarded drams of his chai, for digestion. "So time out, if you've had a fiancée all this time, then what the hell have you been doing with me?"

"Just playing, *deshou*?"

"What is it with all this 'playing' shit? What are we, goddamned toddlers?"

She puffed up her cheeks like some stymied anime character. No way had she understood what he'd said, but his tone was unmistakable.

It didn't make any sense. Here all this time he thought he'd been using Kyoko for his own ends, while it now looked to have been the other way around. What did that do for all his theories about the biologically determined, more or less predictable behaviors of the sexes? Women cheated when they were availed of superior sperm and *could get away with it.* But with only one womb to impregnate, why in God's name would Kyoko have been juicing him, a *white* guy, while she planned to spend her life with the *brown* guy in the photo? No, it definitely did not make any sense.

"So what were you just curious about doing it with a *gaijin* or what?"

She paused to reflect, then said, "*So kamo shirenai*"—maybe.

So that was it then. He'd been just a curiosity to her, a kind of fetish, nothing more. He got up, threw a couple of bills on the table, said, "Congratulations, Kyoko. I'm sure you'll be very happy," and made to leave. He gave her a second to protest, but she didn't.

Three classes remained to the semester. Kyoko skipped the first and kept her head down for the other two. He marked a B+ on the top of her exam in the same red ink he used for everyone else. She'd earned it fair and square too—if nothing else, all their time together had done wonders for her English. They very nearly acknowledged one another as her sumptuous legs took her out of his classroom one last time—and out of his life. The future was plain: she would go off and get married, he would live on as just the faintest blip in her memory, having in no important way altered her destiny.

•

The air-conditioning in Brain and Miho's apartment over the next couple of months—the rainy season and the muggy season—might have sufficed for a morgue. Fortunately, Miho's grandfather was paying every last yen and was himself too close to the slab to fret over such trivialities as money. Working just six hours a week, Brain was accustomed to spending more time at home than most people, but after the emotional strain of that last semester, he'd taken to the apartment full-time. He'd always seemed to require more sleep than most people, which fact he secretly took to be indicative of his hyperactive genius, but lately he was sleeping like he knew it was about to be outlawed any minute. Some days he'd stay in bed as many as eighteen or twenty hours, rousing himself only to use the bathroom, or, if Miho happened to have made something, eat. When occasionally he did manage to upright himself, he limited his activities to lazing around on the Internet or trying to watch TV. Now and then, he took a shower. He even picked up Martina once, but after playing a few notes and deciding he liked neither them nor what they were planning to do, he stuffed her right back in the closet where he'd found her. He wasn't depressed exactly, just sedentary, and with nothing to stir him, his inertia was keeping him thus. Kyoko had sucked the verve out of him. He tried viewing their collision in a positive light. He told himself it had in fact been the best of all possible scenarios. He'd had a hedonistic fling with no strings attached and gotten out alive. But despite his best efforts, he couldn't really see it that way. In reality, the fling hadn't been nearly hedonistic enough. It hadn't even been a fling. All that time, while he ought to have been savoring the unalloyed carnality of his wide-open nurse-ballerina, he'd instead been busy pouring feelings into her, raising the emotional stakes so that now his stupid heart smarted from the loss. Walking away through the bustling arcade that evening, he'd felt like a kid dispossessed of Santa. Since his earliest palpitating intimations of it, he'd regarded sex as that holiest of sacraments, an outward sign, if not of God's grace, then at least of something ecstatically good in the universe. But now he understood, with a clarity peculiar to the damned, that sex was about as inherently sacred as buying a pair of shoelaces or getting your oil changed. It was, in the end, a transaction. You gave something, you got something, and caveat emptor.

Precisely what was to be gained by sequestering himself like this, he couldn't say. Escapism figured into it no doubt, but more than that he felt he'd entered a period of mourning, less for the loss of a lover than for the death of his own heroic innocence.

He couldn't blame Miho for worrying about him. She'd come home from work and he'd be just sitting there on the couch, sunken and disheveled, the curtains drawn and only the anemic glow of some screen or other to suggest he might be other than catatonic. "Did you get any movies?" he'd ask—it was the only thing he could muster any interest in of late. But she wouldn't stop trying to get him to go outside. "Shall we go for walk first?" she'd ask, or, "What if we are taking my sisters to bowling?" He knew her intentions were good, but it was just so much easier staying put. So he'd whine until she pulled whatever DVD she'd rented out of her purse. In the first fortnight of his exile, they'd watched half a dozen classic Hitchcock films and all of Kubrick except the end of *Lolita* and most of *Eyes Wide Shut*—both of which were arousing his bloodlust.

Then one evening some three weeks into his exile, he was sitting at the kitchen table degreasing his forehead with a dishcloth when Miho came in a little later than usual and told him she'd signed him up for a sports club. "You don't have to go," she said, "but at least now you can if you want." Brain opened a parenthesis in the dialogue to congratulate her on a perfect English sentence. It was remarkable how much she'd improved in just a year. He wondered if he'd have made similar strides had he not defaulted on his promise to take up Japanese a year ago. He did cherish that buffer though. He closed the parentheses and said, "*Arigatou* about the sports club. I'll go first thing tomorrow."

"You're not angry?"

"Why would I be angry? I'm actually kind of touched if you want to know the truth." But he knew what she meant. A week ago, he probably would have been annoyed by such an attempt to get him out of the house. In all likelihood he'd have seen it as a ploy to guilt him into it since it involved her paying his dues. But he'd made progress since then. Out in the world, he was such a porous animal, always conveying the babel of human intercourse through his interior, engorged with the sheer volume of it, but here at home in his double exile, he was regaining a sense of his own finitude—and it brought with it a kind of peace. In high school, a Myers-Briggs personality test had taught him that he was an introvert, that he got his energy from the internal world and quiet surroundings. He'd been resisting that emasculating verdict for years, by cranking up the volume for instance, but in point of fact, that music he'd sought to drown the world in had always been his own mixed-and-mastered mind. The suburbs were conducive to that sort of personality. In the city, it was going to take some effort. He would have to work at striking a balance.

Come morning, he got dressed and packed his backpack and put on his shoes and stepped with an albino's restraint into the fervid late-summer sun. The first few minutes all but blighted his resolve, but after the requisite adjustment period, his trudging gave way to an amble. Per Miho's instructions, he gave his membership card to the girl at the front desk (a comely wench, though he felt nothing). Then he went to the locker room and got changed and made his way down the stairs to the exercise room. For an hour he struggled with the free weights, concentrating on his chest, which had sunken even further this past year, and his gelatinized biceps, since they were the first thing people always wanted to see when they were evaluating how muscular you were. When his upper body was sufficiently destroyed, he moved over to the cardio room and did twenty minutes on a treadmill at a leisurely 9km/hour pace. His heart scrapped with him the whole way, pounding against his sternum like some crotchety insomniac against the common wall. But strutting down the street later on, blood pumping like wind through his veins, a fall-presaging breeze blow-drying his damp hair, that same heart seemed to want to thank him for reaffirming its sense of purpose.

What else felt good was finding out once and for all that, in a manner of speaking, he *really was* big in Japan. He'd held his lilliputian towel fast over his privates while assaying the half-dozen publics flopping around the room. He showered calmly enough but failed to fight back a lunatic smile while he sat in the bath anthropologizing. Okay, so he wasn't *big* big, but he wasn't small either. Not the smallest anyway. Granted, a couple of those teenier weenies had just emerged from the ice-cold water of the adjacent bath. In any case, the only appreciable difference between him and most of them was that they had foreskins—and you had to look hard to see them because they wore them retracted. He'd read somewhere that foreskins contained miles of nerve endings and that when adults had their hoods chopped off they registered a marked decrease in sensitivity, so he wasn't wholly without envy, but at least if you're going to be struck blind, it might as well be as a baby— loss only registering as loss if you remember having something to begin with.

He took to going to the gym every morning. Even when his muscles were choked with acid, he'd still go and sit in the bath for a while. In the lambent hours that followed, he'd go home, eat leftovers and take a nap. If Miho wasn't home when he woke up, he'd go online or watch some TV until she was. They'd make healthy love, she'd make healthy dinner, and it was no longer a great project to get him to go for a walk around the block afterwards.

•

All that lasted a couple of weeks, until one afternoon, on the last Monday of the eighth month, traipsing through the cable channels in the moorland between his nap and his wife's return, Brain stumbled on a mine. The MTV Video Music Awards were in session, and sure enough—*Holy fucking hell!*—there was Agenbite accepting the award for Best New Artist. Nick was speaking, gazing into the camera like Narcissus into his pond: "We'd just like to thank everyone at Virgin, and all of our fans around the world, without whom our record could never have gone *triple platinum!* (thundering applause)." Triple platinum? Brain didn't even know what that meant, but it was real good, real fucking shitty-ass good. He tried changing the channel, but his thumb refused to budge. Theo, cocksure: "It's been a long wild ride getting here tonight, but now that we're here, you should all know we intend to stay a while." What the fuck was platinum anyway? All that came to mind were special credit cards and The Franklin Mint, and he sort of remembered it being better than gold, because that was surprising, wasn't it? You never heard about pirates swashbuckling over coffers of platinum. Matt moved in to the mic and even he looked like a preening asshole in his leather vest and his white shirt with the Beethoven ruffles: "First and foremost I'd like to thank the Creator. It's unfashionable maybe, but there you have it. Second, I never expected we'd attain this level of success and I just want to thank everyone out there who made it possible. You know who you are." Matt was wrong of course: Brain had made it possible, but he had no idea who he was.

Brain drank two beers in as many minutes. He took a deep breath, held it and let it out. He'd been through enough now to have a sort of shell, an armor of burns and calluses, and it would take more than a stinking VMA to penetrate it. But Agenbite wasn't through yet. That same night, not minutes before bed, he clicked on a meek little article about audio compression technology and just like that a Dell ad popped up and snipered a 5/8 rat-a-tat-a-tat into his brain. He hadn't heard the song before, but those were the angular contours of Theo's voice, no question. The goddamned song rocked too. He retreated into the innermost atom of the innermost cell in his head, where he found himself lost in a cloudy coagulum of unsheddable tears. He changed the settings on his computer so he'd be notified of incoming e-mails without ever having to access the Internet again. Then he dragged himself into bed, pretended to sleep, and into his fourth hour of mental threshing, had no choice but to nudge his sleeping wife awake.

"Mi, do you think I have a small dick?"

"What? Go to sleep."

"Just tell me. I mean, is it average, would you say? You've seen a lot of them, so I figure you're as good a judge as anyone."

She sighed. "It's nice. I like it."

"Yeah, but is it big though? I mean is it the biggest you've ever seen? No, right?"

No answer.

"Did you ever have any black guys at Pinky? They're supposed to be hung like belugas."

"We had."

"And?"

"Depends on person."

"Well mine's not the smallest you've ever seen though, right?"

"Of course no."

"How small was the smallest?"

"I don't remember. Can we go bed now?"

"Are *gaijin* dicks different from Japanese dicks at all, would you say?"

"It's basically same, *ja nai*?"

"Do they feel the same in your mouth? I won't be mad. Just tell me the truth."

"Are sure?"

"Yeah, I'm sure. What do you mean am I sure?"

"Japanese ones is more harder, I think."

"Jesus. Why don't you just shoot me and get it over with?"

"Not like *gaijin*'s is like tofu, but just Japanese is more harder, I think."

"You know what, you were right the first time, let's stop talking about this right now."

"But you…"

"Just…would you shut up, Mi…please?" A few moments of crickets, then, "I'm sorry I don't satisfy you."

"You do!"

A squall of shushing issued from Brain's lips and the perceiver in him split off from the perceived, thinking *What an asshole he am.* Miho groaned and went to sleep. Brain tried to follow her but failed, fixated as he was on the sweaty stick of string cheese he kept rolling back and forth between his fingers. He folded it in half and plied apart its rubbery segments like some subcutaneous plantain. He called it demeaning Yiddish things like "putz" and "shmuck," and no matter how much he messed with it, he couldn't get it to take a stand. So come daybreak, by way of the usual inverse proportion (sexual desire = $1/$self-esteem), his mind was all groin, and even if the bachelor of arts in him recognized that sex was perhaps only the tip of an iceberg of deeper needs, he nevertheless experienced it in starkest isolation.

So as soon as Miho left for work, he made himself wait for eight antsy minutes, then headed to the train station. Matsuo didn't appear to have any gripes with unfaithful husbands, but for the sake of saving Judeo-Christian face, Brain wanted to steer clear of Akebono-cho, opting instead to test the waters of Tokyo's most notorious pleasure quarter. He got off at Shinjuku Station, pinpointed Kabuki-cho on the map by the exit and memorized the route. Shinjuku reminded him why he never came to Shinjuku. The *gaijin* were out in droves. None of them ever quite acknowledged each other, all of them threatened and threatening, convinced they were doing something original or crazy or inherently interesting, none of which was the case and this place proved it, for you were but one of hundreds of *gaijin* here, and if you still felt special, you might check out the Saint Patty's Day Parade in Omotesando, which was like New York, only with fewer Japanese. Brain walked down a bustling bazaar and turned right at the movie theater. Rounding the corner, he knew he was in the right place. As far as he could see, in three cardinal directions, signs advertised strip clubs and love hotels, "soaplands" and "snack bars," and who knew what all else. It was seedy in every sense of the word, like a hundred Akebono-chos end to end, a vast labyrinthine temple to the primal thrust of man, a Disneyland for gametes.

It wasn't a minute before a sallow old tout read Brain's waywardness and stepped out of the shadows.

"*Gaijin-san?*"

"How much?" Brain asked.

"*Ichi man en*"—ten thousand yen.

"What do they do in there?" Brain asked.

The tout inserted a cracked and dirty index finger into his mouth and slid it in and out.

"Eight thousand *wa?*" Brain asked, and the guy said, "Okay," and led the way over half a block and up a rickety flight of stairs that might have been a fire escape. At the top was a sort of ticket kiosk like at a movie theater. The old woman behind the counter slipped Brain the menu. Brain didn't have to torment himself over the decision. It was the Goldilocks scenario: A was fleshy, B starved, C just right. The tout showed him to the waiting room. The place was decidedly less classy than Pinky, had more of a clinical, antiseptic feel to it, though maybe it was just that the lights here fluoresced louder. What mattered, of course, was the quality of the merchandise, and in that he was not disappointed. Like Miho, she presented herself in a robe, but the similarities ended there. This new masseuse exhibited a harder species of beauty than Miho's, her articulate bone structure lending her features the appearance of being lathed into the sandalwood head, eyes scooped out with a penknife and inlaid with nacre—a masterpiece by any account. They bypassed introductions. Remembering Matsuo's admonishments, Brain meant to keep the engagement as businesslike as possible, and she seemed happy to oblige. She led him into their room, not a cubicle but a proper bedroom with a dressing table and a full-sized bed and a suitcase peeking out from underneath. Did somebody live here? Did *she* live here? She stepped out of her robe and hung it on the door. He beheld the whole sculpture of her now, tall, apple-breasted, a little kneeneed perhaps. She undid his garments, folded them, placed them on a stool, opened a door to an antechamber which turned out to be the shower, and showed him inside. He felt a touch of compunction as she adjusted the water temperature and proceeded to scrub him, for these were the very same motions he'd gone through with Miho back in the dawning of their love, but he reminded himself that these were two different spheres completely, the one for his *kokoro*, and this one for his *chin chin*. Still, when she palmed his scrotum, all life suddenly seemed but a matter of juices and he couldn't help but care about her somehow. Kissing one of her penciled eyebrows, he asked in his best bad Japanese what her name was, and to his great good surprise, she replied in English: "My name is Sakura."

"No way. That's your real name? Cherry blossom? That's too perfect."

"Actually you're right."

"What's your real name then? I swear I won't tell anyone."

"It's very difficult for you to say, I think."

"Try me."

She handed him a capful of Listerine.

"My name is *Wan%$ Hu&#i'e.*"

He spit. "Where are you from?"

"From Shanghai."

"You're Chinese?"

"Are you disappointed?"

"Not at all." To the contrary, he rather liked the prospect of a new sort of notch in his belt. He could see her Chineseness now that he knew. She walked differently, kind of duckfooted, with a self-assured butt lilt and little toe pivots at the apex of each step—a Mandarin gait, or so he'd deem it until he heard otherwise.

"How long have you been in Japan?" he asked.

"Six months."

"Your English is good."

"I hope to go to America."

"That's where I'm from," Brain said, feeling for just the third time in over a year something not wholly unlike patriotism.

The first time had been shortly after starting his job. He'd gone into the Mos Burger next door to the school one afternoon and ordered the grilled chicken sandwich and asked the dude behind the counter if he could melt a piece of cheese on top for him, a modest enough request, but the dude sucked his teeth and refused to let him add it no matter how much Brain offered to pay because, even though the cheese was *right there* behind the glass, they didn't have a policy to cover such a contingency. Willing to accept a Pyrrhic victory, Brain went so far as to say he'd pay for a cheeseburger too if he had to and they could keep the meat and the bun and whatever else if they could just go ahead and melt the cheese on top of the chicken there, but more teeth-sucking ensued. Certain this had to be a language problem he'd come up against here, Brain dialed Miho on his cell and handed it to the dude and let them hash it out, but not only did Miho end up confirming the impossibility of Brain's having that piece of cheese melted on top of that particular sandwich, but she actually went so far as to *defend the dude*, saying that if what you want isn't on the menu then you don't have to eat there and if they make the exception for you then they have to make it for everybody, and Brain was like, "Yeah well wouldn't it be good business though to allow for certain alterations?" and Miho said, "That's American way of thinking," and Brain said, "Yeah, well I guess I'm glad I'm American then."

The second time had been on New Year's Day at Miho's parents' house when Miho's soccer-playing cousin, Ryu, challenged him to an arm-wrestling match and Brain accepted and summarily found himself straining to hold onto the sliver of space between the back of his hand and the coffee table and appealing to the spirits of all those underdogs of the American cinema who'd faced down their foreign Goliaths by strength of will alone, e.g. Rocky Balboa vs. Ivan Drago in *Rocky IV*, Daniel LaRusso vs. Chozen in *Karate Kid II*, the Americans vs. "the enemy" in most of his dad's vast collection of war movies. Of course, will was nothing without muscle, and Brain was months in arrears on workouts.

This latest flagwave lasted only a few seconds. He fought off the impulse to ask *Wan%$ Hu&#i'e* why she wanted to go to America, channeling Matsuo and reminding himself to keep clear about his purpose. *You're here for her body, not her mind.*

After the massage, which was nice but beside the point, *Wan%$ Hu&#i'e* inverted herself and took a seat on his face and he couldn't help but think of that old joke Nick had told him once about the Chinese bridegroom who requests the sixty-nine from his virgin bride on their wedding night and she says, "You want the beef with broccoli?" Brain didn't laugh though. Not now. This was too solemn an occasion. *Wan%$ Hu&#i'e*'s body was such a lithe, young, painted, ligamental thing that it was a bit of shock to find what looked to be a craisin stuck to the left side of her sphincter. He gently prodded it with his index finger, but it wasn't going anywhere, and only then did he realize that this must be what a hemorrhoid is. He didn't mind one bit being her salve, however, and as soon as he was, she let out a little moan, and not a squeaky Japanese one either, not a Miho or Kyoko one at any rate, but a deeper, pitchier, Chinesier thing.

When their time had almost run dry, *Wan%$ Hu&#i'e* flipped over, squirted some lube on his prick, and humped him with her inner thighs while he licked her purple gums and stared in her averted eyes until, huffing and on the verge of spasm, he pinned her knees to the bed with his elbows.

"What's the matter?" she asked.

"Nothing. I just was wondering if you ever...see, the way we're just pretending to...you know, I wonder..."

"You want to put it in?"

"I do as a matter of fact."

"AF, six thousand. Regular, ten thousand. Everything else costs extra."

Brain grinned uncontrollably. So all you had to do was ask! How awe...ful!

"What's AF?"

"Anal fuck."

"Oh, right."

And 'everything else'? Brain wondered, though he stopped short of asking for fear of looking like a Boy Scout. In any event, he'd never fucked an ass before but *man* did he want to. It was so *dirty*. And cheaper than regular sex too! What a counterintuitive bargain that was. A cultural thing, he supposed. He was within a beat of requesting it when it occurred to him that if all this was at least in part by way of evening the score with Miho, then maybe he'd be better off splurging on the vanilla after all. Not only would it cost more of their hard-earned dollars, but there was the procreative possibility there too. Symbolically anyway. The ass was a graveyard.

"I'll take the regular please," he said at last, giddy as a kid ordering from the adult menu for the first time.

She handed him his pants and he felt around in the pockets, pulled out his wallet and slipped her a ten-thousand-yen bill.

She thanked him and put a rubber on him and did as she was told, and it was a hell of an operation on her part because it only took a couple of minutes to get him off. He draped her ankles over his shoulders and licked the bottom of her gangling, yellow feet and rubbed his face with them and drooled and sweated while she intoned and the reservoir tip filled with preliminary emissions and ballooned for the father load.

She handed him the arm and leg holes of his clothes and

unbunched his socks for him. He got dressed and she opened the door to let him out and thanked him and told him to please come again, and Brain chuckled and said he'd need a good hour first and a glass of water, and she said, "Huh?" and he said, "Never mind." He hugged her close to him, forestalling separation, and despite Matsuo's admonishments, told her she was beautiful, because she was, and much as he tried to act macho about the transaction, he couldn't help feeling a great deal of tenderness towards someone he'd shared an orgasm with, even one as expensive as this.

•

After a few weeks, the touts got to know Brain by name, and Brain got to know what he could haggle them for. Brain enlisted girls from Thailand, the Philippines, Indonesia, Cambodia, Korea. Japanese girls went for considerably more in Kabuki-cho, which explained why Keith had taken the band to Kannai way back when, to sample the local fare at affordable prices. The moiety of Brain that had turned Japanese just by living here seemed to buy into the ethos that said Japanese girls were more desirable than those other *Asian* Asians, but the rest of him felt a certain kinship with these more affordable girls, for they, like him, were outsiders. And in another way, he savored the variety, for at last he was having experiences, earning stories by which to chart his existence as a man in time. He thrilled to log in the journal of his memory their various mannerisms, the philharmonic of timbres and pitches, the wildly different attitudes with which they approached their work. Some seemed to hate it outright, kept their eyes on the clock the whole time and turned their heads when he tried to kiss them. Others seemed to figure that if they were going to do it, they might as well try to enjoy it. Most fell somewhere in between. Brain knew there was a good chance some of these girls were indentured to their employers, that they'd had no idea they'd be doing *this* when they came to Japan, but he refused to let himself get sentimental about it. And anyway, he loved them.

Classes started up again the third week of September. As he'd come to expect, there were some knockouts among his students, but experience was making him more discerning and he no longer found all the alternates so irresistible. Even the handfuls of legs and lips and breasts that did succeed at agitating him, he refused to let unmoor him, for he'd come to regard pulchritude as a kind of evolutionary snare, like the nectar bribe of a pitcher plant. At least when you did it with a working girl, you knew the terms. You got laid, she got paid, and then you scrubbed off every flake of each other.

He fell into a routine. He ate and slept and went to work, had sex with Miho every two weeks at best, waging battle on boredom by fetishizing her infinitesimals until they seemed to contain in them all of her infinitely glorious species, a seraglio in each pore. His love for her never quit flourishing in the culture of her devotion, but it was just as natural, was it not, just as scientifically defensible, that her philters should lose some of their potency over time? Moreover, as Agenbite's list of successes grew, as they won their multiple Grammys and released their second post-Brain album—*Within*—to great acclaim, as new singles strafed him in video rental shops and taxicabs, Kabuki-cho sometimes seemed to Brain the only sanctuary in a world otherwise indifferent to his suffering. He received women's bodies there with the same sense of grace he'd once received wafers in the nave, dissolving them on his tongue like the body and blood of an unassailable God, which was what they were to him really, no hocus pocus necessary. But while these communions may have succeeded at displacing some of Brain's felt failures for an hour at a time, their transparently pecuniary nature did little to improve his self-esteem, not in any sustainable way at least, and it wasn't but a matter of weeks before the early elation succumbed to the law of diminishing returns. Rather than make him quit his afternoon errands, however, this growing sense of ennui only made him redouble them, blowing his whole salary and a portion of Miho's—they had a joint checking account and she never asked questions—in search of that vague transformative ecstasy that kept receding from him like some final, unremitting tide.

For a couple of months he stuck to vaginas, until one grim day, riding the train to work, he was ambushed by a salaryman's illegible newspaper across the aisle. Right there on the front page was a black-and-white photo of Agenbite. Brain's stop was next, and as soon as he got off, he scurried towards the newsstand to find yet another photo of the band on the cover of *The Japan Times*. Though his convictions barred him from buying the paper, they had nothing to say about his squatting and reading it.

ROCK BAND TO GIVE CONCERT ON MOON

LAS CRUCES, NM - At a time when most record companies are cutting costs and struggling to reformulate their business models amid historic losses, leave it to Virgin CEO Richard Branson to launch the biggest publicity campaign in history. In a press conference this morning, Branson announced that his company Virgin Galactic has selected rock band Agenbite to be the first musical group to perform on the moon. "Agenbite has exhibited the kind of cosmic bent we were looking for," Branson said. "Clearly they're making music for the new zeitgeist and one need only look at their sales figures to see they have the kind of international appeal that will make this a truly human event, not just an American or Anglophone one." The concert is tentatively scheduled for early September of next year and will take place inside a transparent geodesic dome to be engineered by defense giant Raytheon.

•

Brain didn't remember losing consciousness exactly, only a rapid falling into himself, and now here he was sprawled out on the floor drooling, commuters hopscotching over his head, none of them bothering to check if he was alive or dead. He was alive, wasn't he?

Yeah, because he hadn't seen this coming. At least in hell it was contretemps all the time. Here you just kept getting surprised by it. Here you had this teleological idea that things could get better, that you could progress or evolve or meliorate, that you suffered for causes, but allow yourself for a second to think you were in the clear, and bless your soul you might be right for a time, though you also might be very very wrong. *So they're playing the moon, big friggin deal.* Well, he'd had to try it, but the undeniable fact was that this really was a big friggin deal. Agenbite was going to make history. Which was not to say the whole thing wasn't a cheap gimmick, because a real band could blow minds from right here on terra firma. But the least common denominator would eat this shit up, and almost everybody was that. There'd be a hurricane of money. Matt would build a cathedral out of diamonds, Nick buy up half the NASDAQ, Theo bang whole squadrons of cheerleaders. He tried self-hypnosis again: *Even if it's the event of the fucking century, I really don't give a shit. I really don't. See God, look, here I am, not giving a shit.* He lay there for five more minutes like that, clenched and cursing, then yanked himself to his feet and dragged himself to work. As soon as class was over, he made haste for the one place that might actually take some of the edge off.

Wan%$Hu&#i'e wasn't in today, but her athletic Korean coworker, Sun, was happy to throw a rubber on him and let him penetrate her anus. She got on her hands and knees and he stood at the side of the bed and pushed his lesioned soul into that malodorous cataplasm and she squirmed and made some vague moan-type sounds which expressed either pleasure or distress, he wasn't sure, but either way he found himself swaddled tight and smiling. It didn't take very long at all. When they were through, he took a slightly extended shower and stumbled out into the hoary sun.

He didn't say a word that night, and Miho must have known about Agenbite too because she didn't press him. Within a couple of days, the Agenbite news had swollen into general knowledge.

It showed up in students' homework, and whether the sentences were properly formed or not, Brain marked them wrong. When the students tried to find out why, he told them simply, "Trust me." He also stopped teaching the days of the week because there was no way to do it without including Monday. To think the moon had once been his favorite celestial body. That he'd actually written songs about it ("Pale Mistress," "Velut Luna"). Now he found himself dreaming up schemes to destroy the perfidious thing. To his immense frustration, any scheme he came up with inevitably involved nuclear warheads and more money than he could ever hope to amass. There was the possibility of forging an alliance with a nuclear power, but how many of those were there? And which did he suppose might be interested in pitch-black nights and the end of tides? As a kid, he used to refract the sun through a magnifying glass to roast unlucky earthworms. But where did one get a magnifying glass big enough to roast the moon with? For the time being all he could do was to stop teaching Monday, to disorient his position in bed so that he could no longer see out the window, to try to forget what that action was called when his women dropped their drawers so he could push his dick into their rank asses. And after the third or fourth time, even the ass-fucking was leaving him cold. Cold and hungry. He thought of the *gaki* at the Tokyo National Museum, with their mountainous bellies and their needle-thin necks, and suddenly they weren't grotesque mythologies to him anymore so much as faithful depictions of the way it really felt to be hungry, to be so burningly, insatiably, insidiously void that hunger stopped being an attribute and became a full-fledged state of being. On the off chance that he'd mistaken the physical for the metaphysical, he took himself one afternoon to an all-you-can-eat *shabu shabu* restaurant and gorged himself on boiled pork and beer and got so drunk he could soon be found, by anyone but himself, reaching into the pot of boiling water and juggling meatballs for strangers. He made his bed on the sidewalk and woke at dusk in a puddle of vomit, his teeth chattering, his hands stinging like hell, his hunger unabated.

And so it was that Brain ended up before *Wan%$ Hu&#i'e*, begging her to do the unthinkable.

"You're joking?"

"I've never been more serious about anything in my life."

"Fifty thousand yen," she said.

"Fine," he said. "Just do it quick before I change my mind."

He lay flat on his back and stretched his mouth open as wide as he could. She squatted over him and he wrapped his lips around her hole and waited with a thudding heart and a ramrod erection.

Eighty-one eternities passed.

"Are you gonna do this er…?"

"I'm trying my best. I don't really have to go right now."

"Well can you see if any of the other girls can maybe? I don't have all day."

"Fine." She dismounted and put on her robe and stomped out into the hall.

Man, what are you doing? Why would you subject yourself to this? Everything else you've done up till now was vaguely excusable, marginally normal, but this is some fucked-up shit you're about to get into. Are you sure you want to do this? Of course you don't. But it's necessary. That's the point. You need this.

A knock came at the door and swung it open. Brain knew her straight off: the matronly bitch from the ticket booth. She was late-middle-aged, stately and plump, but evidently she had to shit and could use fifty thousand yen, and she probably hadn't been too terrible looking in her day, and he had to do this, so *Itadakimasu*. She made him pay upfront and he opened his mouth and she squatted over him and he stretched his lips around her slack, mucid pit and waited some more and…

The horror began. A turd materialized, slid through the event horizon, and he felt his mouth filling up with hot liquid and as soon as the gelatinous brisket hit his tongue, he gagged and a plume of vomit fell out of his mouth and dribbled down his chin. He retched and she started to lift herself off of him, to give him mercy, but he anchored her by her sagging ankles and made sure to get his money's worth and take into him that long horrible ingot of burnt beef bouillon and pinworm caviar, and it kept coming, so much of it, and he chewed it up, little seedlike bits crunching between his teeth, and it slid to the back of his throat and stuck there like peanut butter and he used its own hot juice to gulp it down, and it stank like a pestilence, filled not just his nose but his whole shuddering reptilian brain, and he retched and shot off his load and retched some more, and now more than ever did he wish himself dead. And then the old cunt, as if to prove that there was no such thing as worst, she began to laugh at him. "What the fuck do you think you're laughing at, huh? I'll murder you, you fucking cunt!" and he meant it too and she screamed and fled the room half-naked. Some goon came in to see what was going on, but as soon as he entered he was blown back by the funk and pinched his nose and Brain gestured to him that everything was under control, that there was nothing to see here, and he wiped up the mess as best he could with a towel and puked some more and sopped it up, reeled and nearly passed out, went to the shower and sat on the floor and swallowed half a bottle of mouthwash, thinking *If this isn't rock fucking bottom, then I don't wanna live to see what is,* and he meant this too, the abyss was just over there, its lip seductively curled. How this had ever seemed like a good idea, he had no idea. Except that by the time he had his clothes back on and was back on the street, he noticed with great relief that he was beginning to feel better. He really was. Lighter or something. Purged. Chastised. Like he'd descended into hell and risen again and now here he was like Christ in white raiment.

•

As soon as Brain got home, he brushed his teeth for twenty minutes, took another shower and began cleaning the apartment. This was Miho's job normally, and she'd only just done it over the weekend, but the urge was indomitable. When Miho returned from work, she froze in place, a shopping bag swinging from each of her fists. "*Dou shita no?*" she asked—What happened?

"Hi, honey. Leave your shoes on, okay?" He relieved her of the bags, walked down the hall and popped them in the fridge.

"What happened?" she repeated, in English this time.

"What do you mean what happened? I'm taking you to dinner."

"Why?"

"What? You worked hard all day, you deserve a nice meal." He might as well have told her that Martians had colonized their bedroom.

He took her hand and turned her around and slipped on his own shoes and promenaded her around the corner to the Korean barbecue they'd been meaning to try for months, where the windows were bedecked with photos of all the Japanese celebrities who'd eaten there, none of whom Brain recognized, though their larger-than-life signatures looked the part. Miho ordered a plate of tongue. Brain wasn't thrilled about that, but what was taste if not another social construct he'd do well to divest himself of if he was ever going to be happy? If your knee-jerk reactions didn't hold up to scrutiny—and he was no longer sure that any of them did—then what good were they really? Anyway, he wasn't hungry in the least; he just wanted his bowels to move.

"You know," he said to Miho, munching on the tongue some poor animal had bleated its last with, "this news about the band? I think it's great. I really do. I mean, is there a part of me that's jealous? I'd be lying if I said there wasn't, I guess, but the fact is I am a part of this. That band was my brainchild for a long long time, and just because I'm no longer in it doesn't mean my legacy isn't. I mean this could have been Joe Shmoe's band from Kalamazoo and I'd have had no stake in it at all, but this way when those guys play on the moon come next fall, I'll be right there with them. They are my friends after all. We've had our differences, but we were in a *band* together. You can't even understand what that means unless you've been there. It's the closest guys can get to each other while still keeping their pants on. I really think it is. Come to think of it, I should probably write an e-mail to congratulate them. No, I definitely should."

Miho nodded, but a little too slowly. Brain chewed on another tongue, wondered if it could taste him tasting it, and identified that as something Theo might have said, which was fine, which was going to have to be fine.

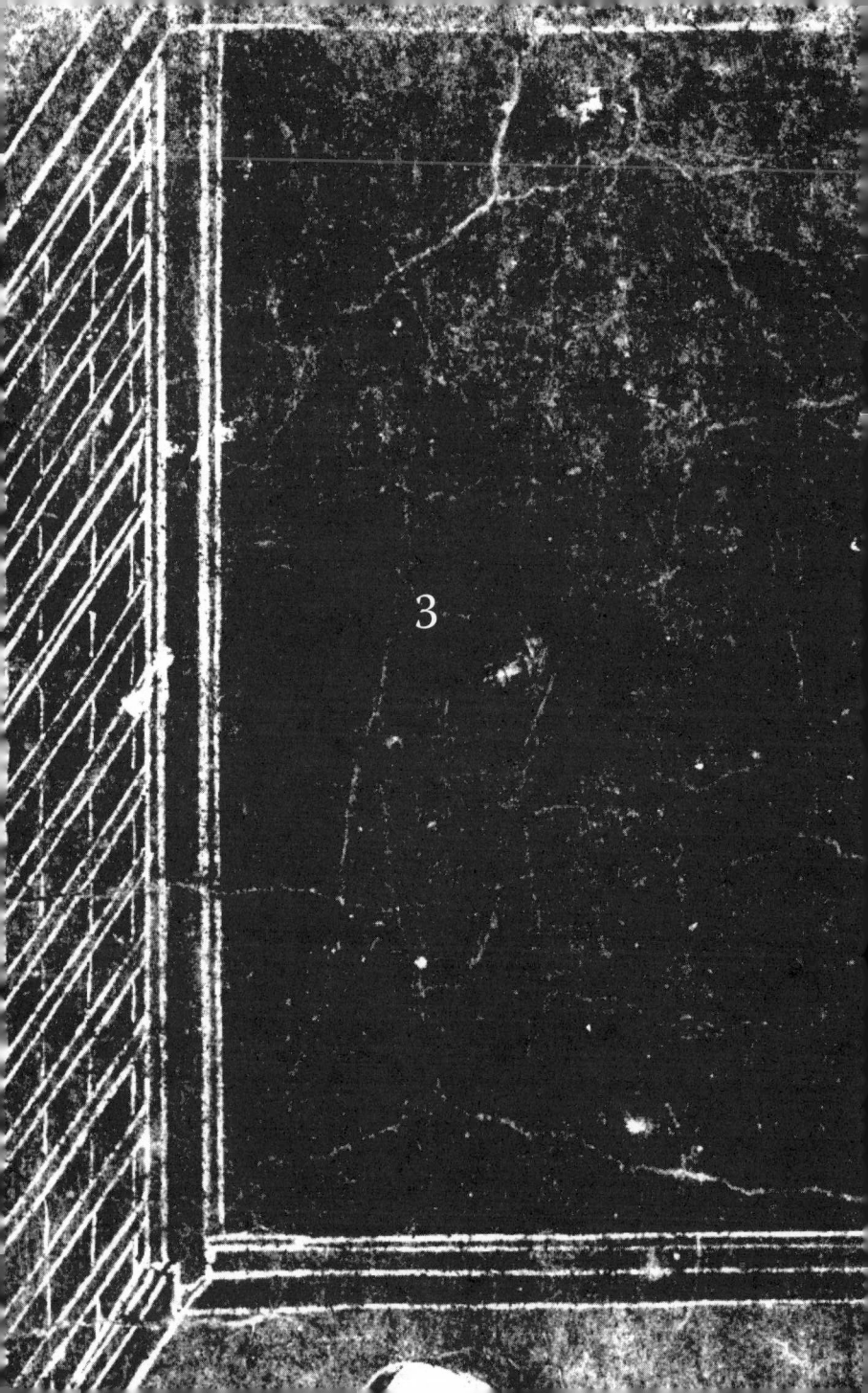

Days **swelled into weeks,** a new year came, and Brain continued to gestate this new version of himself. He routinely helped with the housework and took on a Saturday gig at a language school to help fill some of his idle time. He began teaching the days of the week again, and when students brought up Agenbite in their homework, he started to boast that those guys were his friends. He reoriented himself in bed and acknowledged the moon again, even apologized to her. He never did get around to writing that e-mail to the band, though he did pick up both of their CDs at HMV and listen to them end to end without lighting anything on fire. They weren't half bad, which was to say they *were* half bad, but he told himself he was happy for those motherfriggin ingrates. Miho took to flipping through maternity magazines before bed just in case Brain's attitude adjustment had come with a side of paternal instinct. It hadn't, and sometimes this seemed to him the only evidence that this new easygoing persona of his wasn't the whole story, that his old self, though entombed, wasn't quite dead. Lying in bed between the clamor of days, he sometimes thought he could hear it calling to him: *Hey, you're doing a damned fine job up there. Keep on doing like you're doing and we'll have our day in the sun yet.* But the thing was, Brain rather liked this new incarnation of himself. He didn't want it to be just a means to an end. This new him was simpler, contented itself with surfaces, cast doubt on its own doubts and didn't appear to have an ambition in the world. It didn't even masturbate. On top of all that, it was nice to people.

•

Brain was blending up a couple of smoothies for breakfast one morning when the disembodied woman inside his computer announced that he'd got mail. Expecting it to be just another car insurance or grow-your-penis solicitation, he was surprised to find a few kilobytes from one mulamadhyamikakarika@gmail.com and a subject line that read "RE: ligion."

```
brother, long time no boogey. I write from mountains,
in them or near them or among them. what's this i hear
about your getting married? that's crazy. i don't
mean to congratulate you on something that happened a
long time ago and then follow it up immediately with
a supplication but it looks like my research will be
taking me out east for a while and i'm wondering if i
might be able to crash at your place for a few days?
i'll be in kyoto mostly but i have to be in tokyo the
week after next for orientation. don't sweat it if
it doesn't work for you, i just thought it might be
a good opportunity for us to catch up and for you to
introduce me to the land. but seriously it's no big
thing if not. otherwise, maybe you know an auberge de
jeunesse i could stay at (i forget what you call this
in english???) or even if you just know somewhere i
can pitch my tent? i'm arriving on or about jan 28,
so if you could let me know by then, my breast would
swell with gratitude. i look forward (and in all the
infinite directions of the great everynothing) to
seeing you and your lovely okusan.

beingly,

Ish
```

While the Brain of old would surely have deconstructed every invidious line of that message (his "breast"?) and recoiled at the prospect of his spheres crossing thus, the new Brain simply wrote in reply, "By all means, come stay with us. It'll be good to see an old friend." And so on a bright Saturday morning two weeks hence, a rapping came at the door and Brain looked through the peephole and walleyed Ish looking esoteric as ever with dreadlocks radiating heavenward from his scalp like crude antennae and just as much hair exploding from the bottom half of his face in a way that looked positively scratchy. Brain swung open the door and Ish drawled, "Duhuude," and Brain not only allowed himself to be hugged, but even hugged back. Ish smelled as esoteric as he looked, but that was okay, it was going to have to be okay. "How's it going, Ish? Welcome."

"*Arigatou*," Ish said, slipping off his sandals.

"Come on in. I'll give you the tour."

"*Konnichiwa*," Ish said, addressing Miho, who was standing backlit at the far end of the hallway.

"You found each other. Ish, this is Miho. Mi, Ish."

Ish and Miho shook hands. "*Hajimemashite*," Ish said—nice to meet you. "These are marvelously delicate wrists."

"You speak Japanese," Miho said.

"Not much of it, I'm afraid, but I'm working on it."

Miho poured him a glass of water and set it on the table. "Please sit," she said.

"*Arigatou*."

They all sat.

"So tell us again what brings you out this way? Mi was asking me and all I could say was 'his research.'"

"Oh, it's a whole confluence of things really."

"Like?"

"A Boeing 777. Is that snide? Nourishment, spiritual and alimentary. Basho. Issa. Tofu. Evolution! Our first terrestrial ancestor crawling out of the primordial sludge, which you can bet was a whole lot prettier than the sludge we've got nowadays. The Japanese Board of Education. A café that blew up while I was trying to decide whether or not to apply for this fellowship and looking for an omen. An amorous evening between Mary Spalding and Ish

Barban, Esq. A dose of good old-fashioned wanderlust. My beating bleeding heart. Shall I go on?"

Brain tried again: "What's your research about?"

"Cognitive linguistics, more or less. Sapir-Whorf as it applies to emotions, if that means anything to you."

Brain shook his head.

"Basically what Whorf says is that we dissect nature along lines laid down by our native languages. I'm looking at the degree to which our emotions are part of that nature. In other words, how different language communities divide up the sentimental continuum. Here's an analogy. Like I know in Japan you call the traffic lights that mean go *ao*, right? Well technically that means blue, doesn't it, though they look just like the green ones we've got in the States, no? It's a question of where you split up the spectrum, where one color shades into another. The same naming process goes on with emotions. It's fairly arbitrary when it comes down to it. And then there's the question of whether the continuum itself is even universal. Are there culture-specific emotions? In other words, is language just a mirror or is it a matrix? Do we create it or does it create us?"

"It's interesting," Miho said.

"I like to think so," Ish said.

"Do you know *wabi sabi*?" Miho asked.

"*Wasabi*?" Brain said.

"Do you mean to tell me you're married to a Japanese girl and you don't know what *wabi sabi* is?"

"I might. Refresh my memory."

"The way I understand it—and Miho-san, correct me if I go afield—*wabi sabi* is a sort of aesthetic principle for which there's no real translation in English. I've seen it translated as 'rustic,' but that's not really it, I think. It's more of a feeling than a principle. Something to do with transience and simplicity and loneliness and the beauty of things? The feeling inspired by an old warped earthen bowl."

Miho nodded in agreement.

Brain struggled to keep his curiosity from shading into jealousy.

"Koreans have a word '*han*,' which is another one that's supposedly untranslatable. It has something to do with the great sorrow one feels at being wronged, a sort of grudging, visceral lament."

"What ever happened to French translation?" Brain asked.

"I'll be doing plenty of that too. I'm planning to render *Madame Bovary* in Cockney rhyming slang, if I can get to it."

"It's impressive," Miho said, getting up and refilling Ish's glass. Brain had never heard of Cockney rhyming slang, and he was sure Miho never had either, which was why he found it more than a little annoying that Ish's lingobabble could whip her into such a froth.

"Mi, I wouldn't mind some water too please."

She did as she was told, then announced, "Excuse me, it's very rude, but I have headache, so I think I will lie down."

"Since when do you get headaches?" Brain asked. He looked at her wrists. They really were delicate. Svelte and dove-white.

"Where does it hurt?" Ish asked.

Miho pointed to her temples. "Sit for a minute," Ish told her. She did, and he stood up and got behind her and began to knead her scalp with his fingers. "Do you know what causes a headache? It's when the spaces between our synapses close. Massage is one way of opening them up again. It also helps if you voice some liquids. L's and R's. I realize that might pose some difficulty for you, Miho-san, having to overcome the lallation, but let's try it anyway. Do you know *Row Row Row Your Boat*? It's a mantra disguised as a nursery rhyme."

Miho shook her head.

Ish proceeded to teach her while he applied all sorts of tantric pressures to her head, caressing her temples, blowing on the nape of her neck. At one *merrily* point he *merrily* reached inside her *merrily* mouth with two of his *merrily* fingers to show her *life is* where to place her *but a* tongue *dream*.

Brain ordered himself to keep it together, reminded himself that life was but a tongue dream.

"Any better?" Ish asked.

Miho cocked her head, pondered for a moment, and concluded, "It's maybe a little bit worse."

Ish laughed. "Well maybe you'd better trust your instincts and go lie down then."

Miho thanked him, wished them a good night and excused herself.

"She's lovely," Ish said.

"Wanna do the zombie?" Brain retorted.

The "zombie" was a trick Ish used to do during cigarette breaks in the days before his be*tréal*. Brain would say, "Come on, Ish. Let's do the zombie," and naturally Ish would play along because he was two years their junior and that mattered back then. Ish would take ten deep breaths, then Brain would clutch his neck and strangle him until his eyes went funny, signaling the onset of unconsciousness. Once zombified, Ish would take a turn for the belligerent, lunging at Brain's legs, pouncing and lashing out before finally toppling over, smacking his head on some sidewalk or banister, and finally coming to. It was a demented pastime, and Brain had always derived great pleasure from it.

"I don't do that anymore."

"Come on."

"You still playing music?" Ish countered, broaching what he must have believed to be a touchy topic.

"Not much," Brain said, "but I've been listening to the Agenbite albums nonstop. Amazing what those guys have been able to accomplish, isn't it?"

"I wasn't gonna bring it up."

"Why not?"

"I wasn't sure if you'd made peace with their success or not, but it sounds like you have. That's awesome."

"What's not to be at peace with? I left the band of my own accord, same as you."

"Yeah, but…"

"What?"

"That's a really enlightened view is all. I thought you might have some regrets or something?"

"I don't even know what that word means."

"You've been in touch with those guys then?"

"Plenty."

"I guess you know they're coming through here in a few weeks?"

"Sure, I know that."

Those were lies, and bald as any butler, but Brain was more concerned with the metaconversation that was going on here, the one in which Ish was asking *Have you a scrap of pride left?* to which Brain was responding, with a warrior's zeal in his eyes, that he had more than he knew what to do with.

"So we'll go together then?"

"You bet."

They could sort out the details later.

•

They met up again the next evening after Ish's orientation. Miho had suggested they rendezvous at Hachiko, the bronze dog who sat obediently on a pedestal by Shibuya Station. Evidently the idea wasn't original to Miho, for when Brain arrived, he found himself but one of a dozen or more bundled-up loiterers peeking anxiously at their watches. It wasn't a minute before he was accosted by an overzealous retiree in shirtsleeves, intent on practicing his English. "America?" he asked.

Brain nodded.

"I have been many times to Hawaii."

Had all Japanese been to Hawaii? They always told him this.

"You are from, may I guess, New York?"

Brain nodded. The guy had the right seaboard anyway, and if he told him Philadelphia, all he was likely to know was Rocky, and maybe the cream cheese, which wasn't from Philly at all.

"Do you know story of Hachiko?"

Brain shook his head. Did he want to? Didn't matter.

"Hachiko-chan was very faithful dog. Every day when his owner comes home from work, Hachiko meets him at train station. But then owner is died, but Hachiko continues to come to train station to wait for owner to return. Eleven years he comes. I very like this story."

"It's a good story," Brain said.

"But I think really Hachiko is not coming for love but because people are giving him many kinds of foods. When finally Hachiko is died, they found in his stomach… I don't know how to say… do you know yakitori? They found sticks for yakitori."

"Skewers," said Ish, who'd just materialized out of nowhere beside Brain. "You ready to go?"

Brain said he was, and Ish excused them in a formal Japanese that Brain kind of understood but would have been hard-pressed to reproduce.

"Where do you wanna go?" Brain asked.

"Do you mind if we walk over here for a minute? I just have to take care of something real quick. Supposedly it's right across the street there."

They waited with the rest of the pied mob at the most peopled intersection on the planet. That fogey's take on Hachiko had really bothered Brain. So what if the dog had skewers in his stomach? The most faithful dog in the world still had to eat, didn't it? It had bodily needs as well as spiritual ones. Why'd everybody wanna make everything so binary all the time? When the light turned green—or blue or whatever it was—it was like they were crossing the street in a packed rush-hour train, only minus the train.

"Where are we going?" Brain asked. But already Ish had accosted a pack of swarthy non-Japanese guys who were huddled around smoking cigarettes. He said something in some language he had no right knowing. They laughed and said something back, and Ish pulled out his wallet and handed them a bill and they in turn handed him a zip-locked bag. They shook hands and Ish rejoined Brain. "Sorry," he said.

"Drugs?"

"You really want to know?"

"Would I have asked if I didn't?" But Brain knew where Ish's solicitude was coming from. Even as he smoked his cigarettes and drank his beers, Brain had always prided himself on being a spoilsport when it came to drugs. He liked to think of himself as a kind of rationalist ascetic, prizing self-control over anarchy, praising Apollo over Dionysius, but when Nick—who generally partook of these same views—shared that joint with Ish and Theo in Montreal that time, Brain knew there was little to evidence self-control in how pissed off he'd gotten. Ish had tried to unclench Brain's fists and get him to join them, saying, "It's a rite of initiation for a culture that doesn't have any of those left." In reply, Brain had flipped him the bird.

"No, it's just some psilocybin," Ish said.

"Which is...?"

"The flesh of God, *mon copain*."

"Right. And how'd you know where to get it?"

"This girl Emily told me about it today. She's on the second year of her grant. Actually we're supposed to drop by her place later if that's cool. You'll like her. Sassiest feminist I've ever met."

"I was thinking maybe we'd get something to eat."

"There's an Ethiopian restaurant down thataways."

"Fine by me." Brain had never been to an Ethiopian restaurant, and the idea struck him as not a little oxymoronic since he'd grown up hearing about how hungry Ethiopians were, but anything to forestall hanging out with some drug-addled man-hater, sassy though she may be. And actually the vegetable goulash and slimy flatbread Ish ordered turned out to be pretty good.

They talked about Tokyo, which Ish called "inscrutable" before going on to explicate everything that was so inscrutable about it. As far as Brain was concerned, if Japanese themselves didn't talk about the psychological significance of wearing slippers while using the toilet, then why should an American who'd just arrived in the place? It wasn't until dessert that the conversation took a turn for the personal. "Miho seems great," Ish said, and it was then that Brain's spider sense began to tingle.

"Thanks."

"You must be in a good place right now."

"Yeah."

"Spiritually, I mean."

"I know what you mean."

"What's wrong?"

"I guess I just don't love having my private life put under the lens." It was the most agitation he'd voiced in weeks, and he experienced it with a mix of relish and self-recrimination.

"Sorry, bro. I didn't mean to press your buttons."

"I don't have buttons."

Ish reverted to bookishness, talked in theoretical terms about the dual estrangement of the expatriate. It didn't take long before the abstract circled back around to the particular, but by then Brain had several more beers in him and considerably less paranoia.

"Do you ever miss home?" Ish asked.

"What's to miss?"

"I don't know, family?"

"I'm in touch with my mom every couple of weeks. I don't necessarily mind not talking to my dad."

"What's that about?"

"The usual father-son stuff, the feeling that no matter what I do,

188

I'll never be good enough. It's all old as Oedipus, but it doesn't go away just because you understand it—that's what I learned in my four years at West Chester."

"Seems like our whole generation's got dad issues, no? Mine's upset that I'm not intent on inheriting his legal practice."

Having sliced himself open this far, and anesthetized himself with another lager, Brain felt a muscular compulsion to let the rest of his guts come spilling out. "Do you know what Miho was doing before we met?"

"How would I?"

"Blowjobs."

"Come again?"

"For money."

"What, like a prostitute?"

"Exactly like one. After school. Her friends worked at cafes and clothing stores. Miho guzzled cock." Brain doubled over with forced laughter. His vision blurred.

Ish stroked his beard. "You sure you want to be telling me this? I know you've had a bunch of drinks and all."

"She did a good deal of compensated fucking too."

And now the montage began to roll—burrowing tubers, baths of bubbling semen—and Brain nearly stopped breathing. Despite the recent triumph of his neocortex, his jaw snarled atavistically, sprung to chomp through thighs and chew through arteries. It made him angry, this bodily defiance, and the anger itself enraged him further still, for it gave the lie to this latest tour de force of self-deception that he'd been perpetrating for weeks. He'd really thought he'd burrowed down to his pith this time around, but like skin, the layers seemed to grow from the inside out, reconstituting him before he ever had a chance to know who he was.

"She confessed all this to you or ... ?"

"How'd you think we met?"

"What, you ... really?"

189

"That surprises you?"

"It does, frankly."

"That's why I had to do it, I guess."

"I get that. *Ex-stasis*. But so what's the big deal then? It's not like you were deceived, right? You knew what you were getting into."

"I thought I'd get over it sooner or later but it's like there's this Chinese handcuff thing at work. The closer I get to her, the more her past burns me."

"If you let it."

"I've tried fighting it. It wins."

"Well maybe that's your problem then. Maybe you've got to stop resisting and learn to accept her *en total*."

"Whatever that means."

"Look, Brain, I know to you this probably feels like some heavy shit, but it's not as big a deal as you're making it out to be. It really isn't. We're all prostitutes if you think about it. The whole capitalist system is built on meretriciousness. You sell your body or you sell your mind, and the Cartesian mind/body thing is a fallacy anyway, your mind is just your brain, so it amounts to the same thing really. And anyway, it's not like she loved two thousand guys before you, right? She was working. She probably hated every second of it."

"She thought it was 'fun.'"

"I doubt that. And even if she did, what harm's in that? The point is she fell in love with you, right? And she's not doing that anymore because it would make you jealous? Think about it, Brain. The poor girl's working in a shoestore. She could be making a whole lot more money if she wanted to."

Brain flinched.

"If you don't mind my saying so, Brain, I think what's going on is you're all caught up in your ego mind right now, riding that wheel of suffering, that quavering wheel of meat. It's all a vicious cycle, see. As long as you keep clinging to phenomena of mind and identifying yourself with it instead of seeing it for the red dust it all is, then you're bound up in that fistful of muscle like it was something real. Have you tried *zazen* at all?"

"Is that a food?"

"Meditation. Zen meditation."

Here we go, Brain thought, shaking his head.

"There's no better place for it. We could go check out some temples together if you're interested. I'd be glad to give you a primer."

"Yeah, I don't know."

"And I'm not sure where you're at with this, but for my own practice I've found certain plants to be real helpful." He pulled the baggy from his pocket. "Take these, for instance. This is a hallucinogen, which is like saying it's interconnectedness 101. You've never tripped, right? I didn't think so. Well when you do… when a person does, you lose that sense of subject-object permanence that separates you from everything around you. Your ego evaporates and it's like you literally become one with everything in the universe. You already are, in fact, it's just that the plants help you tune in to that deeper reality. It's a cliché, but it expands your consciousness, it really does. And once you're conscious of that essential oneness, you get filled with this great sense of peace, because what's left to desire when you're already one with everything, do you get what I'm saying? *Tat tvam asi*, the Indians say. Thou art that."

Brain tried for a second to suspend his disbelief, but sex had ruined him for mysticism. "No offense, Ish, but all that sounds like bullshit to me."

Ish shrugged. "That's cool. That's where you're at."

"It's not that I don't respect that vision of things. I just can't bring myself to actually believe in any of it."

"What *do* you believe in?" Ish countered.

Brain considered for a moment. "I don't know. Nothing, I guess."

"Nothingness is a central tenet of Buddhism."

"I knew you were gonna say something like that. But see, it's not like I *do* believe in nothing. It's more like I *don't* believe in anything.

There's a difference, I think."

"Give me a second to think about that."

"Okay, do you wanna know what I believe in? Evolution. I believe in evolution. Darwin. The primacy of fucking."

"That's a start."

"I guess I'm old enough now to look back and identify some patterns in my life, and it's pretty clear to me that there's always been a direct correlation between sexual repression and believing in things—God or music or whatever. I have to think if everybody was getting laid as much as they wanted to, there'd be no need for such things."

"So are you happy now that you've figured all that out?"

"I try not to think in terms of happiness. Nobody's happy all the time."

"Okay, but even if you're right about all that, Brain, even if the spiritual life is nothing more than sublimated libido, does that necessarily make it worthless? I'm not sure it does. I guess you're being descriptive about all this, but draw it out. Dust off the old categorical imperative. Do you really want to live in a Hobbesian world where fucking is the be-all-end-all?"

"Of course I don't *want* it to be that way, but the point is it already *is* that way. We're all animals at the end of the day, and once you've had that kind of revelation, there's really no unlearning it."

"But isn't that what's different about humans? That we have free will? I'm not denying that we have primal instincts, but we've also evolved language and self-consciousness to go with them. Do you think there are any other animals out there tonight discussing the workings of their own brains over dinner? You need language to do that. Language allows us, requires us maybe, to think about ourselves and channel our baser instincts into more worthwhile pursuits. You're pooh-poohing music now, but I seem to remember it making you pretty happy sometimes. Like whenever you'd finish some new piece and you'd pick us up that same night and drive us around and make us listen to it a thousand times and explain to us every little choice you'd made along the way. You drove us nuts, to be honest, but your enthusiasm was infectious, and we all knew what a genius you were. Don't ever forget that, by the way. You were a genius."

"A lot of good it did me."

"See, that's what I'm talking about. You don't think you're revising history at all? It's like you're intent on seeing everything through shit-colored glasses all of a sudden. I can't help thinking it's all coming from some deeply wounded place in you. Maybe you need to take a trip home? Sometimes you can get homesick without even realizing it."

"Maybe."

Ish looked at his pocket watch. "You about ready to go? Emily's waiting."

They split the bill and went outside and Ish borrowed Brain's cell to call this Emily person. She answered, and soon they were fumbling through turnstiles, hanging from straps, descending a vertiginous escalator to a street effervescent with sleet. They took cover under the awning of a ramen shop, drinking green tea from the vending machine and steadily sobering up. Brain's wits returned by degrees. By the second, he'd stopped sharing Ish's can of tea, spit a couple of times and bought one of his own. By the fifth, he was reproaching himself for having confided so much in Ish over dinner and was overcompensating by saying nothing at all.

Then there were footsteps, a growing form in the fog, a yellow umbrella, and the sassiest feminist Brain had ever seen.

She and Ish hugged. "Brain, this is Emily. Emily, Brain. We used to be in a band together."

She reached out a hand and Brain shook it. "Pleased to meet you," she said, with a confident mouth and eyes indeterminate enough to signify an inner life. She was petite, with wavy hair, brown if not black—not at all what he'd expected since everyone knows that Emilys are supposed to be blondes. He'd expected glasses, but there too he'd been mistaken. And wronger still was his forecast of what her face would look like. He'd foreseen fierce lines, cliffs of fall, but in reality her face was warm, dimpled and endearingly flawed. What looked like a chicken pock scar marred one of her cheeks and her ears were decidedly elfin. But the overall effect was one of gorgeous vulnerability. What's more, her teeth couldn't have been whiter or less fucked-up—he'd forgotten how pleasing that could be.

"I brought you guys an umbrella." She passed it to Brain and he opened it, expecting to have to share it with Ish, though when he looked he saw Ish had already snuggled up to Emily under hers. He followed them at a short distance. Aside from having to walk up five floors to get to it, Emily's apartment wasn't bad. It was tight quarters, but so was every other living space in this city. She had the standard six-tatami room, a bathroom and a kitchenette, a poster of Audrey Hepburn in *Breakfast at Tiffany's*—to whom, he realized now, she bore more than a passing resemblance—and a particle-board bookshelf sagging under the weight of books like *The Use of Pleasure*, *Culture and Imperialism*, and *War in the Blood: Sex, Politics, and AIDS in Southeast Asia*. They kicked off their shoes.

"Have a seat," Emily said. "*Mi tatami es su tatami.*"

Brain sat Indian-style, Ish lotus, while Emily went to the refrigerator and busied herself stirring some concoction.

"So, Brain, what are you doing in Japan?" she asked.

"Living," Brain said. "Trying to live."

"Brain doesn't believe in anything," Ish said.

"I wouldn't say that," Brain said, casting Ish a hard look.

"That's right, I forgot. You believe in the primacy of fucking."

"True?" Emily said, looking over her shoulder.

"Ish is a sensationalist," Brain replied. Having recovered his sobriety, Brain considered that, though alcohol might make you see things clearly, they weren't necessarily true things. And even if they were, you didn't necessarily want them broadcast to the whole world.

"So what brought you here in the first place?" Emily asked.

"Brain's wife is Japanese," Ish said.

"I'm capable of answering for myself, Ish, thanks."

"You don't look married," Emily said.

"What do married people look like?"

"Good point."

Brain hadn't had his hair cut in some time—it was nearly at his shoulders again—and he wondered if this wasn't what cast him as single-looking in her view.

Emily set down two glasses on the kotatsu. "It's water with lemon, maple syrup and cayenne. I started drinking it when I did the Master Cleanse like three years ago. I haven't been able to stop since." She took a seat by them so that they now made a perfect equilateral triangle.

"I know it well," Ish said.

Brain took a sip. "Not bad." It wasn't.

Emily sat up. "Hey, do you think I might be able to use you for my research?"

"I don't know," Brain said. "What's your research?"

"Well as a matter of fact, I'm trying to deconstruct received notions of the exotic Orient, specifically by looking at the degree to which cross-cultural relationships are founded on mutual projection shaped by various cultural and hegemonic forces."

Brain didn't catch much of that, but he wasn't crazy about that "as a matter of fact." It sounded accusatory.

Ish translated: "She's studying the Asian fetish."

"That's only one part of it," Emily said.

"Do you have an Asian fetish, Brain?" Ish asked. "Otherwise known as yellow fever?"

"What, just because I happen to have married a Japanese girl?"

"The lad doth protest too much, methinks," Ish said.

"Nobody said you have a fetish and nobody said you didn't," Emily said. "The question is, did you really just 'happen to marry' a

Japanese girl? Or was it prefigured by various forces that you yourself might not even be aware of? I don't doubt that you married your wife because for whatever reason you were attracted to her. But what I'm trying to probe is the nature of that initial attraction. There are lots of cultural and geographic complexities involved in marrying someone from the other side of the world, would you agree?"

"So far," Brain said.

"So it seems reasonable that you must have believed your wife had something to offer you that you couldn't readily find at home?"

Brain nodded, less to signal his agreement than to acknowledge that he was following her argument.

"Granted, if we believe Jung, most relationships are based on projection. We all contain within us our ideal image of a sexual counterpart, what Jung calls our anima or animus. Finding our 'soulmate,' then, becomes a question of finding someone who can comfortably wear our projections, at least in the beginning. What I'm interested in finding out is why so many American men evidently find their ideal projection screens in Japanese women while the reverse is almost unheard of. Japanese women are something like forty-four times more likely to marry an American man in this country than the other way around. Obviously that can't be an accident, right? So what is it then? Is there really something so unique about Japanese women that makes them so attractive to American men, or is this sort of group exaltation the result of certain historical and hegemonic forces manifesting themselves through American men, shaping their romantic desires in a way that has more to do with fantasy than reality?"

Brain wriggled. "Why do I feel like I'm being put on the defensive?"

"Because you are," Ish said.

"There are a million such forces. You can go at least as far back as the Roman Empire if you want to, with the Silk Route and the exoticization of certain fabrics and spices. Then flash forward to

Marco Polo in the thirteenth century, who comes back to Europe from China with reports of Kublai Khan's concubines and the alleged practice of men giving their wives over to guests to do whatever they want with. Flash forward again to the nineteenth century and you get *le Japonisme* and Whistler and Klimt painting women in kimono, Flaubert writing about the insatiable sexual appetite of Oriental women in Egypt, and Nerval talking about the Orient as 'countries of dreams and illusions.' Enter Lafcadio Hearn, the first lifelong Japanologist-slash-rice-king, who arrives in Japan in 1890, overcomes the taboo and marries a Japanese woman, becomes a citizen and spends the rest of his life writing essays about why Japanese women are 'the most wonderful aesthetic products of Japan.' Meanwhile you've got J.P. Morgan's nephew paying a bunch of money to marry a Kyoto geisha and Puccini spinning what started out as a novel about a money-grubbing prostitute called *Madame Chrysanthème* into what becomes the ur-tale of the Japanese woman as the docile, submissive, self-sacrificing girl-woman. Soon you've got the Pali Text Society introducing Buddhism to the West, and Thoreau translating sutras from the French, and a little later Ezra Pound's translating Noh plays. Then before long the Second World War's on. The Japanese lose, of course, which you might expect to put a crack in the romanticization of the Orient, but what it actually ends up doing is undergirding it even more. Then, with the tacit approval of both sides, this imperialist period in Japanese history gets cast as a kind of aberration. The Americans come in as conquerors, penetrating the feminized conquered, and the Japanese, trying to make restitution, accommodate them with prostitutes, eight thousand of them in Tokyo alone, so the West develops this notion of the man-pleasing geisha, which to their thinking is basically a refined prostitute. As lonely as these GIs get, though, they're still Christian by and large and they've come to set up a democracy, not exploit the native women, so there's plenty of moral guilt to go along with all their carousing, which eventually manifests itself as a desire to 'save' these docile, meek, subservient women from their patriarchal, hedonistic cultures, so that soon you've got tens of thousands of GIs taking Japanese brides, many of whom have lost their husbands in war and are dirt poor, so it's not difficult to see what's in it for them."

Brain had been psychoanalyzed once for a course on Freud, and he'd had this same claustrophobic feeling. He needed air.

"So gradually the geisha girl stereotype gets overwritten with the stereotype of Japanese woman as model wife, the unifying concept being that these women exist not as selves but simply to please men, whether by fucking them or making them dinner. We haven't left Puccini territory, see. The myth is so delicious to Western men that it keeps on feeding off itself. Come the fifties you've got a resurgence of Orientalism by way of Alan Watts and the Beats and then the hippies a couple of minutes later. Meanwhile James Michener writes *Sayonara*, which is later made into a movie starring Marlon Brando and which depicts Japanese women as existing to scrub the backs of their American lovers, and each decade since has had its reprise. In the seventies you get *Shogun*. In the eighties, you get the *Karate Kid* movies, most egregiously part II. David Henry Hwang turns the butterfly myth on its head for a couple of minutes with *M. Butterfly*, in which the meek fluttery love interest turns out to have a penis, but it comes back full force in the nineties, with *Miss Saigon*, which is basically *Madame Butterfly* in Vietnamese dress. Vietnam is a whole other can of worms, of course, not to mention Korea."

"Me love you long time," Ish said.

"Exactly," Emily said. "And then, barf, there's this whole resurgence of interest in geisha, sparked by a novel about a Japanese woman told by—surprise!—an American man. And the whole thing comes full circle."

"You left out John and Yoko," Ish said.

"So I did. Probably the most famous Japanese woman-Western man coupling in history."

"Okay," Ish said, "but to take Brain's side for a moment…"

"My side?" Brain said. He was still reeling too much from the attack to have developed anything like a side.

"Couldn't you construct a similar argument," Ish continued, "regarding blondes or big tits or anything else that gets a man off."

"That's the most common rationalization I hear. It's true enough that in its mildest incarnation a fetish really is nothing other than a strong preference. It's characterized as 'partialism.' Then you've got what's called 'low-level fetishism,' in which there's a stronger preference for certain sexual stimuli, but still what you might call a preference. But then at level three you've got 'moderate-intensity fetishism,' in which some sort of sexual stimulus becomes absolutely necessary for sexual gratification. Then in 'high-intensity fetishism,' a partner doesn't even have to be present. The fetishized object itself, a shoe or stocking or veil or whatever, is enough. Of course, if a particular sort of person becomes the object of fetishism, then they need to be in the room, at least by proxy, by which I mean pornography. It's probably no secret to you, Brain, that if you Google 'Asian' and 'pussy' or something like that, you get an awful lot of hits."

"I try to stay away from the Internet," Brain said.

"Where the fetish comes from in the first place," Emily went on, "is a different question, and nobody really has a satisfying answer, but there are competing theories. Originally the term was religious in nature and didn't necessarily have anything to do with sex, but was just a kind of irrationally worshipped talisman. Religion and sex are two sides of the same coin of course. The term gets explicitly sexualized when the science of sexology takes off in the nineteenth century. Freud theorized that the fetish resulted from castration anxiety. The kid supposedly expects its mom to have a penis, and then when she doesn't, the kid's all horrified and the first thing it glimpses on averting its gaze gets sexualized. Of course, you probably didn't have any Asian women in your house, did you, Brain?"

"What? No."

Emily continued with her unsolicited lecture, but Brain wasn't there anymore. He was revisiting a certain memory for the first time in years. Brian Sr. had done a tour of duty in Vietnam in '69, years before Brain was born, and though he never talked about the war, he'd built up a sizable library of books about it over the years. In spite of—or because of—his mother's forbidding it, Brain had delighted in browsing through that library as a kid whenever he got the chance. All these years later, he could still call some of those photos to mind if he tried—agent orange kids with knees in the wrong places, deformed fetuses in formaldehyde, nameless corpses torn up and flipped inside out. But that napalm girl had always been his favorite. She was nine, the caption said, same as him. But unlike him, she was naked, with her arms splayed out at her sides, running down the street with her mouth full of crying and her village in flames behind her. He remembered wishing he'd had a jetpack so he could fly in there, lift her out and escort her through space like Superman.

Emily was still droning on: "There are all kinds of theories about S&M and bondage and the way we play out different power struggles in the bedroom. In the case of the Asian fetish, it usually reveals itself as a manifestation of a conqueror-victim dynamic. Very likely, the reflex to seek out sexual gratification as a response to anxiety or stress originates in childhood as a coping mechanism. The child finds himself in a stressful environment and maybe discovers pleasure as a way of siphoning off some of that anxiety. This behavior carries over into adulthood as a kind of paraphilia."

Not that he was about to lend Emily's bullshit any credibility. It wasn't like he'd flinched from looking at his mother's pussy and his eyes had landed on the napalm girl. He just couldn't exactly say there hadn't been any Asian girls in the house when he was little.

"Did it ever occur to you, Brain, that maybe your wife had her own fantasies about you? Like maybe to her you represent a kind of escapism from conservative, boring Japan. Or maybe she views you as 'yasashii' or chivalrous, the whole ladies-first thing, when really all you're doing is acting out a basic set of more or less rote cultural gestures. Japanese men typically don't pay compliments the way Western men do, they don't dote on their wives in the same way, they don't say 'I love you' fifteen times a day. So maybe she got hypnotized by your apparent charm. So maybe, just maybe, what she married was a projection as much as what you married was one? That's the thing when you're from two totally different cultures and when you don't even speak each other's language that well, there are lots of gaps that get filled in with fantasies. It may well be she thought she was marrying Leonardo DiCaprio or Brad Pitt or somebody. Same difference as far as she's concerned ... I mean, maybe."

"If you must know," Brain said, "my wife was a sex worker before we got married. I never had any illusions about her purity."

"Man," Emily said, "how many clichés are you living?"

"Are you guys gonna help me eat these?" Ish asked, dangling the baggy of shrooms.

"I'll put on the tea," Emily said.

"You in, Brain?" Ish asked.

"Actually I think I'll be leaving."

"I hope I didn't offend you," Emily said.

"You just spent the last fifteen minutes attacking my personal life. How am I supposed to not be offended?"

"I was speaking in general terms."

"Really? Because it sounded an awful lot like you were speaking about me."

"Isn't that interesting?" Emily said.

Brain lost it. "You know what the worst part of it is, Emily? When I first met you tonight, I thought you seemed smart and attractive and nice, and I thought you might even prove the exception to my generally pretty jaundiced view toward Western women, but now you've just gone and corroborated it for me. And I feel bad for you, if you want to know the truth, because it's not even your fault. You can't help your inheritance. Still, at some point we all have to become responsible for our own destinies, so consider it a favor when I tell you that the reason American men tend to be attracted to Japanese women has nothing to do with Marco Polo or Genghis Khan or Yoko Ono. What it has to do with is feminism, which has resulted in our own countrywomen either turning into quasi-men themselves or turning into sirens and tricking us into offering up our nuts so they can chop them off. Meanwhile a lucky few of us escape the penitentiary and find there's this whole country over here filled with elegant, non-obese women who act like women and make us feel like men, and I'm sorry to say it but there's just no going back after that, there just isn't."

Ish shook his hand like he'd just burnt it on the range.

"You'd like to undo the feminist movement if you could?" Emily said. "Send women back a hundred years?"

"I do believe you've hit the nail on the head, Emily. One income per family. Divorce is taboo. Gay means happy."

"So what I'm hearing is two things. First, you married your mom. Second, if you'd only been able to get a girlfriend in the States, then you wouldn't be here at all. It's what I call the loser phenomenon."

"Ha! What about you? What are you even doing here anyway? There must be a few suckers left to marry over there, aren't there?"

"I belong here more than you do," Emily said.

"How's that?" Brain said.

"Emily's mother is Japanese," Ish said.

"Oh."

And now Brain saw it. Her eyes were tucked in at the corners, and she had the tell-tale wisps. But it was too late to reassess. "Maybe that's why I almost liked you," he said, grabbing his shoes and slamming the door behind him.

•

When he got home, he found Miho asleep. He woke her and told her he loved her and was sorry for what a jerk he'd been lately. She said it was okay and he buried his head in the cleft of her neck and held onto her like a life raft, and for as long as he lay there awake, holding onto her in the darkness, he loved her with a purity unmitigated by words. *Just hold onto this feeling,* he told himself, *and everything will turn out okay.*

But by morning, through the agency of troubled dreams, Emily's incriminations had tunneled into his confidence and laid their wriggling larvae, and by breakfast he was being eaten alive from within. *If there isn't some essential truth to Emily's argument, then why'd you take offense like that? Probably does pertain to some of those American dudes cavorting around with girls way out of their league, but if there's some secret fraternity out there, you sure as hell aren't a part of it. They cast you looks sometimes, the brothers, a conspiratorial wink, a knowing nod, but you're through with groups. One's born into them. If you're not careful, they swallow you. Better to be gnawed at from within. Married your mom? How ridiculous. Even if you did propose to her sometimes when you were little. "Oh, sweet darling. Don't you know how I feeeeel about you." She told you about stuff that day after school because you'd been asking questions. Supposed to be your dad who does that. Begged her to show you her thing, plead through the door while she took her bath, but she never did. None of them did. Said she'd show you pictures of other people's. Never did that either. Dad did though, inadvertently. Whole stash of them under that tarp when you were out looking for acrylic paints to decorate your old Strat with. Didn't beat off to them. Something too weird about sharing. Mom went apeshit when she found them. Germans aren't supposed to be hot-blooded but she can be as jealous as any chick on Telemundo. How would it have gone with Ashley Roselli anyway, hypothetically speaking? What if you hadn't been such a nerd and she'd gone for you and you'd gotten married fresh out of high school? Would she have flipped when she found your porn? Would you even need it? Maybe porn's a sign that it's not working out? That's* what they want you to believe. So you can hate yourself more. Still shows up in dreams sometimes, drenched in reverb. So you'd never have met Miho if one of them would've had you, what does that prove? Columbus was looking for India. Where'd all that feminism stuff come from anyway? Sounded pretty good. Women should be able to vote though. And there's something sexy about that liberated bitchiness. You can beat off quicker to the insistent ones. Ish probably fucked her last night. Lucky bastard. Miho knows how to get her way, but you can hardly call her insistent, can you? She's quiet. That's supposed to be one of the things you like about her. You don't look a bit like Brad Pitt or Leonardo DiCaprio, but her eye is unpracticed on Westerners. All that projection stuff might pertain to the early stages, but you're beyond that now, aren't you? Insofar as any couple ever gets beyond that? You do like her, don't you? Of course you do. You love her. You couldn't live without her. Those willowy limbs. That chocolate mole. She smells right too. That's important, they say. You don't necessarily mind that her grandfather gave you an apartment. Is that what keeps you in it? It wasn't what fanned your interest in the first place. That was sex. What's in that pretty head of hers anyway? A whole lexicon you know almost nothing about. Is language just a mirror or is it a matrix? What does that even mean, Asian? Asia's a big place. Lots of different types of women live there. Though the West too, I guess. Miho doesn't look a thing like the napalm girl. You should hope not. The only time her eyes light up anymore is when her friends bring over their newborns. She glows then, the way they do. She's good about not pestering you about it, you have to hand that to her. You'll do it eventually, it might not even be that long, you're just not ready yet, and you can't force these things. Like that other thing you have yet to do, whatever it is. The Thing. Thought it might be ass-fucking or shit-eating. Evidently not. Because you're still hungry, aren't you? Hungry as a ghost.

•

Ish had stayed at Emily's that night, come to get his stuff while Brain was at work and taken a train to Kyoto that afternoon. But he didn't stay away long. It was a mere twenty days before the Agenbite show was upon them, and those weeks were so glutted with thinking that Brain hadn't had a spare neuron to remark their passing. Besides the teeming self-doubts, he'd been cultivating a new interest of late. The day after Ish's departure, he'd gone to pick up Miho at work and he was a few minutes early so he'd moseyed into the bookstore and back to the English section. The very first title he'd laid eyes on was *Essays in Zen Buddhism* by D.T. Suzuki. He wasn't about to embrace synchronicity as a real phenomenon, but he could give himself over to it in a folk sort of way, just as he'd always taken great stock in fortune cookies, without necessarily building his plans around them. He picked up the book and read.

Zen in its essence is the art of seeing into the nature of one's own being, and it points the way from bondage to freedom. By making us drink right from the fountain of life, it liberates us from all the yokes under which we finite beings are usually suffering in this world.

He turned the page.

If we do not cut asunder the very chain of ignorance with which we are bound hands and feet, where shall we look for deliverance? And this chain of suffering is wrought of nothing else but the intellect and sensuous infatuation, which cling tightly to every thought we may have, to every feeling we may entertain.

Reading this was like listening to Ish without having to acknowledge that his insights might be worth anything. He took the book to the register, bought it and stowed it away in his backpack, and over the next couple of weeks, whenever he found himself alone, he'd take it out and read from it. When he got through that one, he bought another by Suzuki, *Zen and Japanese Culture*. He found great solace in a system of thought that so totally shunned the tyranny of logic, which had never done him any good. A monk asks, "Is there Buddha nature in a blade of grass?" and his master barks like a dog or chops the monk's arm off. Brain wasn't an adept yet, but he was moved enough to search the Internet for a Zen temple that opened itself to foreigners.

Come Saturday morning, the day of the night of Agenbite's show at the Tokyo Dome, he set his alarm earlier than usual and was out of the apartment by seven. He'd told Miho he had to work, which was true, though he didn't have to be there until noon. Between the station and the temple, he misplaced himself in a hummocky residential neighborhood. Eventually a series of three wrongs made a right and he arrived red in the face and twenty minutes late, though he was welcomed nonetheless by a giggling, shiny-bald monk in a black robe and white socks with articulated toes. The monk took him inside the temple and briefed him in the fundamentals of *zazen*, including how to sit properly on the *zabuton* cushion, how to set his gaze, how to still the waters of the mind by paying attention to thoughts without clinging to them. For a beginner like Brain, he recommended counting outbreaths, starting over each time he reached ten. When Brain was ready, the monk escorted him downstairs to the meditation hall, slid open the *shoji* screen and showed him into a large, dimly lit tatami room with cushions evenly ranged along a raised platform facing the wall. Against one wall a statue of Kannon, Goddess of Mercy, put forth her thousand arms, a stick of incense burning at her feet, marking time. Another monk nodded at Brain, his robes swishing while he paced the room with a bamboo cane. Of the other meditators, both were *gaijin*, one a lanky guy with floppy, striped sweatsocks, the other an emaciated woman with a mostly shaved head and a nose ring. Brain took up his position on the empty *zabuton* between them and nodded by way of acknowledging them, but neither stirred and he supposed that was to their credit. He molded his legs into the half-lotus position he'd just learned upstairs, cupped his hands by his crotch, imagined his spine dangling from a string originating in heaven, found a broken weave in the mat to focus his unfocused gaze on and set to doing nothing.

For the first few minutes (three? ten?), he fared well enough, but then he caught himself once breathing a twenty-fifth breath, so he started back at one, but then his knee began to itch, and becoming aware of it made itches appear elsewhere—on his scalp, his foot, the roof of his mouth, like bugs or flying sparks—but you weren't allowed to scratch them. You sat it out. Then in his effort to ignore the itching, he lost himself in language, wondering if he really loved Miho and if she really loved him and if he wasn't deflecting his own self-criticisms onto Western women and maybe Emily was right and he really was just a loser. He found his body again with a whack from the monk's cane. He'd been warned this might happen. The guy with the cane was the posture police, and Brain had evidently begun to slouch. He hadn't expected him to whack you so hard though. He straightened himself up and tried again in earnest, counting his outbreaths, letting his words ride out of him, but time passed and the weave swirled, his own heartbeat pulsed the world, and for a time his eyes seemed to float out of his head and around the room, but then the words returned and he was right back inside himself. Then another twenty-fifth breath, and again he slouched and the monk caned him, and Brain grinned for the attention, though his co-meditators still refused to acknowledge him. He was all too ready when the incense ran out and the monk rang a bell and freed them to be slaves to their egos again. Could a human being never be happy? Sit one down for too long and he wants to stand up. Stand him up for too long and all he wants to do is sit.

Brain went to work a couple of hours early and busied himself reading Suzuki. The workday passed like a workday passing.

But when he got home that evening, he had to do a double take. No, his senses hadn't deceived him—no more than they ever did. Here, on the kitchen linoleum, was Ish on his knees and Miho seated in a chair over him wearing his favorite skirt, the pink-and-gray camouflage one, and there were her bare, pink, spindly feet cradled in his hands, her head back, her eyes closed.

"Howdy Brain," Ish said, as if Miho's bare, pink, spindly feet weren't cradled in his hands, which they sure as hell were—insofar as anything was anything.

"What the fuck?" Brain said.

"Miho has one of her headaches again," Ish said, "so I thought I'd try a little reflexology. There are coordinates, you know. The Chinese have them all mapped out. Press here and it corresponds to the liver. Here you've got the lower lumbar. And here is supposed to be the head." He pulled out a tube from somewhere and squirted some oil onto Miho's bare, pink, spindly feet.

You thrust your knee into his face and drive the bridge of his nose into his brain. Then you check to see if he's alive, and if he is, you knock him to the ground and get the cleaver from the drawer and hack off his scrotum, drop it in the blender and purée it with some ice, and when it's nice and slushy, you put the cup to his lips and make him drink the whole friggin thing, and then you let him plead for his life for a while before hacking off his legs, arms, nose, and ears until all that's left of him is his torso and his featureless face and little blood spouts here and there, and then for the grand finale you scissor off his eyelids and make sure that the last thing he sees of this world is you fucking Miho, pulling out your cock at the last second and jizzing all over the moribund stump of him.

"So we'll leave in like half an hour?" Ish said.

"I think I may not be going with you after all, but you guys go and enjoy yourselves." He tried to mean it.

"What's wrong?"

"I just don't feel so great." He really didn't. It may have been psychosomatic, but his salivary glands were swollen and he felt lightheaded and heavy all at once. Even if he had felt well, though, he couldn't have brought himself to go. It was one thing to pretend he was happy for his old bandmates, another to testify to it with his body. The hardest part was knowing he'd left the band of his own accord. He'd sacrificed his rightful place in the history of music for a girl, and now here was Ish taking that same girl on what amounted to a date to see that same band he'd breathed life into, playing to a sold-out crowd at the biggest stadium in one of the planet's most populous metropoles.

After they left, Brain chewed up some aspirin and spent the evening trying to sleep and writhing and giving up and going to the karaoke joint near the station to drink cheap alcohol and sing to himself. He shuddered on finding a full seven Agenbite singles in the songbook. Then he thought of Kyoko and wondered what she was doing now. Was she happy? Did she ever think of him? Was she a mom? Was she dead? He felt like some kind of scarecrow with wind whistling through his ribs, and he thought about how loneliness was just a conceptualization and wondered what else he was when he was nothing but that. He paid his bill and went for a stroll under the scimitar moon. It was after one AM when he returned home, and Ish and Miho weren't back yet.

Whatever the Agenbite message boards might have said, Brain Tedesco was no idiot. He could see what was happening, and for some reason he knew he'd speculate about forever, he was inclined to let it. Even with the formidable costs of domestic travel, Ish came to visit often after that, usually unannounced. Brain would return home from work and Ish would be there, cooking a vegan meal or taking a shit in their Washlet. He'd claim to have some conference or other to go to, though as far as Brain could tell, he never actually went to one. He was there even when he wasn't. His clothes would wave at Brain from the line, a foreign toothbrush would turn up in the holder, Miho's cellphone would vibrate while they watched TV and she'd sheepishly get up and go answer it in the other room. Brain's ego urged him to do Ish violence, but he overrode it, acquiesced to every humiliation, for he was determined now to float in the stream of life without putting up any resistance. He was so tired of fighting. And if he drowned, well he was drowning anyway.

•

As Agenbite's "Music of the Spheres" concert approached, evidence of it was everywhere. It had hijacked all the media outlets, and you couldn't go out in public without hearing talk of it everywhere. It was being billed as the biggest concert of all time, and one could see why. They were playing the moon for Christ sakes! Brain's students wouldn't shut up about it. They wore the t-shirts. Brain was so doggedly oblivious that it was from them he had to learn that Bono was setting up projection screens throughout the African continent, that IMAX theaters would carry it live in 3-D, that they'd be playing at 4:17 Eastern Daylight Time to commemorate Neil Armstrong's first small step for mankind—which meant they'd get the better end of the bargain over here since it'd still be dark out and they'd get to watch the concert on the moon with the actual full moon as a backdrop—and that they were blocking off the main street in Shinjuku to traffic Saturday night/Sunday morning so that people could gather and watch the epochal event on the giant screen across from the station.

Brain braced himself for the worst day of his life. He consciously deprived himself of sleep in the days leading up to it so that he might sleep through the event and wake to a new day. But the concert was still two days out when, walking home from the station after work one evening, he remarked the absence of light inside the apartment. Normally Miho would've been home for a couple of hours already, her silhouette preparing dinner. Had she said anything about going out with friends? Or staying late to do inventory maybe? A nap would be unlike her. He unlocked the door, opened it and called, "Hello?" but there was no answer. He flipped on the lights. The phone wasn't blinking. The notepad was still on the same bedoodled page. He checked his cellphone—no messages. He dialed her cell, but there was no answer, so he left a message: "Mi, it's me. Just calling to see where you are. Call me back when you get a chance. I love you." He cooked himself some spaghetti, threw a strand at the ceiling to make sure it was ready. He heated up some canned clam sauce. When he was finished eating, he wrapped his leftovers and put them in the fridge. He did the dishes, then sat in bed and tried to read the rest of Suzuki, but he couldn't get any traction on the words. *Should I call the police?* he thought. *What if something's happened to her?*

But Brain was no idiot.

He called her again, left another message: "Mi, it's me. Wherever you are, please just call me and let me know you're safe. I love you."

She didn't call, and he didn't sleep, and it was going on ten AM when at last a timorous knock came at the door. He peered through the peephole. It was Ish, sure enough. Brain opened the door.

"Brain, man, hi."

"I think the best way to go about this is for you to say what you've got to say and then leave me alone. So do that, okay?"

"Brain, I don't ... this isn't easy for me."

"It's a piece of cake for me, Ish."

"Look, Brain, none of this is anybody's fault. God knows nobody meant for it to happen. You have to believe me, Brain. We tried to fight it, we really did. But it was just bigger than the both of us."

Brain closed his eyes, looked for some calm back there, found only a smear of brazenest red, like some whore had kissed the insides of his eyelids goodbye.

"She wanted to come down here with me, but she was afraid of how you'd take it. Look, Brain, I know how bad our timing is, what with the concert tomorrow morning and all. And God knows we feel absolutely awful about it. You have to believe me when I say we didn't mean for any of this to happen."

"What difference does it make whether you meant for it to or not? It happened, right?"

"We were powerless to stop it. We never did anything in this apartment, I should tell you that."

Brain winced. "Am I supposed to be grateful?"

"Look, I respect you, Brain, and the last thing I want to do is hurt you like this. I'd like it if we could go on being friends, though I don't expect that. It's natural that you might feel some animosity towards me, and I deserve it. If you want to fight me or something, I can't blame you, though the truth is I don't know what the point would be. Her mind is made up."

"When did this happen?"

"She's been fighting it for a long time. The whole thing's been really hard on her."

"Spare me the bullshit, Ish."

"Really though. The hardest part for her is hurting you, Brain. You might not believe that right now, but she really loves you. Just not in the way you love her maybe. You're like a sibling to her."

"She said that?"

"She always says that."

Why this was the worst part, Brain had no idea, but on hearing the word "sibling," a wrecking ball swung down and demolished what was left of his heart.

"So you two are gonna live here or what?"

"You can stay here for a while of course. Miho feels really bad about that too.

She's going to be staying with me in Kyoto for the foreseeable future, so you've got time. She hasn't told anybody about this yet, though she's planning to tell her parents soon."

"Is there anything else you want to say to me, Ish?"

"Not really, just... Brain, I really can't tell you how sorry we are. We never meant for this to happen."

"Fine. Now I think you should go."

Ish reached out to put a hand on Brain's shoulder, but Brain deflected it. "Ish, I'm about two seconds from sticking a knife in your face. Leave."

Ish did the smart thing and took himself away, leaving Brain alone with this new and terrible clarity. She was gone, it was that simple, their story together aborted like a third-term fetus. Something pushed up the back of his throat and he let it spill over the shoes

212

in the entranceway. He left it where it lay and went back outside in his bare feet. He took the stairs and walked down the street and made a right and went down the bigger street. It was bright out and he sneezed, which felt good, and he wanted to do it again, but he couldn't make himself, so instead he pressed shut one of his nostrils and blew out the other one. A ribbon of warm snot hung from the tip of his nose and he bent over and tried to shake it loose and then the vomiting came again and he toppled over into fetal position there on the pavement. Pedestrians passed by, but none stopped for him, and he began to sob then, quaking like an overheated car and moaning herdslong. What the fuck? How could your life be so normal one day and so fucked up the next? He couldn't pretend to be surprised, and yet he was surprised. Surprised that the thing he'd thought would happen had actually happened. He'd never *really* thought she'd do it, did he? Else he'd have done something to stop it. A Japanese woman no less. He hadn't been the perfect husband maybe, but he'd have died before leaving her for anyone else. Had he really meant so little to her? How could she have done this to him? *A sibling? Oh God!*

Then he caught himself and started counting.

•

He walked to the temple on bleeding feet, counting to ten over and over again. It was far, probably took hours, but time didn't register anymore, much less pain. When he got there, he went inside the temple, and a monk he'd never seen before said, "May I help you?" but Brain ignored him and walked down to the meditation hall and turned on the light and took his spot and stared at the wall. The monk followed him but he must have thought this was an eminently Zen thing to do because he didn't bother Brain about it. Now that Brain's body wasn't walking anymore, his mind grew restless, kept on walking—*How could she? I can't believe she*—and then the monk he'd never seen before did him a favor and whacked him on the neck with the cane and Brain straightened up, but his mind kept on moving—*Why are you shaking? Are you shaking?*—and the monk came to whack him again, but this time Brain saw the shadow on the wall and when the cane came whirring at him, something came loose in him. Without a thought to impede him, he caught the weapon and wheeled around, wrested it from the monk's hands, popped to his feet and swung it at the monk's chubby head, and the contact couldn't have been more gratifying, he'd hit him right with the cane's sweet spot. The monk grunted and felt his head, checked for blood and found some. Brain wound up and swung the cane again and this time it whistled through the air and caught the monk in the neck and a red seam appeared and split and the stunned monk struggled to get the cane back, but Brain was as strong as a thousand men now and he drew it back and hacked down on the crown of the monk's head and the monk reeled for a second and collapsed in the corner, nodding his head and looking impressed.

Brain bounded up the stairs and ran out the door and through the trees that surrounded the temple complex. He climbed a svelte pine with his bare feet, his heart fluttering like a hummingbird's wings, the evergreens redolent of Christmas, and he felt wonderful all of a sudden and knew this had to be it, *satori*, the freedom Suzuki had preached. He checked his back. Sure enough it was sweating. This was it. He'd had his cataclysm, the brightening of his mindworks. He was a bona fide Zen warrior now. *The fighter is to be single-minded with one object in view: to fight, looking neither backward nor sidewise. To go straight forward in order to crush the enemy is all that is necessary for him. He is therefore not to be encumbered in any possible way, be it physical, emotional, or intellectual.* All this time he'd been looking at the master's finger while the master had been pointing at the moon, but now there was no question, he was looking at the moon, and it was sneering at him.

He walked, bled, laughed at shadows.

He arrived at Club Pinky, bundled his wits, and knocked on the door.

"Brain-san," Matsuo said. "Long time no see. Where is your shoes?"

"I didn't feel like wearing them tonight," Brain said. "I need to ask you a favor."

"Okay."

"You know you once said if I ever needed anything, I could come to you?"

"Yes."

"Well I need to borrow something."

"What?"

"A gun."

"A gun?" Matsuo said. "Why you are needing a gun?"

Brain had thought it out. The best approach would be to appeal to Matsuo's paternal instincts. "There's this creep stealing Miho's panties off the line and peering in our windows at night. Miho's getting really scared. I don't plan to use the gun, just to scare the guy away."

"I see," Matsuo said. "Maybe I can investigate for you?"

"No. I appreciate it, but I think I'd really like to handle it myself. You know, *as a man*."

"I see. Let me search what I have. Come inside. Do you want to drink something?"

"No thank you."

Matsuo came back a few minutes later with a gun (9mm? 35mm?—Brain had no idea). "It's okay?"

"Is it loaded?"

"You know how to shoot gun?"

"All Americans know how to shoot guns," Brain said. Matsuo seemed to buy this and handed over the piece. It fit Brain's hand like lambskin. He was a little surprised at how heavy it wasn't. It was light, glinting and filling his head.

"You are not planning to shoot this guy?"

"Of course not. I just thought it might be effective to shoot a couple of bullets in the air, let him know I mean business."

Matsuo went rummaging through a drawer, found a box of bullets and handed it hesitantly to Brain. Brain pocketed it. "Gun is illegal in this country, you know, so must be very careful."

"We'll be careful," Brain said.

"You will watch the concert in Shinjuku tonight?" Matsuo asked. He was only making conversation. Brain had told Matsuo about how he used to play in a band, but he'd never told him it was *that* band.

"I'll be there," Brain said. He thanked Matsuo again, stuffed the gun inside his pants like a codpiece, and, a little uncomfortably, walked.

•

Hours passed him by like so many Toyotas. The sun sank down in a swirl of glorious pollution and the moon rose towards its apogee. Agenbite was up there by now, making preparations, tuning their instruments, watching the Earth rise, hundreds of thousands of miles away and assured they were out of his reach. But he had a plot of his own now. He couldn't hit them directly, but he could still get at their audience, which was the source of their power anyway.

When he arrived in Shibuya, he crossed the street and found the swarthy guys.

"Good evening," said their leader.

"I'll have one of those bags of mushrooms," Brain said.

"What size?"

"Large?"

The guy went in his backpack, pulled out a baggy. "How's this?" The baggy twirled from his fist like some shimmering, circumvoluting planet.

"That's perfect," Brain said.

The guy said some numbers and Brain gave him some paper. Money didn't mean as much when you had death in your pants.

He walked to Kabuki-cho and went to find *Wan%$ Hu&#i'e*. "I'm not going to do any crazy stuff," she said. He nodded and took out his wallet, found his ATM card and gestured that he wanted a pen. She brought him one and he wrote his pin number on the signature panel and handed her the card. "There's not much in there," he said.

"What do you want me to do?" she asked.

"Pay off your employer," he said. "Go to America if that's what you want and do something with your life. The clock is always ticking." He left without waiting for a reply.

He went into the Mos Burger and ordered a grilled chicken sandwich with cheese melted on top. The dude behind the counter sucked his teeth. Brain took the gun out of his pants and ordered again, and now the dude gave Brain the kind of service Japan was famous for. Brain didn't pay, and he wasn't asked to. He thanked the dude, and then just to be sure they were on the same page, he pointed to the telephone on the wall and shook his head side to side. "*Hai*," the dude said, bowing his head—they were on the same page.

He put the gun back in his pants and as soon as his sandwich was ready, he took it to the adjoining dining room and sat among all the college kids who'd normally have been waiting for the trains to start up again, but who tonight were waiting for history to be made. He took out the baggy, laid a bunch of mushrooms under the bun, and took his first bite. It tasted like shit—and no one knew as well as he did—but he kept eating until he'd eaten the whole bag and washed it all down with a melon soda. He thanked the dude behind the counter, and the dude bowed nervously and told him to please come again.

The streets around Kabuki-cho had emptied out for the most part. Nothing was open but the sex clubs, and Brain didn't have that kind of lust in him anymore. He walked aimlessly until he happened on a Korean church. He was glad to see the door was open, because what good was a church that locked its doors? He genuflected and took a seat in the front pew. The place looked like St. Pius, where he'd gone as a kid, only it was a little smaller. He thought of Sarah Milliken for a moment and cast her out with the devil. The stained glass windows might have been pretty if it weren't so dark out. Votive candles flickered in crimson cups.

Brain approached the altar, screaming in case the Christian God was hard-of-hearing—which would explain some things.

"Hey! Here I am, Father. O *Merciful* One. No I don't believe in you, but I'm gonna talk to you like you were real anyway, because what the fuck else am I supposed to do? What do you want from me anyway? That's what I want to know. What am I supposed to do down here? You're supposed to have it all planned out, right? I mean it. I really don't get what you want from me, and I'm getting a little fucking sick of waiting for you to tell me. Here's the brief plot synopsis. You put me down here and give me irritable bowels, asymmetrical ears and a shitty personality, so I give my life to making art, then I meet some chick who finally gives me hope, who makes me feel something beautiful, and I give my soul over to her, but I've still got all these fucking issues to work out and I don't fucking want them, but they're my fucking cross, so whatever, I'll bear it if I have to. And now I've done that and I'm ready to just love her and start a fucking family and whatnot, and what do you do but pull the fucking rug out from under me. So where does that leave me? What am I supposed to do now? Tell me that. I didn't sign up for this. I hope you're getting a kick out of it. Listen, if I'm supposed to serve you, then just tell me how to do it already because I'm pretty desperate right now and you can probably have me if you want me. So show yourself, why don't you? Let's have it out, man to man, man to deity, ghost to ghost, however you want to do it. Float in here like the good witch and talk to me already, because I'm fucking dying here. You realize that, right? That I'm about fifteen minutes from popping a bullet in my brain? All I'm asking for is a little guidance.

I need you to pick me up like in that crappy poem about the beach and carry me a little ways. Even if you're not real, by all means come down anyway, show yourself and offer me some comfort because it's really fucking uncomfortable right now. It's cold and dark and I feel like crying and I can't even make myself do that. Why would you let this happen to me? When I finally had a shot at happiness, at doing something decent with my life? Come out of hiding already, I beg you. I'll give you till the count of ten. *Ten, nine, eight, seven, six...* I'm serious, Father. I won't ask again. *Five, four, three...* I hope you realize that I'm about to do something totally insane and once I've done it there'll be no coming back and it'll be on your fucking head not mine. *Two, one, half...* Thanks a fucking lot."

He put his head down on the pew, puked and fell asleep.

•

He wakes to Japanese and Korean hieroglyphs dancing about his face, jumping off his nose and vying for his attention. He swats them and sits up. He starts. Jesus has come unstuck. He's floating there a good three feet in front of his cross, and the crazy thing is he still looks pretty much dead but he's breathing. He's definitely breathing. His ribs are moving in and out and his abdomen is undulating the way the TV screen does when you vibrate your skull with an electric toothbrush. The cross behind him is a fluid thing, bending this way and that in some imaginary Golgathian wind. Brain senses some motion over on the altar and turns his head to find that it too is breathing, this monolith of marble is sucking in breath and letting it out. He stands up and makes to leave this place, but the pew goes limp and he gets caught up in its folds and falls to the floor and now he's looking up and all the saints in the windows are breathing at him too. He struggles to his feet and makes for the breathing door while the pews on either side close in on him.

The first thing he sees when he gets outside is a pachinko parlor.

Words dance on the marquee:

PACHINKO&SLOT
PASSAGE
Because the thing which a ball appears most in Shinjuku.
SUCH A THING IS.
Our supporter in this store. As for this store.
The way that a ball like the sun bursts open
is the order of this store.
Love a ball is, **ORIENTAL PASSAGE**

Brain doesn't have the first clue what that means, and yet he does too, Japanglish makes a numinous kind of sense to him all of a sudden, and if he has to think, he wants to think like that, because Suzuki says words are liable to detach, so he figures you might as well encourage them. He walks towards the crowd, immerses himself in it and it dawns on him now that words are all a part of this great plot against him, that he's been thinking inside of it, falling into its traps. And this narrative sense, this storytelling propensity in him, that would have to go too. He doesn't like the story it's been telling.

He walks among the gathering masses and immerses himself **fuck that, cut the leash. So many people about, sexy the clothes which look at the band. Large celebration festival. Neon smell reaching and the girls have shone beautiful and young. Tainted meat entirely. It is constituted. You and your very money. Give your all the miserable lives to that pursuit. Monads entirely. Because of those those may obtain. Truly, they cooperate here and there over long time, but it dies independently. In order to be possible to obtain the heritage and to hurry with your bedside for** the people therefore you tighten with your life screw, it sits down, sees and prays. Is the thing which is the human remains has chosen that, what kind of good is? A state which is exquisite, the pain. Include that. Feel this. *Brain notices a couple of businessmen exiting the front door of an office building. He squeezes in the door before it shuts* fuck you, stop succumbing. You speak Japanglish now. Japanglish speaking is by what you are. At least the dad was honest. Strict view of life, was his truth, you were informed entirely, it was war. You take those, the wife while having sexual intercourse, the specialist and of substance you are polite mutually. That then a certain way. *He gets in the elevator, presses the highest number.* She left me. It is that. And that is my defect completely. Because you knew him entering here, her, and to clean from her feet. The girl that is loved. It does with anything because of her. The fucker of mothers. She was relied on. *He emerges, finds the stairwell, ascends to the roof.* She was relied on. As for that it is believed very. There is a despair. Why it doesn't have my plan? This is rage, don't you think? Then I who catatonic am felt very why? Because something which my now can do? Her telephone? She is a nip in the air. Hiho, I think that we would like to express exactly. Very inferior it seems the woman who is not. I relied on. You don't feel? The sufficient energy which is not. Inside it dies entirely. *He peers over the ledge and sees the screen, the fabric of heads.* Obtaining you obtain, just. I probably will die, and it has been about probably to become everyone. It shakes. Desire the fact that now it has sexual intercourse eagerly. The next way in order to observe at that it chops up thing very, mixes, that does the beverage in him, in that mouth attaches the bomb very, blasts that head. Is sexual intercourse somewhere? You pull out that, can make the fear of God. That coarse item, I coming out blaze. We are large, it had gone. There were we together to that. It could not divide us. I very am regrettable. As for me then very it was happy. I do not know I why was perplexed to the road. As for us, when then understanding mercy should be shown better, little it comes here really, suffers from the meat, becomes, and is controlled and obtains everything which should and is not. Put us in here, observe at that you struggle. So I now belong to Satan perhaps. So, his ambition, that mistake it was, it possessed? I have ambition. We begin the band together perhaps, fuck the fallen asses. The laughing is murder. *He fingers the gun in his pants.* Fuck you, this is not a story, there is no here story. As for me it is possible to do that. As for me it is from my pocket to pull this gun, places on your clean temple, can blow your unpleasant brain. This gun takes your life. Now you see that, don't you think? That is not avoided. That now is in the story, or the story which is not done you must go out. You look at that, don't you think? Without that without this that or. *Brain sees the big screen, sees Richard Branson introducing the band, sees the gathered masses.* Fucking! These very people. Such many goddamned people. The way all these it is beautiful, murder and their corpses. The people gather, before various diversified it is possible those there under the large screen where the large quantity it should see is possible and it reaches here with the earth and the commentator and the astronaut it has the band which plays. Intermittent shock of the movie screen where the band on the suit of the astronaut to whom the appliance which around those in the dome of type is bound with the string has been attached and will be exact is large, is obtained there floating, it leaps to the top and bottom and smiles. This is the day when your life is largest, when those the gun which is here, here is there. And your monopolized ones it is possible and it is not possible and therefore when the book of history has remembered Agenbite, it has been about to remember Brain Tedesco. That fairness destiny is believed, chance and the disorder which that are unlimited series entirely exactly, but there is a destiny, it is not possible to think exactly, destiny now interwinds, it interwinds. *Brain stands on the ledge. His toes curl over the edge. He totters.* That thing which stops your body is proper. If it does not die, it is not possible to do that. That it cannot know those which are everything which you can do high all everyone. Everyone so stimulated concerning this. There is a design of the astronaut where everything is obtained in those, moon pie and udon of tsukimi and sells cheese there. That is very happy day for all these fuckers. It is beautiful, excessively. Contact of the fall of the air of feeling the very school which season of your taste so far is always therefore the girl and dream concerning those contacts and then my generally known friend touches her excessively, that very coarse item which obtains, it leads away. My now has, to that of my bullet which bores the hole you want. Whether or not as for me there is there, you do not know, but being, or, while the people remove love from me, passing my life which suffers nobly there is amicable roughness. And I God loved her. As for me. I submerge. *Brain Tedesco, son of Broomall, Pennsylvania, twenty-six years old, holds the gun before him like a monk's cane. He aims at the fabric of heads. He cannot miss. One twitch of his finger and people die. One slip of a foot and he does.* **The hole my, concerning that, between here of the hole my entirely concerning, there movement of those people because of the my use work history music.** *He raises a leg, dangles it in the void.* **Before my confusion and because the left my friend hole my here and at the time of the gun my substance we want entirely the Christine pristine feel and there permanently. Starting approximately there are those. There as for those then is, flies to weightlessness**

Brain was yet alive when there came a diabolical roar and a flare so brilliant as to suffuse Shinjuku with an eerie daylight. Before he could make out what had happened, the narrator in his brain had resumed its former position. "Something had gone terribly wrong," it said. "A technical malfunction of some kind." He saw it now. Raytheon's breakthrough dome roiled with aqueous flame. Enclosed on all sides, the fire licked itself into a raging furnace. Between those fierce tongues, instruments buckled, particular faces twisted into universal death's-heads. When the footage at last cut out, the crowd turned their gazes upon the actual moon. They were crying, breathlessly lowing. He'd never heard so many people cry at once, and he was a little surprised to find that he was one of them. He got down and took a seat on the ledge, peered out at the vast expanse of eyeballs, a moon reflected in each pupil.

He fancied for a moment that they were looking up at him, that he was their leader and they were looking to him for guidance, imploring him to say something to help them make sense of what was happening and carry on with their lives.

But what would he say to them?

Well, for one thing, he would tell them that he was listening, that not a one of their pleas would go unheard. He would tell them that their pain mattered to him, that he suffered it as his own. He would tell them what he wished he'd been born knowing: that even love required moderation, but if your problem was one of size, if you were born with a heart too big for your one scrawny life, then you could at least start by loving one person to overflowing. And he would tell them what, with his love gone and his only friends turned to ash, he himself finally understood: that life was jazz, there was no fixed score, and you'd damn well better stay awake.

And in case he'd minced his words, he'd sum it up for them:

There is no Thing.

There is nothing.

We are free.

ACKNOWLEDGMENTS:

For putting up with me, keeping faith (or pretending to), and various other kinds of help along the way, my deepest appreciation goes to:

Mayumi and Reina, Mom and Dad, The Honda Family, Joseph J. Feeney, S.J., Sheree Bykofsky; Bruce Rutledge, Josh Powell, and all the other good people at Chin Music Press; Nathan Belofsky, O. John Brown, Michael Carroll, Susanna Lack, The Japan-U.S. Educational Commission, Tajiro Iwayama, my teachers and cohorts at The New School, Clockwork, Pilgrimz of Soul, Daisuke Suzuki, Joseph Cardinale, Chris Kelsey, Desi Poteet, David Odhiambo, Tim Denevi, Tammy Pavich, Mike Brennan, Michael Kenig, David Vicic, my many penguin friends, and Providence, whatever it is or isn't.

Also, in memory of Ian MacMillan, teacher, bullshit detector, friend.

•

KAMI BOOKS 2009

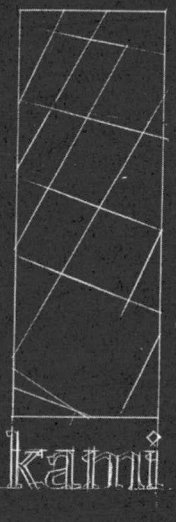

kami kami

PAPERBACK
SERIES

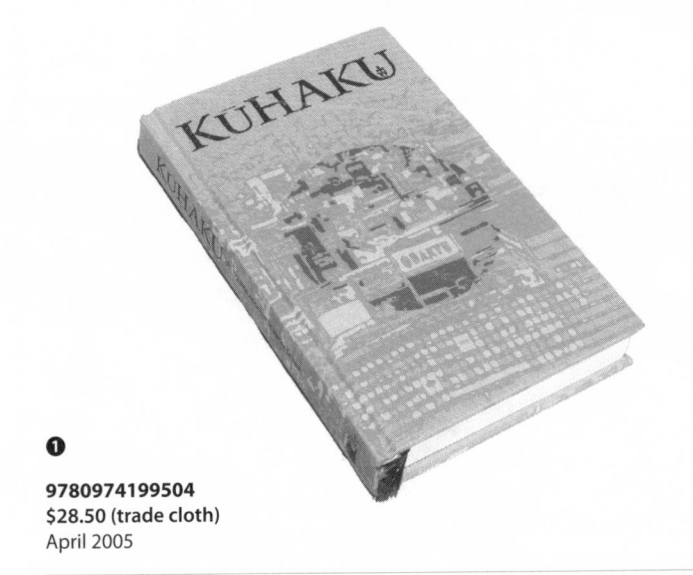

❶

9780974199504
$28.50 (trade cloth)
April 2005

Kuhaku & Other Accounts from Japan

The first offering from Chin Music Press is the literary equivalent of a knockdown pitch. Sixteen stories and essays by different writers destroy the many stereotypes about Japan. With artwork from Craig Mod, kozyndan and Peyote.

"Inconclusive in the best possible way, by turns pointed and generous, *Kuhaku* paints a shifting portrait of a shifting place."

— Ellis Avery, *Kyoto Journal*

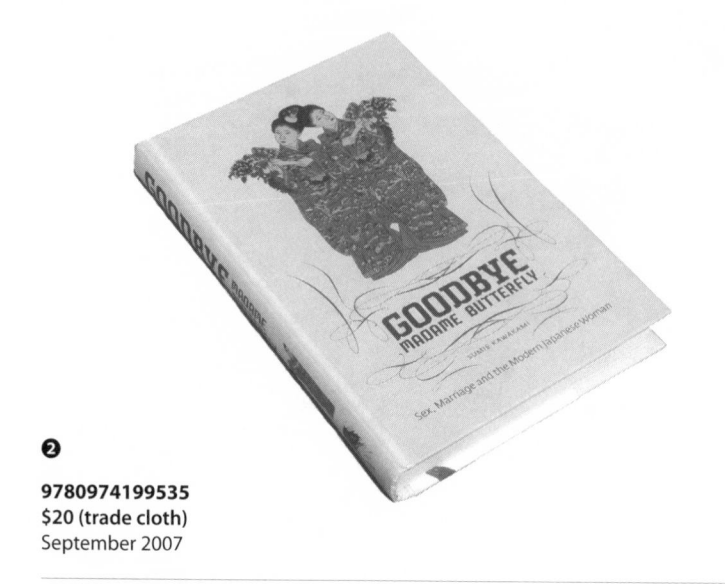

❷

9780974199535
$20 (trade cloth)
September 2007

Goodbye Madame Butterfly:
Sex, Marriage and the Modern Japanese Woman

by Sumie Kawakami

"An eye-opening, detailed look at the private, intimate lives of Japanese women… This is an intelligent and authoritative work, covering everything from adultery to sex volunteers and the role of fortune tellers in Japanese romance. It is at once illuminating and entertaining, credible and so engrossing you will find it difficult to put down."

— Robert Whiting, author of *You Gotta Have Wa*

3

9780974199566
$22.50 (trade cloth)
June 2009

Oh! A mystery of *mono no aware*

by Todd Shimoda with artwork by LJC Shimoda

Oh! was selected for National Public Radio's summer reading list. NPR reviewer Lucia Silva called it "a triumphant kick in the pants for anyone who doubts the future of paper-and-ink books."

"Can an aesthetic concept developed in Japan 300 years ago be revived and made relevant to a contemporary American audience? This is what Todd Shimoda so masterly achieves in his fascinating novel *Oh! A mystery of 'mono no aware.'* This is a journey through a delicate world of emotions and poetry on the part of a young Japanese American from Los Angeles who in his search for his native roots uncovers the complexities of being human in a world framed by skepticism and rationality. Structured as a thriller with a most unexpected finale, Shimoda's novel unravels like a Japanese scroll—one cannot put it down until the last scene comes into full view and, with it, the realization that the realm of feelings (*mono no aware*) is far from being an innocent enterprise; it carries risks that one must be ready to pay in order to fully understand. This is a brilliant novel—it makes the reader feel the pleasure of thinking."

—Michael F. Marra, professor of Japanese literature, UCLA